PRAISE FOR

Winter in Full Bloom

Winter in Full Bloom will grab your attention right away and it won't let go until you finish each satisfying word. Anita Higman has written a beautiful story with well-rounded characters that reminds us what it means to be family.

Kristin Billerbeck, author of The Scent of Rain

At a poignant crossroads in her life, Lily Winter heads off to Australia to track down a family secret, armed only with a clue given by her mother, an eerily cold woman. In Melbourne, Lily finds who she was looking for, aided by a handsome stranger with a few skeletons in his own closet. But she ends up with more questions than answers and her faith is tested in ways she never expected. The results transform not only Lily but her entire family.

With a touch of humor, romance, and heartache, Anita Higman pens a beautifully written story of hope and healing drawn from the lives of wonderfully complex characters. *Winter in Full Bloom* will stay with you long after you read the last page.

Suzanne Woods Fisher, bestselling author of Stoney Ridge Seasons

Anita's Australian-inspired novel is as warm as a koala, creative as a platypus, and filled with more twists and turns than a billabong. G'read, love!

James Watkins, award-winning author of thirty books including
Writing with Banana Peels

Winter in Full Bloom had me from the first paragraph. *Why is this woman who hates flying on a plane headed for Australia?* Then throw in trying to redeem her truly dysfunctional family, and Anita Higman's heroine will capture your heart.

Neta Jackson, bestselling author of The Yada Yada Prayer Group series and its sequels.

WINTER

IN

FULL BLOOM

ANITA HIGMAN

MOODY PUBLISHERS
CHICAGO

© 2013 by
ANITA HIGMAN

The author is represented by MacGregor Literary, Inc.

Edited by Cheryl Molin
Interior design: Design Corps
Interior image: Botond Horvath / Shutterstock.com / 90744185
Cover design: John Hamilton Design, LLC
Cover image: Stephen Carroll / Getty Images
Author photo: Circle R Studios Photography

Library of Congress Cataloging-in-Publication Data

Higman, Anita.
  Winter in full bloom / Anita Higman.
    pages cm
  ISBN 978-0-8024-0580-7
  1. Family secrets—Fiction. 2. Adoption—Fiction. 3. Family reunions—Fiction. I. Title.
  PS3558.I374W56 2013
  813'.54—dc23

                                                                    2013015831

This is a work of fiction. Names, characters, places, and incidents either are the product of the author's imagination or are used fictitiously, and any resemblance to actual persons, living or dead, businesses, companies, events, or locales is entirely coincidental.

We hope you enjoy this book from River North by Moody Publishers. Our goal is to provide high-quality, thought provoking books and products that connect truth to your real needs and challenges. For more information on other books and products written and produced from a biblical perspective, go to www.moodypublishers.com or write to:

River North Fiction
Imprint of Moody Publishers
820 N. LaSalle Boulevard
Chicago, IL 60610

1 3 5 7 9 10 8 6 4 2

Printed in the United States of America

Winter in Full Bloom
*is lovingly dedicated to my son-in-law, Alex McMullen,
whose Irish ways not only beguiled my daughter, but enchanted us all.
The Irish touches in this book,
including the bagpipes, come from his merry influence.
(You play them delightfully, Alex.)*

"If winter comes, can spring be far behind?"

PERCY BYSSHE SHELLEY

PART ONE

the adventure

CHAPTER
one

I sat on a 747, trying to talk myself out of a panic attack.

The jet still sat on the tarmac, but already I could imagine—in electrifying detail—the fiery crash and then the watery pull into the briny depths of the Pacific Ocean. *Lord, have mercy.* What had I been thinking?

Fool that I was, I'd left the sanctuary of my own home, which was safe, and hygienically clean, I might add, to board this death trap. Too late now. I'd taken a leave of absence from work, stopped the mail, given all my indoor plants to my neighbor, and said a dozen goodbyes to my daughter, Julie. The trip was set in stone—the igneous kind that the geologists liked to talk about at work.

While I sat there sweating, my mind got out its magnifying glass to examine my inner motives. All in all, the journey had a grab bag full of miseries attached to it. For me, getting on the plane proved that my empty nest had driven me over the edge like the biblical herd of pigs. Since my Julie had left the house, was I trying to find a person to fill that void . . . that vacant place at the table . . . the perpetual silence of the house and the clocks, ticking away the rest of my tedious life? Probably. And yet finding my sister in Australia would be no less than wonderful, whether Julie was at home or not.

I looked out the small plane window at the heavens with my anxious puppy dog eyes and could almost hear the Almighty chuckling. *Yes, I know, God. I must keep You entertained.*

But back to the fear at hand. I rechecked my seat belt and pulled it so snugly I felt my pulse throbbing in my legs. My stomach busied itself doing the fandango. What had I eaten in the airport? A double bean burrito with a side of green chilies. Not a good travel choice. Did I already have motion sickness? The plane hadn't even taken off yet. If I were to exit the plane right now, would they give me a refund? Probably not. I'd already used the restroom, crumpled the magazines, and troubled the flight attendant for a ginger ale. *Lord, I need a friend. I need backup.*

"You have to ask yourself: what am I most afraid of?" It was the voice of a child.

I turned toward the sound. "Excuse me?" Straight across the aisle sat a child no bigger than a thimble—a girl with moon-shaped eyes, a Pooh Bear T-shirt, and a wad of gum she was chomping as if it were a lump of tough meat. *Surely this child isn't backup, Lord.* I think God enjoys showing off His sense of humor.

"You're scared to fly. Right? I was too, but I got over it." The girl blew a bubble and let the purple gum pop all over her face. She gathered up the gum and put it back in her mouth for another round.

"How can you tell that I'm afraid to fly?"

"All that sweat. Dead giveaway. And you look like you've just swallowed a Boogie Board." She exploded into giggles.

I had no idea what a Boogie Board was. And in spite of the silliness the kid talked as if she were thirty, although she couldn't be more than nine or ten. I had to know her secret—how she managed to rise above her fears. And something about her little turned-up nose and soft brown eyes reminded me of Julie when she was little. "And so how did you get over it . . . the fear of flying?"

The girl looked at me, her big eyes gobbling me up. She lost all the playfulness when she said, "I watched my grandma die of cancer. Her body stopped working, but she was still in there. It was a bad way to die. When I get old I don't want to go to heaven that way.

Maybe dying on a plane isn't so bad. I mean, I know God doesn't ask us, but we might as well give Him a list of our pref—choices."

I wasn't sure if her reasoning reassured me or alarmed me, but I leaned toward her and said, "I'm sorry about your grandmother."

"Yeah, me too. She always played dolls and Mario Kart with me. Every kid needs a grandma like mine."

"So true." If only my Julie would have had a grandma like that. When the girl said no more I turned my attention back to the plane, which now taxied toward the runway. My body wanted to flee. Each time I took in air it didn't seem to be enough, so I breathed in more.

Did I smell fuel? My head went so buzzy I'd only heard half of the flight attendant's speech. What was that about oxygen masks and exit doors and life vests? Oh, my. I fanned my face.

I clutched at my heart, which was now beating itself to death. Would I pass out? Throw up? Go crazy? All the above? The cabin felt like a cauldron. Maybe the air conditioner was malfunctioning. Maybe deep within the belly of the plane other more important electrical devices were failing. Things that kept the plane aloft— things that kept us from plummeting to the earth in a fiery heap. I mashed my damp bangs away from my face.

"Just so ya know . . ." The little girl crossed her legs. "I also found out that you can't die of a panic attack."

Her tone came off so pragmatic I looked at her again just to make sure the words were coming out of her petite mouth. "How do you know I was having a panic attack?"

She cocked her little Freudian head at me. "Classic symptoms."

Who was this kid? And where were her parents? I unbuckled my seat belt. "I don't think I can do this." I jumped up and bumped my head on the overhead storage.

"We're about to take off," the girl said with maddening calmness.

I collapsed back onto the seat and rubbed my throbbing head. The contents of my stomach threatened mutiny. "I'm going to be sick."

"Here." The girl handed me a little folded bag. "It's a fresh one. Never been used."

I was in a tin can with wings, and there was no way out. The plane took off then. I gripped the armrest as the jet tilted upward at a steep angle. I was now officially airborne. My body felt a little weightless, but it might have been because I was sitting on the buckle of my seat belt, which made my posterior go numb.

"Know what? You remind me of Eeyore."

It was that kid again. How could anyone make chitchat at a time like this?

I said nothing to her, since I was busy concentrating on my terror, the vibration of my seat, and the roar of the jet. After she glared at me for a full minute, I asked, "Why do you say I remind you of Eeyore?"

"You're wearing Eeyore clothes, and it's almost spring where we're going," she singsonged as if she couldn't imagine anyone so ill-informed.

I'd forgotten. If it's nearing autumn in America it's almost springtime in Australia. I'd barely thought of it. Perhaps the girl was right about my connection to Eeyore. Wait a minute. Did Eeyore even wear clothes?

"Just so ya know . . . taking off and landing are the two most treach—"

"Do you mean treacherous?"

"Yeah. That's it. Those are the two most treach-er-ous parts of the flight." The girl wiggled her eyebrows while continuing to thrash on the wad of gum. "If we were going to die, it would have been back there. Of course, we could also crash on landing."

"Good to know. Thanks." I continued to grip the armrests since I was somehow convinced that my gesture helped the pilots keep the plane in the air.

"Just so ya know, I'm Jenny." The girl held out her hand. "What's your name?"

"Mrs. Winter." I let go of one of the armrests to shake her hand. "You may call me Lily."

"So, why was it so important for you to get on this flight?" The dainty psychiatrist turned her big, round eyes at me again. "Talking about it might help."

"Oh it's a very long tale of woe. I'd hate to bore you."

"Hey, what else have we got to do? It's better than thinking about our plane catching fire and bashing into the sea." Her finger made a little nosedive into her palm.

Cute. "True." But I feared the telling of my story would be my undoing. Where could I begin, anyway? Maybe with the visit I'd had with my mother. "Are you sure you want to hear this?"

She nodded her head with wild abandon.

"Well, okay. My dark story starts with a recent visit I made to my mother's house. It'd been ten years since the last time I'd seen my mother."

Jenny pursed her lips. "Nobody does that. Everybody has to see their mom, right?"

"Well, it certainly wasn't my choice. But when I got to my mother's house, the visit turned out to be as shocking as sticking my finger into a light socket." I frowned. "Don't ever do that, by the way."

"I know." Jenny rolled her eyes. "I'm not a *child*."

"Right. Okay. Well, in my story I also meet a woman named Dragan."

She giggled. "Sounds like dragon."

"True. Dragan was my mother's housekeeper, and believe me, her name fit her well."

Jenny sat up poised, resting her cheek on her index finger. "I wanna know more." She smacked her gum, waiting for me to go on.

"All right." *Lord, be with me.* I rested my head back on the seat, inviting the memory of that infamous day into my life.

First a jumbled mess of sensations trickled in, making me shud-
der. Then mist burned my eyes, thinking of Mother's notorious secret and a lifetime of deception. The smarmy residue from being in
her house stole over me like a dark slithering fog. Soon that day—
the one that changed my life—began to unfold in my mind, so
intensely that the remembering and the telling of my story became
one and the same. . . .

CHAPTER *two*

Standing at my mother's front door, the seconds ticked by like a hundred frenzied clocks. I glanced around the old place, trying to ignore the negative self-talk in my head and Houston's sweltering August heat, but it was no use. I'd already surrendered to both.

The old plantation-style house still looked the same—its pillars like guards and its darkened windows like eyes that always stared at me without really seeing. Hmm. Suddenly, empty nest with my Julie off in college felt lonelier than ever.

More seconds passed. Mother didn't seem to be at home. Guess my thirty-minute drive across the city was in vain. But maybe that was best. It had been ten years, after all, and ten years was enough time for a goodbye to harden into something permanent. After hearing my pastor's stirring message on reconciliation I had vowed to reach out to my mother—even though she didn't want it—not just for my sake, but for Julie's sake. For now, though, I'd have to let go of my promise.

As I turned to leave, a deadbolt unlocked behind me. Oh, no. The front door moaned its way open as if wailing over my arrival. I hugged myself.

A stranger stood in the doorway, looking as lost as I felt. "May I help you?"

"Does Iris Gray still live here?" My voice made a flutter. "I'm her daughter."

The woman adjusted her red-rimmed glasses and blinked like the slow shutter speed on a camera. "But Mrs. Gray doesn't have any children."

"I'm afraid she does." I smoothed my dark pantsuit. "I'm Lily Winter . . . her only child."

"I'm Mrs. Dragan Humphreys."

What an odd name. Sounded Hungarian or something. The woman wore a faded Hawaiian muumuu, and her hair looked like a tossed salad, which gave her a bedraggled air. As my gaze wandered downward, I saw that she wore tattered red flip-flops too. Well, at least they matched her red-rimmed glasses.

"Your mother never mentioned you." The woman sort of impaled me with her words.

❦

"What? Wait." Jenny suddenly interrupted my story, waving her hands. "What did that dragon woman mean? Your mother *never* talked about you?" My tiny flying companion looked at me with her hand over her gaping mouth.

"I know. Hard to imagine. Even with our estrangement, it is shocking that my mother never mentioned anything about me."

The girl took my hand and squeezed. "You poor thing."

Where did Jenny come from anyway? So much sensitivity in such a little package.

"Is that why you're going to Australia? You're running away from home?"

"No, adults don't run away from home." Although maybe she had a point.

"It's a pretty good story so far. Does it have a happy ending?"

"I don't know." I sighed. "I'm still living the story."

"Oh, yeah." Jenny leaned toward me and drummed her fingers on the arm of the seat. "I'm not sleepy yet, so maybe you better tell me some more."

"All right.

"My mother's housekeeper, Dragan, pulled her glasses down to the tip of her nose. 'I guess I can see the resemblance,' she said to me. 'You have the same gray eyes as your mother and that sad Mona Lisa smile.'

"I could suddenly see the woman's eyes more clearly now. You'll like this part, Jenny. Dragan's eyes were like pale marbles. But one orb appeared slightly different from the other."

Jenny leaned into the aisle. "Oww, that's pretty creepy. Keep going."

"Yeah, well, it made me uneasy trying to figure out the colors and which eye to look at. Finally, I just asked the woman, 'Is my mother at home?'"

❧❦❧

"She's in the study." Dragan paused and then opened the door wider.

I stepped inside. "So, are you my mother's housekeeper?"

"Yes and no." Dragan closed the door behind us. "Your mother and I have a special arrangement." She placed her palms together, prayer-like. "I know how unorthodox this might sound, but Mrs. Gray pays me to be her friend."

Normally I would have laughed at such a bizarre comment, but being in my mother's house kept my bursts of emotion in check. "Oh? I see." Most normal people wouldn't be able to imagine hiring a stranger to be one's friend—and yet in my mother's case it was plausible. She'd always needed a friend more than a daughter.

Dragan seemed to study me for a reaction.

I smiled convincingly and trudged behind her toward the study. A trace of alcohol swirled in her wake, and when she glanced back at me, I saw the tapering of her eyelids.

Our footsteps clacked and flopped across the marble floor, making strange echoing rhythms through the entry. Even though I'd grown up in the house, I'd only visited the study occasionally. It had been my mother's sanctuary, a place off-limits to animals and children. A place she retreated to when she could no longer tolerate the world. Or me. But perhaps my mother had softened over the years and the tendrils of compassion had attached themselves to her heart.

Dragan opened the door to the study and then, with the cadence of crisp snaps, she flip-flopped away down the hall. I tiptoed through the doorway, and all my good intentions threatened to scamper away like scared little mice.

I paused to get my bearings. The study looked the same—paneled walls accented with wainscoting, shelves of books, and an eclectic array of French Provincial furnishings. The afternoon light made phantoms on the walls, and like an enchantment, a grim and lonely feel still shadowed the place. Musty odors completed the overall anti-festive ambiance. I swallowed a chuckle and then hesitated mid-stride like characters do in cartoons, knowing that my mother's disposition was as stagnant as her surroundings.

"I could hear your whispers through the vents . . . you and Mrs. Humphreys," my mother said from behind one of the high-back chairs.

Her face was hidden from view, but the voice belonged to my mother. It was raspier than I'd remembered, but the brusque tenor sounded the same as a decade before. Suddenly my bones felt incapable of holding me up. I sensed it then—our meeting would be a farce, but without the comedy.

"What are you doing back there? Come here. I want to have a look at you," came the voice.

I walked over to the chair opposite from my mother and sat down. I looked at my hands; they'd taken on a life of their own, strangling each other until they throbbed. "Hi, Mother. It's been a long time."

"Let's see you. Your complexion has improved, and your long hair isn't so straggly. But you're still thin and pale. But of course, all that dark clothing you're wearing makes the pallor more pronounced. In fact, you look ill. My doctors say I have a weakened immune system, so if you think—"

"I'm not sick." I looked up at her. Mother's eyes had faded some, but they were still as intense as ever. Streaks of iron gray ran through her dark hair, so many, in fact, that it was hard to know which color was more dominant, but the whole bundle was drawn up into a painful-looking bun. Her nose appeared more angled, and with her piercing stare, the whole effect was one of a fearsome eagle studying its prey.

My body shriveled like dried fruit in the hot sun. I felt desperate, almost reckless in my hopes for a chance to reconnect with my mother. I huddled down onto the chair, gripped the cushions, and waited for the judge's decree.

"I've been expecting you." My mother lifted a tiny glass of clear liquid—most likely schnapps—to her lips.

"You have?" I smiled, glad for any sign of goodwill.

Her eye twitched. "Well, let me see if I can guess why you've come. Your daughter has gone off to college, and you're feeling useless. Empty nest is eating at you. And so you thought you'd visit your old mother. See if we couldn't be pals."

Mother either talked in riddles or cut to the chase. "Yes, some of that is true, but I hoped—"

"I heard about your husband's death a year ago. My gout kept me from the funeral. But I'm sure I wasn't missed."

"Of course you were missed."

"Bah. If you're going to lie, girl, learn to do it with style or not bother." She took another sip from her glass.

Talking my mother out of one of her certainties was as easy as getting an amendment to the Constitution. So I let it go.

"Tell me again . . . your husband . . . what did he die of?"

"Richard died of a heart attack."

Mother tucked the corners of her dress under her legs and then smoothed the fabric, which looked a lot like wall tapestry. "Hmm. You should have fed him a healthier diet. Less junk food . . . more prunes."

A wall clock chimed, and I jumped.

CHAPTER
three

"**So, now that your daughter** has gone away, and your spouse is dead, what are you going to do with your life? You're thirty-nine years old, alone, with no promising future. You probably still live in that shabby little house your husband left you." Mother shook her head. "You never did use your expensive education for a real career. You just wanted to marry and have a *child*."

I sighed. "I don't know what God has planned for me. Not yet anyway."

"Bah. Leave God out of this. You're old enough to make your own plans." She set her glass down and pulled her afghan up over her knees.

I tried to batten down the hatches of my emotions, but I'd been born too flimsy to stand up to my mother's hurricane-force blows. I could no longer look at my mother, so I stared out the window into the solarium. A wooden table sat in the center of the glassed-in room, covered with botany journals, microscopes, and sketches of flower parts. There would also be small instruments of torture, for dissecting. With all her multiple gardens, no flowers were ever displayed in the house for their beauty. "Have you made any new discoveries with your flowers?"

"You mean angiosperms. No, nothing new there, but I did recently purchase a night-blooming Cereus cactus. Amazing specimen. It blooms just once a year, you know, and if you miss your one chance . . . well, now that would be a real loss. Wouldn't it?"

Irony had more weight than I could carry. My mother's worship of flowers was never-ending, probably because they had no hearts. No sins to number. Or remember. I fingered my charm bracelet to remind me that life outside her walls was still good—that the sun still rose in the morning and my darling daughter, Julie, still loved me.

"I see you fidgeting with some trinket on your wrist. What is it?"

"Julie gave me this bracelet when she left for college recently. Each of the tiny silver charms represents our favorite things, like her rollerblading or my reading. And—"

"Yes, well, I'm sure." My mother gave a one-finger pat, pat, pat on the chair, which was meant to silence me as if I were her trained poodle. I'd never forgotten that gesture. My heart constricted, no longer wanting to beat, but it kept on pounding just the same.

"Well, let's have a look at it." She motioned to my wrist. "The bauble."

I removed the bracelet, handed it to my mother, and immediately started picking at my fingers, a habit I must have started in the cradle.

The hinges on the study door creaked, and I glanced back. The door was ajar, but perhaps I'd left it that way. Or was Dragan eavesdropping just outside the door? Hmm. I turned my attention back to my mother.

She put on her reading glasses and rolled the bracelet around in her hand. "So, little Julie's all grown up."

Was this the moment I'd waited for? I gave myself the luxury of hope. "Julie plays the guitar and the piano, and she sings like an angel in church. She's grown up so beautiful and wise and funny too. She's getting a music degree at Sam Houston State University, so she's about an hour drive from Houston. I miss her, even though she's not that far away. Mother, you would love her. Maybe I could have her come visit you. Julie has missed having a grandmother in her life. She needs you. We both need you and love you and—"

"I don't think so." My mother closed her hand around the jewelry.

"I would like for you to keep the bracelet as a gift." I hadn't planned on giving away my greatest earthly treasure, but I really did want my mother's love—her understanding. Her "knowing" of me and my Julie. Life seemed to be an unfinished puzzle without it.

My mother clutched the bracelet to her heart as if she'd just found a misplaced heirloom, and then she set it on the coffee table between us. "Please take it back. We both know that the bracelet comes with strings. You want me to have a relationship with your daughter."

"But she's your granddaughter. Doesn't it feel unnatural not to be a part of her life?" Not to be a part of my life? What would it take for her to see me, love me? How long could I survive such an onslaught of rejection? Guess that was one of the reasons I'd disappeared from her life for so long.

"What are you insinuating? That I'm heartless?" My mother raised an eyebrow. "So, is this the real reason you came today? To call me names?"

The anticipation of good things faded. "I meant well." Some people loved the theater, but Mother didn't. She hated displays of emotion, which were sentiments for the meek in spirit she'd say— fools who had no business inheriting the earth.

"I don't appreciate your gift. You should have brought me some more schnapps instead. It has such purifying qualities."

I retrieved the bracelet and ground my nails into my palms, trying not to cry. It was no use, though. Tears splashed onto my lashes anyway.

"Are you trying to manipulate me with your tears?" I didn't answer her. What was the point? I instead walked over to the large window that overlooked my mother's solarium. Then I placed my palm on the pane, letting the warmth from the glass seep into my skin. I left my hand there. I didn't know why exactly. It was a windowpane ritual I'd performed my whole life as if I'd wanted to connect with something but didn't know what it was.

❧❧❧

"Sit down." Her tone became a hiss.

If I returned to my seat I was bound to dislike myself for a long time to come. Nevertheless, I surrendered to the force—my mother—and sat on my trembling hands.

"You, Lily, are just like your father . . . an unpredictable ocean. No matter how calm the water is on the surface, the waves come to shore full of bluster and drama. And to tell you the truth, I've never felt at peace near the ocean."

"I see." I caught her meaning, and I felt my insides curdle like sour milk. I was officially mutating into a child again. "I know I didn't turn out to be the daughter you hoped for, but why do you hate me so much?"

"Hate? Why do you always have to pick the most potent spice in the rack when a little salt will do? That is so Lily. What do they call it these days? A drama queen." Then she closed her eyes—something my mother always did to be rid of me. "And . . . you still look just like her," she said in the barest whisper. "Just like her."

"I look like whom, Mother?" Who could she mean? Whoever it was, the person seemed important.

And then I noticed something just below my right hand—a small decorative glass dome sitting on the table. Just under the clear glass were two seeds. Nothing more. So tiny. Were they mustard seeds? How peculiar. Would the mysteries never end? I touched the dome and then pulled back. My thumbprint remained on the surface of the glass. Is that all I would leave in this house? *God help me.* If there wasn't going to be any affection between us, maybe there could be a connection, no matter how small. I would try again, for Julie's sake. "I look like whom, Mother?"

Mother's eyes drifted open. "Her name is Camille Violet Daniels."

"Is she the woman I look like? Who is she? Is she still alive?"

My mother slumped in her chair, the color draining from her face. "Yes, she's still alive."

"What's the matter?" I leaned forward, thinking I might need to call 911.

"Maybe it's time." A bit of drool dribbled out of the corner of my mother's mouth, and she daubed at it with her hand. She gazed off into the solarium still murmuring, "Maybe it is time." She gripped the arm of her chair until her knuckles went ashen. "I'll answer your question. Camille Violet Daniels is your identical twin. She is your sister."

"My sister. An identical twin? Is it true? How could it be?"

"It's true."

The moment turned fantastical as if I were Alice, falling down the rabbit hole. "But why don't I remember her?"

Mother took on a faraway gaze, but then suddenly her attention snapped back to the room. "Because you were only one year old at the time when she was taken from me."

"Taken? But who would do such a thing? Where is she?"

Mother closed her hand around the doily on the armrest and pulverized it in her knotted fingers. "That is one of the reasons I never told you. I feared this infernal avalanche of questions."

I tried to compose myself. If I wanted to know more I'd need to proceed with caution. To upset Mother now meant severing any chance of knowing how to find my sister. So, her name was Camille Violet. How beautiful. She'd been given a floral name too. And perhaps she'd gotten married, since her last name was Daniels. I thought of all the nieces and nephews and how Julie would love to have cousins. Perhaps they all lived nearby. "If I have a sister who's still alive I want to meet her." I would want to know her, welcome her back to the family.

"I doubt there's any chance of finding her." Mother drank the last of her schnapps but continued to hold the empty glass as if it were full. "Camille lives in Melbourne, Australia."

Australia? "How did she end up so far away? Are you sure?"

"I received a card from her six months ago. There was no return address, but in her brief note she mentioned her name, the country and city where she lived, and the news that she was well. She also mentioned that she attends St. Paul's Cathedral. So apparently she's wrapped up in the same spiritual nonsense you are."

Australia. The word echoed in my mind. Then a distressing dimension adhered to the first. In order for me to find my sister, I'd have to fly—something I feared. I'd barely traveled out of Houston while Julie was growing up, and certainly hadn't flown to the other side of the earth. Camille might as well live on the moon. How would I ever be able to meet her?

"All right. You know the truth." Mother squeezed her eyes shut again, but this time a small amount of moisture escaped the corner of her eye. There was so much about Mother I still didn't know. She remained the island, and I the tiny boat, ever circling, but never finding an inlet.

"But you haven't told me the reason she lives so far away."

Her eyes blinked open. "I said that is *all.*" She reached for her crystal bell and gave it a jangle. "Dragan will see you to the door."

"But don't you care that I need to know—"

"Is *cuma liom!*" she said.

I wasn't sure what it meant, but Mother always broke into Gaelic when she really got her Irish dander up. And that was it; the audience with my mother came to a halt. I rose from the chair, knowing that no temptation, no enticement would ever get her to change her mind, so I was left holding what she called my infernal avalanche of questions. I had a sister, a twin, and if anyone were going to find her it'd have to be me.

"Goodbye, Mother." I stepped out of the room with what crumbs of dignity I had left.

Dragan didn't show me to the door, but then I hadn't expected her to.

Questions flowed like rain on a dry riverbed. Why had I been separated from my sister? And why was it a secret? Why were we denied the chance to grow up together? Having an identical twin sister to play with, a bosom friend, would have been amazing fun. Even being teased about wearing the same clothes and knowing that people would constantly get us confused sounded like delight. No doubt a thousand whys were going to plague me, and yet just to know I had a sister, an identical twin, made me feel completed in some way. Whole and connected.

I shut the front door and breathed in the air, so light and clean, so unlike the oppressive atmosphere inside the Gray mansion. I always became a different person inside her house, all my wit and courage dissolving as if dipped in a vial of toxic fluids—the kind my mother used in her Frankenstein-esque floral experiments. Except for when Julie was little, she hadn't seen me under the influence of my Mother. Perhaps she would have thought I'd disgraced myself with excessive groveling.

I headed to my car with a lilt in my step and a vow in my heart that even if the quest to find my sister took me to the other side of the world, I would find what my mother had hidden from me all these decades.

Yes, I would find Camille Violet Daniels, even if it were the last thing on earth I did!

❧❧

"And so, Jenny, that's how I came to be sitting in this seat and flying on this plane all around the world." I flopped back in my seat, exhausted from the remembering and the telling of it all. I looked over at her little face, wondering what profound words she would cook up this time. Jenny yawned. "Wow, your mom is kind of weird."

I chuckled.

"Your story is sad-happy like having to eat broccoli before you can get to the chocolate pudding."

"Yeah, maybe a little."

"I hope you find your sister. I always wanted one."

"Me too."

Her eyes fluttered shut for a second.

I grinned. "You're looking a little sleepy."

"How can you tell?"

I cocked my head at her. "Classic symptoms."

"Good one." She grinned. "Yeah, I'm going to sleep now." She pulled the gum out of her mouth and held it out to me.

I automatically reached out my hand and let Jenny drop her gooey glob of bubble gum into my hand.

Jenny smiled. "Nighty-night. Thanks for telling me about your sister." She pushed on her nose, making a little piggy face, and then snorted. "I guess you aren't really running away, after all."

"Good night." I had no idea in the world why I accepted used gum from a stranger in my clean hand, except that Julie used to pass me her gum when she was little. And I'd always hold out my hand in the same way. Reflex, I guess, and, well, wishful dreaming that it had been Julie.

Jenny's abrupt exit from our little exchange startled me. "Good night," I whispered to her again. "Sweet dreams." I was sorry to see her snuggle down onto her stack of Piglet pillows. Her chatter had kept me distracted, and even enchanted. I placed her gum into a tissue and wiped off my hand.

Now I would be alone with my thoughts. As scary as it felt to look outside, I scooted over to the window seat and lifted the cover on the porthole. Wispy clouds whirled by as if the plane were spinning inside a cotton candy machine. Far below, America's patchwork of farms became visible here and there.

Soon the Pacific Ocean would heave and swell beneath me as if it were the great unknown, yet somehow I wasn't as frightened at the prospect as I had been. I doubted I'd ever go to sleep, but maybe I could read a novel. Perhaps my journey wouldn't be quite the hardship I'd imagined. Maybe Mother was right; I always picked the most potent spice in the rack when a little salt would do.

❧❧❧

Twenty-two hours later, after a tedious layover in LA, two sleeping pills that worked like espresso, more plane crash statistics from Jenny, a stiff neck, drool, a flight that lasted as long as the breeding cycle of small marine creatures, I finally landed at the Melbourne airport. Not well, but alive.

Then after dragging myself through immigration, baggage claim, and customs I hailed a cab. My driver turned out to be Greek and proud enough of his heritage to give me all the details as we careened to and fro along the Tullamarine Freeway. The taxi smelled of cigars and baklava, and everything including the man's laugh had a Greek accent.

"Many, many people here are Greek. So, where is home for you?" the man asked.

"Texas."

"Ahh. I love Texas. John Wayne is my favorite actor." He exploded with laughter.

I wasn't exactly sure how John Wayne was connected to Texas, but the man seemed friendly enough, and he got me to my hotel without any real damage to me or the luggage.

Later I checked into the River Loft Hotel and Apartments, and plunked myself down on the bed. The room looked clean and tidy, but maybe a little too barren for my taste, since it once again reminded me of my solitary life, without Julie and without a husband. I stared at my hands; they were cradling each other as if they were the hands of two lovers, holding each other. It's probably something Eeyore would do if he didn't have hooves. I laughed. Jenny would have liked that one.

Moving on. Someone at the front desk had said that St. Paul's Cathedral was just across the river. Sounded so easy, but what if my sister no longer attended there? What if it were the last clue in finding Camille? But if she did go to church there, someone would have information. Where she worked. Where she lived. Her family.

Every pore of me wanted to sleep, but a flight attendant had warned me about jet lag—to stay awake until night, to trick my body into a new rhythm. And really, I didn't want to wait to find my sister. No matter the level of exhaustion, I wanted to start the search right away. I changed into black slacks and a black silk shirt—apparently for now, black was the color of my life—and freshened up a bit. I wished now I hadn't brought so many dark outfits.

Once outside I felt revived again, although when a cloud shadowed the sun the breeze turned surly right away. What had someone warned me about on the plane—four seasons in a day? I untied my windbreaker from my waist, slipped it on, and then gazed down at the Venetian-style boats floating on the Yarra River. Outdoor cafés lined the streets, and people chatted as they sipped coffee. Pigeons took advantage of the free comestibles, and the sounds of live music and performers filled the streets. The city was alive with energy, and it was hard to imagine that Lily Winter could be a part of it.

I joined the throngs of people that streamed over the bridge like the very river that flowed beneath us. Then I followed the crowds through the tunnel and up onto the other side. The people encircling me were foreigners who appeared to be from all over the world. Standing there, taking it in, I had never felt so alone and yet so invigorated in my life.

After the light turned green, I crossed Flinders Street and headed east, trying to follow the directions from the hotel's front desk. I walked awhile, admiring everything along the way—the unique dress shops, the hustle-bustle of shoppers, the Flinders Street Station, and the smells of bakery goods and open-air markets.

When I looked up, suddenly it was there before me—the spires of St. Paul's. The cathedral rose in front of me, grand and majestic, its pinnacles reaching toward the heavens as if they were hands raised in praise. I felt dwarfed in my humanness, but not dispirited.

I wanted to shout to the bustling crowd, "Don't you see it? How can you not be in awe?"

This holy place would surely lead me to my sister. My pace sped up until I broke into a run and then raced up the concrete steps of the church. Someone opened the doors, and I breezed into the narthex. Off to the right was a cozy gift shop, and behind the counter stood an elderly woman who seemed happy to see me. I stopped to ask her the question I'd been practicing in my head for hours. "Hi. My name is Lily Winter. I've come all the way from Texas to find my sister. I heard she attends church here. Her name is Camille Daniels. Do you happen to know her?"

CHAPTER
five

The woman blinked, her face a parade of bemused expressions, and then said, "I've never heard of her before."

My spirit spiraled into an abyss I'd reserved just for this moment. "Really?"

"Let me ask Rowan. He's been here a lot longer, and he knows most of the members. Yeah."

"Thank you so much." I clung to the slender cord of hope she handed me, but knew it could be cut off easily with a shake of Rowan's head.

The woman smiled and headed to the back room.

In the meantime, I turned and glanced around the church, trying to revel in the majesty—the gothic archways of stone that stood like great sentinels of the faith, the old smells that whispered of ancient mysteries, the stained-glass windows lit with sun, and the holy awe of wonder it all instilled. But I would have to put off my awe and explorations for another day. In the meantime I counted the seconds until a man named Rowan would come out of the back room. Perhaps he would do no more than smile and wish me "G'day."

My foot woodpecker-tapped on the floor. The back room couldn't be that large. Had she forgotten about me? *Oh, please, God, let a man named Rowan know my sister.*

After waiting an eternity—which may have been encapsulated into a minute or two—an aged-looking gentleman, wearing a cardigan, a bowtie, and a benevolent expression, hobbled out of the back room. "Joyce told me you've come all the way from Texas to find your sister."

"Yes. Her name is Camille Violet Daniels, and she attends here."

The light in Rowan's eyes dimmed under his bushy brows. "I'm so sorry. I can't think of anyone by that name."

Rowan had no idea he'd just severed my lifeline. "Actually, she's my identical twin, so maybe you've seen someone who looks a little like me, or maybe a lot."

The older man studied me through watery eyes. "I hate to make you sad by saying this, but your face doesn't ring any bells."

"I don't know where else to go." I realized how pathetic I sounded. "This was my only solid clue in finding her."

Rowan tugged on his bowtie. "Well, I could check the records just to make sure. I don't know everyone who attends here. But I'm not able to do it right now. Perhaps in the arvo . . . uh, afternoon. Yeah."

"Yes, of course." I reached out and touched the sleeve of his sweater. "Thank you for your kindness." I wanted to ask him what was so pressing that he couldn't have a quick peek right this minute, but I didn't want to be rude. "If you come across anything at all I'll be here for three weeks. Here's my cell number and my sister's name." I handed Rowan the slip of paper with all my information.

A sign on the counter, publicizing one of their services, caught my attention. Evensong—perhaps I could attend at some point. I had never been Anglican, so I didn't know what the word *evensong* meant, but it seemed as pleasant as a spring breeze, and because my sister may have had some connection with the church I wanted to experience the worship she'd known here. I would participate in evensong and I would imagine where she always sat and sang or took communion or read from the prayer book.

Rowan raised his hand. "You never did say how you and your twin got separated."

"I don't know really. My mother didn't explain it to me." I squeezed back the tears, determined not to shed a single drop until I was on my way.

"Oh?" He scratched his head.

"Thank you again." I left Rowan standing there and fled out the door before he could ask any more questions.

I felt a need to walk off my disappointment, and the folks at the hotel had mentioned a garden not far from the cathedral. As wearied as I felt I couldn't seem to slow down. I kept up my brisk pace in the direction of the gardens, crossing the Yarra River again and the busy streets. The church bells rang out in the distance. Perhaps it was a reminder for me not to give up.

I passed a group of men playing the bagpipes of all things, a museum on the other side of the street, and then I came to a sign that read The Royal Botanic Gardens. I slowed my stride to an amble as I gazed around. The city's playground of greenery turned out to be grand, full of exotic trees and flora unknown to me. I'd caught the gardens in the midst of embracing spring and every shade of heaven.

A pathway curved its way here and there through gasping beauty. My favorite—eucalyptus trees—grew everywhere. The leaves chattered like children. I had no idea what they were saying; I just breathed in their scent and strolled on. Julie would have loved these gardens. I fingered the bracelet she'd given me and wondered what she was doing. Was she eating enough? Had she made college friends yet? Did she miss me as much as I missed her? I hoped not, since I didn't want her to live like I had—as if her wings were clipped.

The wound of my lonesomeness, though, felt gaping and ready for more salt, and I was usually the person with the shaker who could do the job thoroughly. I couldn't imagine anything softening the pain, except maybe finding my sister. And yet now my hope dangled on a rope so thin it felt like a worn thread.

A bird let out a mad shriek in a nearby tree, startling me, and then a young woman brushed by me, wearing a balloon-bottom skirt, fishnet hose, and a floppy hat. Interesting attire. I imagined myself in an outfit like that and chuckled.

After I passed another flower-laden hedge of yellow, a lake came into view with a vast lawn in the foreground. The pond glistened like diamonds strewn on the water, and swans—black and sinuous-looking—glided across the surface as if they were duchesses in search of their tiaras. People were scattered like random bits of confetti on the green, where they played and chatted and soaked up the sun. And in the distance a couple decked out in their wedding clothes posed for cameras. Lovely.

I removed my jacket and sat down on one of the wooden benches. The tears I'd saved were on the verge of spilling over, but instead of weeping I opened my purse and pulled out a bag of marshmallows. On a defiant whim I stuffed a big puffy confection into each cheek. Pillows of sugar. Ahh. They were sweet and soft and amiable, and all the things that empty nest was not. Of course, if I kept eating wads of them I'd eventually resemble one. For some reason that thought opened the floodgates, so as I chewed, tears streamed down my full cheeks. I lived a sad little life that no longer made sense. What was I doing here? Was I on a fool's errand?

"Want to talk about it?" someone said from behind me.

I jumped at the male voice near my ear and whirled around to see who spoke with such familiarity. "Excuse me?" My voice got muffled through the sugary fluff.

"My friends say I'm a good listener. Yeah." The man sat down on the other end of the bench even though the park appeared to be full of empty spots. Then he set some sort of music case down on the seat between us.

I finished chewing. "You're a stranger, so—"

"And your mum told you never to talk to strangers." He gave me a decisive nod. "Good advice, Love."

The man probably expected me to grin over his Aussie endearment, but I daubed at my eyes and blew my nose instead. The stranger didn't appear to be hideous, now that I'd had a chance to give him the once-over. He seemed to be early forty-ish, and he had a nebulously attractive thing going—sort of an older James McAvoy look with a scruffy five-o'clock shadow. Not too bad. But I was in no mood for banter. "I'm not used to perfect strangers being so familiar."

"Well, I've never been called perfect before, so I thank you."

I frowned. How could he possibly think that was funny? Hmm. I was a breath away from getting up, but before I left he needed a lesson in manners. "If a woman looks sad and she's sitting by herself, conventional wisdom says you should walk on by because she wants to be alone with her thoughts."

"Yes, true, but I'm not all that conventional." He rested back on the bench with a lounging manner and then crossed his legs at the ankles.

Still I didn't gift him with my smile, since it was obvious that he'd benefit more from a good smack on the head. Being the fine Christian woman that I was, though, I restrained myself.

I glanced at him out of the corner of my eye again. Even though he looked wrinkly, his shirt and slacks weren't too shabby. Maybe I'd stay for a moment longer. It was the first real conversation I'd had with an Australian man, so I hated to get a dull view of the male population right off. "You're not representing your Aussie countrymen very well."

"You're American, aren't you? Guessing from the accent, you're from Texas. You're on your own, but you're not here on holiday. Something else entirely has brought you to Melbourne. Yeah."

"Yes, it is something else entirely . . . and it's entirely none of your business." Like the box turtles I befriended as a child, I pulled back inside my armor.

"Maybe it would help my cause if I introduced myself. I'm Marcus Averill. Although some people around here tend to call me Avers. Aussies like to shorten things up."

The only thing that needed shortening was the conversation, but since I didn't want to be thought of as a rude American, I shook his hand. "I'm Lily Winter."

"Lovely name. Yeah. By the way, the lily is an emblem of beauty and virtue."

"Thank you." I cleared my throat from all the sticky sugar. "You didn't pronounce the city as Mel-born like I did. Why is that?"

"Because here we say Mel-bun, not Mel-born."

"I've noticed that people pronounce things differently, especially the word *yeah*."

"True. It's like Aussies invented some new vowels just for that one word."

Exactly.

He gazed over the gardens. "Soon the park will be in full bloom. You'll see colors that even artists have trouble re-creating on their canvas."

"Oh?"

"You know, every winter it's hard to imagine how it will be . . . all those tightly closed buds just waiting for a little spring. And a bit of love and attention."

Time to amend the conversation. "So, what are those yellow flowering trees I saw all along the freeways? They're everywhere. I saw one of the blooms up close, and it made me think of tiny fuzzy tennis balls."

Marcus grinned. "It's the wattle, the national flower. In fact, that's where we get the national colors . . . green and gold."

"Oh." I loosened the grip on my purse. "You said you had a cause. What did you mean?"

"Well, it was my personal campaign to meet you."

"Oh." Well, at least he seemed consistent in his audacity. "So, I'm wondering . . . are all Australian men so forward and rude?"

"I reckon. Truthfully, they can be a bit rough around the edges sometimes, although you'll see more of that in the bush than in the city. But then I'm not from Australia. Or as they say here . . . Stralia."

"If you're not from here, where are you from?"

"Texas."

"You're kidding. Right?"

"Born in Dallas." He stared up at the sky as if there were some revelation written there. "Just look at those clouds off to the west . . . a wash of Prussian blue near the horizon. It's the color of deep twilight or . . . the color of a storm brewing."

For a moment I saw the layers of blue and coasted with my own thoughts. Before I could catch myself, I murmured, "I wonder what's just beyond the horizon."

"Well," Marcus said. "We'll just have to use our imaginations . . . won't we?"

Back to reality, I pushed on past the weather report. "You don't seem to have any Texas accent."

"Pity, isn't it?" He looked at me over nonexistent glasses.

That time a smile crept out before I could filter it. Now he'd made me curious, so I set my purse down and stayed a bit longer to ask, "So, why Australia?"

"I could ask you the same thing. Texas is on the other side of the world. Not a random choice to come here."

I looked at my hands, which had made a limp little vessel in my lap. "I'm here to find someone." The last thing I'd planned to do was tell this Marcus fellow my business, and yet I did anyway. It must have been the solitude talking. And he could probably tell. I wore my lonesomeness as if it were Quasimodo's hump.

"I honestly wouldn't have guessed that one."

Marcus fingered the mysterious case sitting between us, so I thought I might toss him a friendly bone of repartee. "So, what's in the case?"

He touched the container with affection. "The Great Highland Bagpipe. It's broken at the moment. Some things aren't easy to mend, but when they're precious enough, it's worth the effort." Marcus smiled.

The man was a walking innuendo. "So, you're a bagpiper?"

"Among other things. But it's only a hobby."

Hobby. The word seemed as foreign as the place I sat. I didn't have any pastime interests, didn't bother cultivating them. Julie had been so much a part of my life that I'd never taken the time for them. They'd always seemed pointless, or were they merely ill-defined like a blurry photograph? "You have to know yourself to have hobbies...be a friend to yourself," I let slip out.

"Yes. Yes, you do." He rested his arm over the back of the bench and leaned toward me. "I have an idea. Maybe I can assist you in your search. The person you're looking for."

I thought for a moment, not wanting to throw away any chance for help, especially if it were divinely sent, but I also didn't want to engage the services of someone who seemed what my mother would call half-baked. Or worse. "I don't know you, so, I'm not—"

"But if you had dinner with me tonight that would no longer be true. Hey, I know a place that has kangaroo on the barbie. You haven't lived until you've tried it."

CHAPTER
six

The little bit of child left inside me cringed at the thought. "It's a nice offer, sort of, except I can't imagine eating Roo."

"Who?"

"You know, Roo from Pooh . . . never mind." I suddenly had serious doubts about a man who'd never heard of Roo, but since he had a twinkle in his eye he may have just been kidding me. Marcus would be an interesting book to read if you didn't mind starting from the back. "Thank you again, but I'm not here to date. I'm here to find my sister."

"Aha. Now we're getting somewhere. I'm sure I can help. I have a laptop." He crossed his arms, looking smug.

"I do too."

"But I'm familiar with Melbourne, so you could move faster with my help. Remember, a friend in a foreign land is better than a jewel in your shield."

I frowned, puzzled. "Is that from Proverbs?"

"No, I call them Marcus-ites. You know, bits of wisdom assembled from all the rocks in my head."

I grinned.

"I'm sure you don't have an infinite amount of time here. You probably have to get back to your job in Texas. I'll bet you do something inspiring."

At first I thought he was being sarcastic, but his expression looked so earnest, I replied, "I'm an executive secretary for an oil company. I've never heard anyone refer to what I do as inspiring." In fact, I hadn't had one good day there in years, let alone an inspiring one. "But don't you have to get back to work?"

"I'm between jobs."

When he wasn't looking I scooted to the edge of the bench. "So what are you, a bum?" *Hence the rumpled clothes.* My snippy retorts were building. Perhaps jet lag was creeping up on me. Maybe I just needed to eat something besides marshmallows.

Marcus winced, but didn't look offended. "Well, I like calling myself an entrepreneur with limited prospects . . . at the moment. But you haven't insulted me. So, no worries."

"I'm not that worried." But he had revved up my curiosity. "So, how do you live then? How would you even pay for my dinner?"

"It sounds boring, but I live on a trust fund among other things." Marcus seemed to gauge my reaction.

"You should get a job. You haven't lived until you've tried it."

I stuffed my marshmallows back into my purse. The last thing I needed was somebody tagging along like some homeless pooch.

Marcus shook his finger at me. "You know, you have a biting wit hiding under all that angst. But sometimes people spend more time hiding than living." He crossed his arms and looked out at the lake.

Humph. "More Marcus-ites?"

"No, Love, just the truth." He grinned. "So, am I getting under your skin?"

"No, but you're getting on my nerves."

Marcus chuckled. "I wasn't quite finished with what I was saying earlier. The trust fund I spoke of was set up with my own money. I don't live off my family's funds in case you were wondering." He scrubbed his knuckles through his short dark hair, which left it even messier than before.

"Oh. I see. Sorry." Guess my mind had run with that one. "So, how could you know I have angst or that I'm hiding anything?"

"Well, aside from the fact that you were weeping when I found you, you're a picker."

I started to argue with him, then looked at my almost bloody fingers, which had yet to heal from the last picking.

"Parrots get that way, only when *they* pick, it's their feathers."

What a sad thought. I twiddled my thumbs. "So what happens to them? You know, to the parrots?"

Marcus looked at me, his eyes full of what looked like regret for bringing up the subject. "Since you enjoy eating soft and sweet things you're going to love lamingtons. Be sure and buy some while you're here."

"What does that have to do—"

"Okay. All right," Marcus erupted. "The whole 'you spend more time hiding than living' thing was a tactless remark. Sometimes I *am* too direct. Too presumptuous. A bit arrogant. Insensitive. And lousy at combing my hair. You're welcome to toss in a few more here. But I promise you, Lily, if you'll go out to dinner with me . . . I'll be fully reformed."

The word *no* felt tantalizing, but something stopped me. "So you'll be fully reformed between now and dinner? Unlikely."

"I attend services at St. Paul's. I do some volunteer work for them too. Surely that puts me in a better light."

"It might count for something if it were true." I did admire a man who gave of his time and talents to the church. Fascinating turn of events, since I could now catch Marcus in his duplicity if he were lying. "I was just over at the church." I arched an eyebrow. "What time is evensong?"

"5:10."

"Lucky guess. You happened to notice the sign as you *loitered* on by."

He slapped his hand over his heart. "Woman, you wound me."

"Okay, one last chance. What's the man's name who works in the gift shop?"

"Mmm." He tapped his chin, frowning. "Not an easy one."

I pretended to pick up my bag as if to leave.

"Rowan," he said, quickly, grinning. "Top bloke."

He must know Rowan, and he was teasing me again. Humph.

"So, does my redemption draweth nigh?"

What if Marcus really could help me find Camille? What if God had sent him? *But, Lord, why couldn't You have sent a servant who was a little less ridiculous?*

"God works in mysterious ways, Love."

I restrained my surprise. "I was just *thinking* about God."

"Well?" His face lit up as if the last of my lingering doubts had been divinely vanquished.

"Real Australian men call women *Love*, but you're from Texas."

He laughed. "I call women *Love*, because it never fails to bring a smile to their faces. Except to yours."

"All right." I took in a deep breath. I would say yes to his dinner invitation just to stop his silly debate. It was like being inside the head of Oscar Wilde.

"All right, what?"

"Dinner. But I'll pick the place, and we'll meet there. That way—"

"That way if my intentions are ungentlemanly you can make a safe exit."

"Exactly. How about The Yarra Bistro." It was a small eatery I'd noticed on my walk to the cathedral. It would do.

"I know where it is . . . Southbank. I'll meet you there at 7:30."

"Six thirty. We Houstonians eat at a civilized hour." I couldn't believe I'd agreed to go out with a stranger—such reckless behavior had never been in my repertoire of conduct. Julie would be appalled. Well, maybe not. She might applaud. She'd always told me to get out more. In fact, she'd been ecstatic when she heard about my trip, and I supposed she would be equally happy that I wasn't spending all my time alone. I glanced over at this James McAvoy look-alike again, still dubious as to why a man, any man, seemed interested in me. I was bound to be as much fun as an IRS audit.

"All right. Six thirty it is." Marcus looked at me, his blue eyes appraising me in a new way. "You know, there's something else about you. More than the attraction I felt when I first saw you."

The statement was so frank and flattering I wanted to blush, but I was too mature for anything so girlish. I doubted my blood vessels could manage such a workout.

"You look familiar to me." Marcus rubbed the stubble growing on his chin. "You do."

"Familiar? What do you mean?" A bud of hope opened itself to me. I'd only told Marcus that I was looking for my sister, not my twin. Had he seen someone who looked like me?

"Well, sometimes I've seen a woman play her flute on the Southbank promenade. She isn't as slender as you are, but her face and raven hair are the same . . . and those gray eyes of hers . . . very much like yours and as memorable as the melodies she plays."

I hurried past his flattery and asked, "So, you really have seen a woman on the streets who looks like me?" Without thinking, I leaned over and tugged on his sleeve. "Please tell me."

Marcus seemed to study my face in a more serious fashion, and then he nodded. "Yes. In fact, you two could be identical twins."

CHAPTER
seven

I sat tucked away in the corner of The Yarra Bistro like a scared little bird in its nest. Story of my life. But the more Marcus's claims about my sister ran through my head, the more I fluffed my feathers. "You two could be identical twins," he'd said of the woman who played her flute on the streets of Melbourne. Could it be Camille? Right after dinner I would start my search along the river walkway—which was the place where Marcus claimed the woman played her flute.

Hmm. I tapped the face of my watch. Marcus was a full fifteen minutes late. Did he forget? Maybe he wasn't coming? Maybe he'd changed his mind about our date. Which would be fine. Absolutely fine. It might be best when all things were considered. And yet Marcus had been the first flare of hope after my first clue had fizzled. Meeting him in the gardens felt ordained. Then again, maybe Marcus was really a plastic worm, and I was the gullible fish. I barely knew the man. Could it be he'd lied to me and no mysterious woman who looked like me played on the streets of Melbourne after all?

Maybe I'd been had.

I fidgeted with my hands, rubbing the faint tan line on my finger where my wedding band had been. The ring now sat in a small box hidden away in my bottom drawer at home—along with my old socks, the ones that had gaping holes but I couldn't throw them away.

Hmm. Back to my Marcus musings. I gave myself the luxury of picking at my fingers as the endless pros and cons battled it out in my head.

Finally my thoughts went weary and landed on something more peaceful—the hemlock tree, which I'd spotted in the botanic gardens. Even though I'd never seen a hemlock tree in Houston, my Nanny Kate had always talked about the species at Christmastime. She'd said the reason the hemlock tree curled at the tippy top was because the trees wanted to discourage people from cutting them down to use as Christmas trees, their logic being that an angel on top would surely look askew if placed on its tilting crown. The silly tale had stayed with me. My personal survival tactics weren't nearly so romantic as the hemlock tree. Strange the things a person thinks of when about to be disappointed by humanity.

By a man named Marcus.

A waitress popped over, refilled my water glass, and asked, "Do you want to go ahead and order?" Her black eyes held a mixture of weariness and kindness.

"Thank you, but no." I placed my hand on the other menu in case she tried to take it. "I'll wait a bit longer. Hope that's okay."

"No worries." With a flip of her long tresses, the waitress headed to another table.

I gazed out the window and, without thinking, touched the glass as if I could draw my sister to me as easily as that gesture. If only. I left a fingerprint, just as I had on my mother's glass dome in her study. She'd placed two tiny mustard seeds under the glass. What had been the meaning of it? Was it symbolic—representing Camille and me and the faith that someday we'd be reunited? No, it was too wild a stretch.

Outside on the street, a man who looked like Marcus juggled three small balls in the air. My motto had always been to never trust a juggler—too unpredictable. His silly circus nonsense made several children laugh, though. I leaned closer to the glass and squinted. It was Marcus. Okay, so the scene came off charming, but what was he doing out there instead of in here? Did being on time mean nothing to him? I had no place in my life for irresponsible behavior, no matter how endearing.

Marcus ruffled the bushy curls on a kid's head and with a leisurely gait strolled inside the bistro. After a moment or two he found me in the corner.

"You're late," was all I said, even though I wanted to tell him he looked almost handsome in his navy sports jacket.

He pointed to a clock on the wall, which read exactly 6:30. "I'm right on time. Didn't you say 6:30?"

"I think I said 6:00." Marcus twitched a bit as if to disagree, but then he said, "I will never argue with a lady. I humbly apologize." He leaned down and offered his hand to me. "Get your purse and jumper. Nobody eats inside here on such a memorable evening."

"Jumper?"

He grinned. "Your sweater."

"Oh. Funny word." *But funnier man.* I scooted out my chair and allowed him to help me up. "So, how do you know it will be a memorable evening? It hasn't even happened yet."

Marcus bowed like an earl. "I'm here, Lily, to make certain it's memorable."

I felt too tired to get feisty about his smuggery, so I grabbed my things and let him lead me outside into a breeze that was whippy enough to sail us away if we'd been on a boat at sea. "It's usually too hot or humid to eat outside in Houston." I put on my heavy sweater. "But here it's almost too breezy and chilly."

He placed his hand at my back and maneuvered me to a table with a nice river view. "You'll get used to the weather," he said.

I buttoned my sweater all the way up to my neck. "I won't be in Melbourne long enough to get used to anything."

"Are you sure about that?" Marcus pushed in my chair as I sat down. "Melbourne has a way of getting into your heart."

"Oh, that."

Marcus grinned.

When ordering time came, I said, "I'll have the chicken." It was what I wanted, or what I thought I wanted, but why did that seem so tasteless and predictable? Guess I'd become the very thing I was going to eat—a chicken.

"Why don't you get something a little more exotic?" Marcus asked. "You can have chicken in the States."

"You're not going to let me glide along in my happy comfort zone for five minutes, are you?"

"Not if I can help it."

I smiled, and the muscles around my lips were glad for the new workout. I gestured for him to order. "Okay, you may order, but no kangaroo and no emu."

Marcus looked up at the waitress. "We'll both have the lamb chops and potatoes."

Sounded good, sort of. I tried not to think of all the adorable lambs from nursery rhymes and the ones that I sometimes counted to get me to sleep at night.

The waitress winked at Marcus, but to his credit, he ignored her flirtations.

"That's a pretty heavy meal for my first night here. I'll be so bloated you'll be able to float me down this river, belly-up."

Marcus laughed.

Guess that wasn't a very ladylike thing to say.

"You'll sleep like a baby. I promise." Marcus used his finger on the tablecloth like a pencil, as if he were in the middle of a sketch.

"Do you mind if we talk about my sister for a while?" I pulled a small notebook from my purse. "I'd like to enjoy myself, but it's not really why I'm here. I want to stay focused."

"All right. I understand." Marcus leaned forward. "Tell me what you know about her."

"Well, her full name is Camille Violet Daniels, but I suppose her last name would have been the same as mine when she was born, which was Gray."

He steepled his fingers together. "Did you go online and look up all the Camille Danielses in the area?"

"Yes, but I couldn't find anything."

"She's probably just unlisted."

"Yes, I thought of that." Just to feel as if I were making some headway I printed my sister's name at the top of the page just like in grade school. "It's understandable for her to be unlisted, especially if she were a single woman. But I have no idea of that either."

Marcus looked up as if concentrating on those tiny bits of information. But then he brightened and said, "You know what? Now that we're talking about it, I do remember something else about this woman. Sometimes before she plays, she stops to talk to a man. Maybe it's her husband or boyfriend. Don't know. I've never met her, but sometimes I've stopped to hear her play. It's quite mesmerizing."

I took a few notes and wrote the word *mesmerizing* below her name. "What kind of music does she play?"

"She plays Irish music. Occasionally she'll break up her performance with a lively jig, but mostly her sound is sort of earthy like flickering lights in a deep forest. And you find yourself wanting to follow those lights wherever they lead. . . ." His voice drifted.

Mesmerizing? Flickering lights? That was my twin sister? My, my. It didn't seem like me at all. Apparently Camille was the dancing light in the family, and I was the troll guarding the forest. I almost laughed. Could Marcus be a little bit in love with Camille along with her music? Maybe that's why he'd latched onto me. It was like being near her and her music. Maybe he wanted to find Camille for his own personal reasons.

A distant gaze crossed his face, as though he were staring off into a faraway serene and lovely place. A place her music created, perhaps.

I found myself wanting to go there with him. More than ever I longed to meet this woman Marcus spoke of, and in some ways I wanted to be more like her. "And so do you get lost in her music too?"

"Hmm?" Marcus seemed to come back to himself. "Of course. No one is immune to her playing."

He tilted his head, studying me in a way that made me uncomfortable. Perhaps he misunderstood and thought I was jealous of my sister and her gift. But then maybe I was—a little.

"Do you have any idea why your sister lives here?" He seemed all business now. "Even the smallest detail of her story could be valuable."

The time had come—I would either need to trust Marcus or cut him loose. I had nowhere else to turn. "Okay. Here's all I know. Camille is my identical twin, and she was taken from my mother when she was one. Now six months ago my mother received a card from her. There wasn't a return address, but she mentioned that she lived here in Melbourne. Oh, and she attended St. Paul's Cathedral."

"That's quite a story," Marcus said.

"Don't you believe me?"

"Yes." He crossed his arms. "I know you stopped by the church. Did they have any information on her?"

"None. I was so disappointed."

The waitress stopped by with a loaf of rustic-looking bread on a board with a slab of butter shaped like a kangaroo. How clever.

I cut off a slice of bread and then passed it to Marcus.

"So, Joyce and Rowan couldn't find Camille on the membership rolls there?" he asked.

"Well, Rowan didn't have time to check his records, but he did say he would, and he'd call me if anything turned up." I whacked off the kangaroo's tail and buttered my bread, heavily for a change, and took a big bite. Guess I was hungrier than I thought.

"Maybe your sister attends the services but never joined," Marcus said. "I attend, but haven't joined yet."

"Why not?"

"Because my church membership is one of the last things I have left from home. Long story. Too long for this evening." He busied himself trying to smear chunks of butter on his bread.

Sometime I would ask him about his long story. Perhaps on another evening. "So, you've never seen even a glimpse of my sister at your church?"

Marcus shook his head. "St. Paul's is a large cathedral, and there are different services. We could easily have missed each other."

"Okay. Sure. That sounds reasonable."

He caught my gaze. "Do you mind if I ask you something personal?"

"Depends on what it is."

"Your mother said Camille was taken from her, and yet you said it in a matter-of-fact kind of way. That really is an amazing admission." Marcus shifted in his chair. "Was your sister abducted? Were the police involved?"

"No, I don't think so. That's such a dramatic scenario my mother would have mentioned it. Well, I'm not sure. You see, my mother and I aren't close. The information I gave you is all she would give me. I begged for more, but she wouldn't say any more about it."

"Really? Nothing?"

"Trust me, when her wall goes up, it's over."

Marcus gazed out toward the river. "I do understand . . . more than you know."

Something in his expression told me he really did know what I meant, which made me wonder about his past, his family. Could it be similar to mine—a secret room with the key thrown away forever? "When I say my story out loud to you, it seems so shrouded in mystery. My daughter, Julie, thought so too. We went back and forth with ideas on what could have happened all those years ago, but until my mother decides to give me more information, I'll just have to work with the meager clues I have." I dusted off some of the bread crumbs from the table. How could eating bread cause such a mess? In seconds two little sparrows—which looked like a set of salt and pepper shakers—gobbled up the crumbs.

Marcus took a sip of his water. "I'm surprised you haven't hired a private investigator."

"I don't have the money for one, at least not if the search went on for months. My daughter is in college, so some of my savings is going for that right now. My mother does have plenty of money, but she isn't as interested in Camille as I am." *At least I don't think so.*

"Not interested in her own daughter?" Marcus's brow furrowed then, almost to the point of anger, which was an expression that seemed as awkward on his face as spots on a kangaroo. "That's so sad."

"It is. Tragically sad. I agree. But then that was the kind of mother I had growing up." I'd better not elaborate too much. No need to unload all my dirty laundry on him in one evening. He'd surely suffocate.

"You turned out well in spite of a difficult childhood."

"Thank you. I hope so."

A gust swept through, churning our tiny world. I pulled out a scrunchie and tied back my long hair, but Marcus left his spikey windblown mop the way it was, which looked amusing as well as surprisingly attractive.

"You know, I'm sure you've thought of all these angles, but since you said your maiden name was Gray and your sister's last name is Daniels, there are only a few possible scenarios. Camille was married or adopted . . . or she changed her name legally for some other reason."

"Adopted? I just assumed she'd married at some point. My mother said Camille was taken from her when she was one, so that doesn't sound like she gave her up for adoption. And why would she? My mother is a harsh woman, but it's hard to imagine that she could be that heartless. I mean, keep one identical twin and give the other one away." In spite of the strangeness of the thought I jotted down a note about the possibility of adoption.

"So, do you have any memories of your sister?" he asked. "Guess it's unlikely at one year old."

"I've tried to remember, but I'm pretty sure it's just wishful thinking." I doodled on the pad of paper.

"So, do you play an instrument like your sister?" Marcus tore off a piece of his bread.

"I play the piano, but I haven't practiced in years."

"What made you give it up?"

"I don't know that I have given it up forever, but my husband, Richard, who passed away, used to say I was banging and not playing. I think it made him edgy, so I stopped."

"Pity."

"A pity to please my husband?" I asked.

"No, a pity your husband saw your music that way."

"Oh." I looked down at my random scribbles, which to my sad surprise were little hearts with angry lines marking through them.

"So, you're a widow."

"Yes. I am. But I have the one daughter that I mentioned . . . Julie. She's in college, so now I have an empty nest. I love her dearly, but she's gone, at least from my daily life. That's my saga." Well, not all of it.

Marcus stroked his whiskers. "That can't be all there is to Lily."

"My life has been distilled into a handful of facts. But now it includes a desperate search for my sister." I took a sip of my water. "I can't tell you how much I want this performer to be her. I'm scared to get my hopes up, though. I mean isn't there a chance this woman you keep talking about is just someone who looks a little like me? I have such a generic face."

"Are you kidding?" He gave me a tsk-tsk. "You don't have a generic face, and once someone gazes into those smoky gray eyes of yours, well, they're decimated."

I laughed. Spreading it on a bit thick, Marcus.

"How is it you've learned to give yourself no credit? To see your-self in such a negative light?"

I sighed. "My mother always said that thinking highly of oneself was a sure sign of foolhardiness."

"Hmm." Marcus ran his finger along the rim of his glass, mak-ing a musical sound. "Even though I don't see you as fake in any way, one could make the same argument about false modesty."

"Is there another Marcus-ite in there somewhere?"

"No more of those. Fresh out."

"Well, you're right. I'm not guilty of false modesty," I said. "When I run myself down I do it with my whole heart."

Marcus chuckled, and it rose merrily like bubbles on the breeze.

I laughed along with him, since his chuckles were contagious. "You're awfully pleased with yourself."

"Why shouldn't I be pleased?" Marcus asked. "I found an open-ing in a garden wall."

"And what do you see on the other side?" I smoothed a wrinkle from the tablecloth, not knowing for sure if I wanted to hear what he would say.

"I see a lovely garden . . . with flowers yet to bloom." He gave his head a shake of certainty.

"Humph."

"Well, that's not a very inspiring sound. I'll bet you'll never hear that word sung from a hymnal."

I grinned. "Don't mind me. I think it's just the jet lag talking. By the way, I wonder where the food is."

"The service seems slow compared to American standards, be-cause meals aren't rushed here, they're relished."

"Another Marcus-ite?"

"No. But I'm sorry you're hungry. Do you want the last slice of bread?"

"I'd better not."

"It'll spoil your dinner?" Marcus asked.

I rested back in my chair and looked at him. "I see how this is going between us. It's so obvious. You're like this . . . I don't know . . . this sports jacket, and I'm the itchy black wool sweater buttoned up to my neck so tightly that I can barely breathe. You're the man who can enjoy life, relish things . . . make water glasses sing to your touch. While I'm the woman who will always be the flower that's never quite ready to bloom."

"You're twisting my words." Marcus shook his finger at me. "But I will say this . . . except for those marshmallows I saw you eating earlier today, you seem to hesitate to do anything that might bring you pleasure. Why is that?"

"Because my husband was unfaithful." The words slipped out as a murmur before I'd had a chance to censor myself. *Lily, what have you done?* I jerked up, nearly knocking over my chair. "Maybe I should go. I'm sorry. I just—"

"But why?" He reached over the table and placed his fingers over mine.

"Because what I said to you just now about my husband . . . I've never said those words to another living soul. Because I'm mortified. You've got me hypnotized or something. I wouldn't normally say anything like that." Especially not to a stranger.

"I wish I *could* hypnotize you. I'd make you stay." He let go of my hand, and the warmth drained away. "But as it is, I'll just have to ask you nicely. Please Lily, please don't go. You shouldn't need to feel embarrassed by what you said. It was just an honest moment between two new friends."

CHAPTER
eight

Marcus's words were just above a whisper, and his eyes, well, I had yet to see him that serious. There didn't appear to be any signs of mischief left in him. I eased back down in my chair. "I still think you've got some power over me that I don't understand yet."

"I can't imagine how. I'm not nearly as exotic as you seem to think I am, and I assure you the only true authority I have over this life is what I order for breakfast."

I grinned. Marcus did have a way of putting me at ease. Maybe that was his sway over me—a disarming earnestness.

Marcus played with various items on the table, lining them up like toy soldiers. "This is when I go quiet and let you talk. If you want to talk about your husband, I want to hear you out."

"I shouldn't have brought it up, but . . ." I fiddled with my napkin, roping it around my little finger like a noose. "There is a relief in saying it out loud, telling someone."

"That makes sense."

I waited for Marcus to say more, but he went quiet again. Maybe life would feel lighter to talk about it. "I think I have forgiven Richard, but it's difficult to forget. That kind of disloyalty taints everything like black dye on white linen."

The water in my glass shimmied when I picked it up to take a quick sip. "Richard . . . I always thought it was such a gallant name. He was supposed to be my prince, the one who would rescue me, protect me from harm, but what he did was far from noble.

When he gave away his heart and body to another woman after he'd promised to be faithful, well, my hero became a villain." I held the water glass so tightly I thought it might shatter in my hands. "It still makes me feel awkward to unload all this baggage on you. I barely know you."

"How is it any different than telling a counselor you've just met? Except that I won't charge you anything."

"I suppose that's true." But how would it feel to say all the words out loud? Would it lessen the pain or rub it raw again like sandpaper on a wound not yet healed? I had no idea. "Well, the woman Richard had an affair with was from his office." Succumbing to my stress mode I hid my hands under the table and began picking at my fingers. "I found out about the affair from a note hidden in his desk at home, and then I decided to confront him. But before I could ask him the whys surrounding the affair . . . well, Richard died of a heart attack."

"That must have been a difficult time."

"It was. All of this happened a little over a year ago, but the pain hasn't gone away. I guess it's because I was grieving over his death, but I felt angry too, for what he did. Angry at the woman. Maybe even angry at God, since I couldn't understand why I'd been left with grief as well as so many questions about our marriage. It made me wonder if what Richard and I had all those years was real. Had he loved me, or was he waiting for the right moment to escape? Had he planned on leaving me to marry this other woman? I knew Richard and I didn't live a fairy-tale life, but it seemed like a good marriage. I thought so anyway. I just wish we'd had a chance to talk, so I could have asked the question all women want to know in my position . . . the big why."

I glanced down at my dark clothes. Maybe the reason I wore funeral-type outfits was that even after I'd said my goodbyes to Richard, something still felt unresolved. Something felt unburied. Too many questions still lingered in the air.

Amazingly, Marcus was still listening as intently as before. "It does help for someone to hear my story. It wasn't easy holding it in all those months."

"I'm sure it wasn't."

Before either one of us could say any more, the waitress arrived with two plates of lamb chops and potatoes.

After my troubling disclosures, my stomach seemed in a quandary whether it should churn or cheer over the food.

Marcus said grace, a lovely prayer, in fact, which included me and my quest to find my sister. Nothing was said about Richard. We turned our attention to the food as I tried to forget that this man across from me now knew my most painful secret.

The lamb did a savory melting thing in my mouth, and I closed my eyes for a moment. In some small way I came a little closer to Melbourne in that bite. The noise around us sounded more like laughter. The breeze felt more refreshing than chilling. And my spirit embraced the moment. "I've never eaten lamb before."

"What do you think?"

"I like it. Not at all like chicken."

I thought Marcus would chuckle but instead he stopped his eating and looked at me. "Since you told me something very private, I'm going to give you something in return. I'll tell you why I left Dallas and moved to Australia."

"Yes, I'd love to know." I speared a bite of potato, glad to be using my ears instead of my mouth.

"Well, the truth is . . . my family has disowned me." Marcus set his knife and fork down but didn't quite look me in the eye. "You see, my younger sister died a year ago, and I'm the one who killed her."

CHAPTER
nine

That tasty morsel of potato stuck in my throat like a pebble. A big one. I stifled the urge to run. "Oh? That's pretty heavy, Marcus." I managed to keep the tremor out of my voice. "Maybe you'd better explain."

"I'm not a murderer, traditionally speaking. I know it's what you're thinking, and yet what else do you call it when the passenger in your car dies, and the accident was your fault?"

I calmed myself and swallowed. "While deeply tragic, I'd still call that an accident."

"Well, it's not what my family calls it." Marcus looked away toward the river and the boats and the tide of tourists strolling along the promenade.

A couple next to us effervesced with laughter. Their heads dipped and touched, and the outline of their forms almost made the shape of a heart.

The pleasant vignettes seemed to ease the taut pull of Marcus's revelation. But he really had allowed me to see into a window of his past. I could tell that the confession had diminished the playfulness in his demeanor and replaced it with a burden that I could not imagine. "Do you mind if I ask how the accident happened?"

Marcus pushed his food around on his plate but didn't eat it. "I wasn't drunk, but I was very tired, which is just as bad. I shouldn't have been driving. After I had dinner that evening with my family, I needed to go home to bed. But my little sister, Ellie, wanted to go to the movies, and she didn't want to go by herself. My parents weren't in the mood to go, and I didn't want to disappoint her. We all had trouble saying no to her, because she was such a good kid. Anyway, she had her own car, but she asked me to drive. She still wasn't all that sure of herself as a driver.

"But it didn't matter," Marcus spat out his words. "I should have listened to my gut. I was tired. Too tired to be driving. I fell asleep, and the car drifted off the road. Ellie screamed, and I woke up, but it was too late. The car hit a light pole. I was only cut and bruised, but my sister died there in the car with me by her side... while we waited for the ambulance. It was as swift and horrific as that. And I cannot go home. I can't blame them for the way they feel. I think God has forgiven me, but my parents, well..."

I reached out to him, touching the edge of his sleeve. I gave it a little tug to get him to look at me. "I'm sure they knew you wouldn't have wanted to hurt your little sister for anything in the world. Didn't they feel differently about you after they had some time to think and pray and grieve?"

"I'd like to say they did. But my father would ignite into quite a fury every time he talked to me, and my mother lived inside this dark haze I couldn't really understand. I'd never seen either one of them like this, but then nothing so horrible had ever happened to our family. At one point, my father told me that keeping some distance for a while might help the healing."

Marcus took a deep drink from his water glass. "I had this friend who'd moved here some years ago and loved it. I thought, why not? I figured I could go for a visit and see how I liked it. I fell into step right away. I've been here not quite a year. Of course, I brought all the sadness with me surrounding my sister, but I figured at least my parents might recover now. There's been some consolation in that."

His story moved me as much as it grieved me. An attachment toward Marcus, like the first tiny roots clinging to the soil, took hold in my heart. "Do they know where you are? You know, in case they're worried? Even if they're angry with you, you're still their son."

"The day I flew out I told them. They have my address and phone. But there's been no communication from them, so I've let it go. I assume when I hear from them someday, if I ever do, it'll be time. But you see, Ellie was always their favorite, and I understood that. Everybody adored her, including me. She was funny and sweet and full of life. I was always a few steps behind her in every way even though I was twenty years older." Marcus took a bite of his lamb.

"What do you mean, a few steps behind her?"

"Well, I've never fit in with my family the way Ellie did. Some kids seem like they belong to their parents, and then there are kids like me. A little offbeat. Sometimes I can relate to children better than adults. When I was a teenager I thought I'd been adopted, but I wasn't. I'm just different."

How very true. But now instead of agreeing with Marcus about his peculiarities I wanted to defend him. "I'm sorry your family did that to you. Surely, though, in the end, they wouldn't want to lose both their children."

"It's what I hope for, pray for." He daubed at his mouth with his napkin. "But I will say this . . . you don't really know people until there's a tragedy. Even family. Suffering has this way of stripping us all bare of any pretenses. There can be no more pretending."

I thought of my mother. If Camille really had been taken from Mother against her will—although I couldn't imagine how—it would have been a terrible heartbreak. I know if anyone had taken Julie from me it would have been unbearable. Maybe Mother's grief had turned into bitterness over the years, which would explain her attitude. "You're right, calamity works like fire, bringing impurities to the surface, but sometimes all that's left are the impurities."

"The voice of experience?" he asked.

"Yes." Maybe God really had brought this man along to help me. Marcus of all people could understand my strange family drama.

We ate quietly for a few moments as the sounds of the evening surrounded us. Finally I said, "Thank you for sharing that piece of yourself. I'm sure it was hard for you to tell me."

"Surprisingly, it wasn't that difficult." Marcus smiled, revealing some of the buoyancy from when I'd first met him. "I trust you, even though we've just met. Why is that, Lily?"

"Honestly, I have no idea."

"I'm sorry if my story put a damper on the evening."

"Nonsense," I said. "It was just an honest moment between two new friends."

Marcus smiled. "Maybe we should hurry a little. I wouldn't want you to miss your sister after coming so far." He sliced off another bite of lamb.

"Thanks." I gave him my best smile. "Really, Marcus. Thank you."

"You're welcome."

When we were finished, Marcus paid for the food and escorted me out of the bistro. The performers had just started to show up along the promenade—magicians, musicians, and comedians all delighting the crowds.

"I didn't expect to see so many people. So many performers."

"It's the balmy weather," he said. "Brings them out like turtles on a sunny rock."

I laughed. "Balmy?" Was that another twinkle in his eyes? I tucked my sweater around me.

Marcus took off his jacket and put it around my shoulders. "You need this more than I do. I'm used to the weather, you're not. I don't want you to get ill your first night here."

"Thanks." I snuggled into the warmth of his jacket and vowed to be more prepared the next day for the wildly fluctuating temperatures of Australia. I could barely comprehend that I, Lily Winter, was in such an exotic locale. I'd never done anything outlandish in my life. Maybe I'd stayed up late for a Johnny Depp movie marathon or splurged on a little black dress that was searching for the perfect evening, or ate my way through a bowl of chocolate cake batter when I was feeling particularly lonesome, but those were indulgences, not colorful life events. I knew mostly ordinary days in a life that appeared not too far from trifling.

Marcus steered me away from a group of musicians playing chamber music and then after a short walking distance he stopped. "This is it. This is the spot where I've seen her play. Right here. The woman who looks just like Lily." He smiled at me.

I scanned the area, searching and praying. *Lord, please let it be.* But we waited and nothing happened. No woman suddenly appeared to play her flute. So, we waited some more. The woman, whom I'd willed to come, did not, and my optimism drifted away like one of the gondolas floating on the river. My disappointment weighted my whole being like a terrible yoke.

When Marcus saw my forlorn expression he whispered, "Sorry, Love."

Not too far from our spot the chamber orchestra began packing up their instruments. "Just a moment. I want to ask one of the musicians about Camille."

"Good idea," Marcus said.

I hurried toward the cellist, a young woman who appeared friendly enough. I dropped twenty dollars in a colorful basket, which sat in front of the group, and then said to her, "Excuse me. I'm looking for someone."

"Yes?" She set her bow into the case.

"Have you seen a woman play a flute here in the evenings? She stands just over there." I pointed toward her right, closer to the river.

The woman's smile morphed into a puzzled frown. "Is this some kind of joke?"

"No, not at all. What do you mean?"

"But you look like her. Just like her." The woman gave me a good long look, taking me in from different angles. "Except, I guess your hair is longer."

"Really?" My heart sped up. "This woman . . . she's my identical twin sister. At least I think she is. Her name is Camille. Do you know her?"

"Never met her. But she does play here sometimes. She was here a couple of nights ago. But I think I heard her coughing. Maybe she's ill." The woman snapped her instrument case shut and looked like she was ready to move on.

Why was everyone always in such a hurry? Perhaps I'd become a still-life painting. I talked faster. "So, you don't know if her name is Camille or when she might come back? Any details about her at all?"

"No, I'm sorry. But she does play beautifully. I'm envious of her, I'll tell you that."

"Oh?"

"You're American, aren't you?" she asked.

"Yes. I've come a long way to find her. All the way from Houston."

"I love Texas . . . cowboys." The young woman's face lit up.

"We have a few cowboys there." The taxi driver had mentioned John Wayne. Guess Australians had seen too many old westerns.

"Here we call cowboys and cowgirls jackaroos and jillaroos."

"That's cute."

"Well, if you want to find your sister," the young woman went on to say, "I'd come back every evening. You're bound to catch her eventually. Good luck."

"Thanks for your help."

"Sure." The woman turned back toward her group.

When I glanced around, Marcus stood nearby. I told him, "I'm ready to go. I guess you heard all that."

"I did. So, are you encouraged?"

"Yes, and I'm going to be right here tomorrow evening."

"I'll come with you. That is, if you want me to." Marcus's expression was a question mark dotted with hope.

"I do, but are you sure? All this endless standing and waiting can't be that fun for you."

"Trust me, there's no hardship in being with you." He gestured toward his jacket, which I was still wearing. "I almost forgot," he said. "Look in the left pocket of my jacket."

When I did, I pulled out my charm bracelet and gasped. "How did . . . ? Where? Oh no. I rolled it off my hand and forgot it."

"I happened to see it as we were leaving the restaurant."

I held the bracelet to my heart. "Oh, if I had lost this I would have been sooo disappointed. My daughter, Julie, gave this to me. The charms represent our lives . . . our loves." I lifted it to show him the tiny charms and explained the significance of each. "I suppose someday I'll add a silver flute to my bracelet. At least I hope to."

"It's going to be fine. You're going to find Camille. God didn't bring you this far for nothing."

I rolled the bangle onto my wrist. We strolled back toward my hotel, and I tried not to think about how ill Camille might be. How many evenings would I have to show up to finally meet her? And what if I used all of my evenings waiting for her and then found out it wasn't Camille after all? The word *devastating* came to mind, but I remembered the two mustard seeds under the glass dome in Mother's study. "Marcus?"

"Hmm?" He seemed to have wandered off somewhere. Maybe he was thinking about his parents again. Poor man.

"I was curious about something when you talked about you and your sister. Do you mind if I ask you a question? Please tell me if I'm being nosy."

"Ask me anything." Like a gentleman he held my elbow as we crossed the street.

"When you said you were tired that night of the accident, I just wondered if you suffered with insomnia . . . like I do."

"Yes."

I stopped on the sidewalk and touched his arm. "What keeps you awake? I know you must think about the accident, but you said you were tired before that. I just wondered about it."

Marcus stared at me blankly for a moment as if he were looking through me into a place where I couldn't go—where he was truly alone. "All right." He offered me a surrendering nod. "Instead of walking outside here in the cold wind, let's go back to your pub through Southgate. It's a complex of shops that's more enclosed. I can show you something that will help you to understand."

"Yes, please." For some reason I really did want to know more, to understand. My curiosity surrounding the man, as well as my empathy, was growing by the hour. "Pub?" I suddenly thought to ask.

He smiled. "People use the word *pub* here for hotel."

"Oh." When we'd walked past a few businesses—a jewelry store, a café, and various clothing shops—we came across a quaint bookstore.

"Shall we?" he asked.

"Okay."

He escorted me inside and led me to the children's section. I noticed a few of Julie's favorite books spread out face forward on a big oak display. Books I'd read to her so many times that we'd loved all the pretty off like the velveteen rabbit. I ran my finger along the brightly colored books and let the wonderful memories trickle down like a soft rain. "When Julie was five she called all her picture books 'story lovies.'"

"That sounds adorable." Marcus picked up one of the hardbound picture books and handed it to me.

I looked at the title. *When Monsters Come Out to Play.* Mmm. "My daughter and I both loved this book." I gave him a sheepish grin. "I still do. What a whimsical concept, that monsters get lonely, and they're just looking for someone to play with . . . someone to be their friend." I opened the book to the first page. "And the man's use of watercolor is so distinctive and lovely. I've never seen anything else like it." I looked at the author-illustrator's name with affection—Miles Hooper. "Little does Mr. Hooper know . . . well, this was my miracle book when Julie was five. It's how I got her to sleep. It made all of our lives so much easier back then. In fact, I could kiss that Hooper fellow, whoever he is."

Marcus grinned then—a big satisfied grin that looked both enchanting and curious. "The author does know. That is, he knows now. And a kiss was far more than I'd hoped for this evening."

"*You'd* hoped for. Wait a minute. What are you saying? *You're* the author? You're Miles Hooper? You're kidding, right? You're not kidding . . ."

CHAPTER
ten

"Miles Hooper, my pseudonym." Marcus stuffed his hands into his pockets, looking like a boy caught with his hand in the cookie jar.

So, while Marcus was busy looking hangdog I was hyperventilating, knowing that Miles Hooper was actually conversing with me. My goodness. Would I ever recover from such serendipity? And how wonderful to do something so creative with one's life. Of course, wouldn't any job be more creative than being a secretary? But knowing Marcus was Miles explained so many things—his talk of color and imagination and the angles of the sunlight.

"Miles Hooper," Marcus continued to say, "has been my pen name ever since I started writing at age seventeen, which is why I had a trust fund with my money. The Monster book did well for me and was made into a TV movie for kids. After that experience, writing became my life."

"It's incredible." I held the book to me. "I'm blown away. But why didn't you tell me before?"

"Because I don't do this anymore. I'm no longer Miles Hooper."

"Really? Why not?" And then I realized Marcus was trying to tell me more about his sister, or his life without her. I glanced around, glad that the shop was quiet. "Is it about Ellie?"

Marcus nodded. "A few years ago I got writer's block. Terrible stuff. Nothing seemed to work. I threw most everything out, and the stuff that didn't get thrown out was published, which sold maybe thirty copies. Probably bought by some of my fellow writers who felt sorry for me."

He released a mirthless laugh. "That's an exaggeration, of course, but the publisher was not amused with my sales. And who could blame them? They'd sunk a fortune into my books, packaging them so they were irresistible to kids, marketing them to the hilt, and paying for special placement on the bookstore tables, end caps, that sort of thing . . . just to see the books fail."

"So, this is what made you stop?" I took a step closer to him, hoping for more of the story.

"No. There's more. For some unknown reason, the inspiration came again. When it arrived I recognized it right away. But it was like putting a feast before a starving man. I became a madman working until all hours . . . too scared to stop. I thought the muse might disappear again like it did before. I worked so hard I became perpetually exhausted." He sighed. "And that's the reason I was so tired that night. And why I'll never write or illustrate again. Because one of the sweetest, dearest persons I ever knew is dead because of me and my lunacy."

My fingers ached from holding the picture book so tightly. I wanted to give Marcus a hug, but didn't. Mist stung my eyes instead. "I'm sorry. It's such a sad story."

"I didn't mean to make you sad. You wanted to know why I was tired that night, and I really did want to tell you. To show you a piece of my life. Or what used to be me. There's just a shadow left of Miles. No more."

I put the book on the shelf. "Thank you for that. For showing me."

"No one else knows here, none of my friends. It just didn't seem necessary to tell them. But it felt important now for some reason."

"I'm glad you did."

"This life is a dangerous place to be, at least with me at the helm. Not sure any woman deserves that." Behind Marcus's smile there seemed to be a dozen doubts and queries.

Before I could respond a clerk popped her head around the corner of one of the shelves and said, "We're closing soon."

"We're just going." Marcus led me out of the store, and we walked in silence for a while toward my hotel. "Selfishly . . . well, I hope what I've told you tonight doesn't change anything between us. Although I would understand if it did."

"It changes nothing. I promise." *Except to endear you to me even more.*

"Good."

When we were in the lobby of my hotel Marcus pulled me to the side, to a quiet area near a cluster of couches. "It was a very fine evening, Lily."

"Yes, it was. Thank you for dinner, for helping me with my sister, and for sharing your heart, well, for everything." Amazing, how an evening could start out one way and end another. "Here, don't let me forget this." I slipped his jacket off my shoulders and helped Marcus put it back on.

"I'll let you get to sleep now. It probably feels like the longest day of your life."

"It does, but not in a bad way."

Marcus hesitated and then said, "Until your sister performs in the evening you'll have some time on your hands in the morning and afternoon. I'd love to show you some of the city if you're up for it."

I thought for a moment, but not too long. "I would like that."

"I could pick you up at 10:00. It'll give you a chance for some extra sleep and a leisurely breakfast."

"Sounds good."

Marcus backed away but didn't take his eyes off me. "Don't worry. I'm not going to hold you to that kiss."

"Kiss? What kiss?"

"The one you promised Miles Hooper in the bookstore. You know, because I'd written the miracle book that got your Julie to sleep every night. But it would be cheating you, of course, since you didn't know Miles was me when you promised a kiss." There was that twinkle again.

I'd grown accustomed already to his playful blue sparkle, but there were other "looks" attached to it—perhaps shyness and a boyish anticipation?

"I wouldn't feel cheated." I stepped over to him, rose on my tiptoes, and gave him a brief but genuine kiss on the cheek. "Good night. Thanks for the evening." *You really did make it memorable.* But then I flushed hotter than a summer day in the Outback, since I not only surprised Marcus but I shocked myself with my display of affection.

His face lit with surprise and something else. Gratitude? "Are you sure I don't just have you mesmerized?"

"Maybe a little." But then maybe I didn't mind so much.

"Good night . . . Love." He grinned. "See you tomorrow." And then he turned and walked out of the hotel lobby.

I didn't whirl up to my room like a cloud on a windy day, but it wasn't quite the slogging gait I'd anticipated earlier in the day. In fact, so far, nothing I'd experienced had been anything even close to what I'd expected in the Land Down Under.

So, God, what do You have planned for me tomorrow? A little later, while snuggled under a white down comforter, I fell into dreaming with that very query on my lips.

Chapter
eleven

The next morning, I rose late, feeling stiff and groggy and jet-lagged. My back ached. My neck ached. I suppose all of me ached—that is, I ached to find what I was searching for—whom I was searching for. I stared at the bathroom mirror and leaned in to get a good look at myself. Would this be the day I found my living reflection? Only God knew.

I texted Julie and dressed in several layers, which seemed to be the best way to handle Melbourne's four seasons in a day. No matter how tired I felt I was determined to enjoy myself on my little outing with Marcus, but I had no idea what he'd cooked up for our adventure. Guess he wanted it to be a surprise. There was no skirting around the truth, though—the man I thought was a bagpipe-playing bum had already grown on me like Spanish moss on live oak.

After breakfast I made my way downstairs to the lobby, where Marcus was already waiting for me.

He rose from the couch and greeted me with a smile warm enough to take the chill off any morning. "Hello. You look nice."

"Thanks." *So do you.* His slacks were pressed to perfection, his polo shirt was Ralph Lauren, and he was clean-shaven. Nice. I clutched my purse strap for support. "So, where are you taking me?"

"Do you like chocolate?" Marcus asked.

"Who doesn't?" Funny how the thought of chocolate added a pleasant lilt to my voice, but then chocolate is, after all, a woman's best friend.

"I know just the place. In my opinion, Melbourne has the best chocolate shops in the world. Some of them are nestled in the laneways."

It sounded like a tasty adventure.

A cluster of guests scurried in through the lobby doors and brushed by us, laughing. "So, tell me, what are laneways?"

"They're alleyways crammed full of cafés and galleries and bustling with life." Marcus made circling gestures with his hands. "You'll love 'em. But before we go there, maybe we should check in with Rowan at St. Paul's. Maybe he found some time to look over the membership records for your sister."

"Rowan did say he'd call if anything turned up."

"Did you get any phone messages?" Marcus asked.

"No."

"Well, just in case he forgot, it wouldn't hurt to swing by the cathedral."

"Good idea."

Marcus knelt down in front of me. "Your shoe, my lady."

"My shoe?"

"You've come undone."

I looked down at my shoelaces, one of which had indeed come untied.

Marcus gestured for me to place my shoe on his knee, and after I obeyed, he gingerly tied my shoestring. "Falling is easier than you think, Love."

He stared up at me. His expression waded into waters deep enough to drown in, but before I could even think to respond, he gave my shoe a pat and stood. "Shall we?"

"We shall."

Marcus placed his hand at my back and escorted me through the sliding glass doors of the hotel. Even though I barely felt his hand through my layers of fabric, the encounter caused an awakening inside me, like the first tentative signs of spring after a long winter. Yes, it was an apt description, and one I didn't shy away from.

Marcus gave me bits of data about the area as we strolled along the river, which turned out to be much more than just a waterway. The longer I stayed the more I could feel it—the Yarra was the center of life, the heartbeat of the city—and I felt glad to be a part of that pulsing vitality.

As we crossed one of the bridges and headed toward St. Paul's, Marcus said, "Since you seem to like touristy information, you might like to know that this bridge we're walking on is called Princes Bridge, and it was constructed in 1888. The bridge was named after Edward, the Prince of Wales, and there's another one similar to it in London."

"Ahh. Well, it's beautiful. And I especially like the balustrade and the old lamplights. So ornate. Makes me think of something out of a Dickens novel."

"I can almost see the police dashing past us as they chase after the Artful Dodger."

I grinned. My glance at him lingered. Marcus had turned out to be more than I'd imagined. Funny how first impressions almost always came up wrong. Perhaps I'd judged too quickly. In the midst of my musings about Marcus, my mind wandered back toward my sister and the missing puzzle pieces. If only we could find her, so much would be answered and made right again. Could our paths have already crossed on the streets, and I'd missed her?

We approached St. Paul's Cathedral and trotted up the concrete steps. Once inside we made our way to the gift shop counter. Rowan was there, and he lit up when he saw Marcus.

"How are ya?" Marcus shook Rowan's hand.

"Good." The older man adjusted his bowtie. "Thanks for helping out the other night with the teens. I'm not very experienced around young people. They've got this new language and so many techy gizmos I don't always know what to say to connect with them. But they like you."

Marcus leaned on the counter. "Probably because I'm still a kid."

Rowan laughed.

"They'll warm up to you," Marcus said. "So, how's the missus?"

"She's well. Thanks." Rowan turned to me. "It's Lily. I remember. And I did look up your sister on the membership rolls. Camille Daniels, right?"

"Yes, that's right." I held my breath. *Please let it be good news.*

The light left his face. "But I didn't find anything under that last name." Rowan lowered his gaze. "I know this is important. I'm really sorry."

"Do you have a schedule of all your services?"

"Yes." Rowan reached under the counter, pulled out a small blue sheet of paper, and handed it to me.

"Maybe my sister attends here, but she's not a member yet. Perhaps I can come to your services and try to find her that way."

"That's always a possibility." Rowan tugged on his bowtie as though it were strangling him. "But I wish I could have been more help."

"It's all right." I smiled, since everything on the poor man's face went crinkly with sorrow. "Thank you."

"I know you did your best." Marcus splayed his fingers on the counter. "Thanks, mate."

"Hope you find her," Rowan said in a gravelly whisper. "I'll pray that it'll come good."

"Thank you." A pipe organ revved up in the cathedral—someone practicing perhaps—with one of my favorite hymns, "Holy, Holy, Holy." The majestic and sacred tune, announcing God's glorious presence, could not be ignored. I was glad for the reminder. I would need Him every step of this journey.

"Beautiful, isn't it?"

"Never get tired of hearing it."

Rowan raised his hand, palm facing us. "Well, then . . . cheerio."

"Cheerio." I waved back.

As we stepped away from the counter, Rowan said, "Glad to see you have Marcus to help you. It'll make the search easier . . . and more enjoyable."

"Thanks, mate." Marcus gave Rowan a hearty salute. "I'll pay you later for saying that."

Rowan chuckled.

On the other side of the big wooden doors, away from Rowan's eyes and ears, my enthusiasm faded a little. "I'm so ready for that chocolate now."

"I'm sorry, Lily. I didn't mean to start your day with disappointment."

"Of course you didn't. We did the right thing. I don't want to leave any stones unturned while I'm here." I held up the schedule of services. "This is good . . . to have this complete list. You know, just in case the woman we find on the streets isn't Camille." A jazz band revved up across the street, startling me. Along with the traffic noises and clatter of humanity I didn't even hesitate when Marcus offered his arm.

"I'm pretty confident that this woman is your sister, but you're right. There's no guarantee. I don't mind attending the services with you. If you'd like me to."

"Of course I would, but you don't have to do that. I feel as if I'm abusing you." But I hoped my words wouldn't make him go away. Rowan was right—the search for my sister would have been so much lonelier without Marcus.

"I have the time, and I feel it's a privilege to help you. It's a worthy pursuit."

I touched the sleeve of his jacket. "Thank you so much." I'd been saying that to Marcus a lot lately, and meaning every syllable of it. I slid the church schedule into my purse.

"All right then." He slapped his hands together. "Time to get some serious chocolate in you."

I stayed close to Marcus as we zigzagged through several blocks crowded with people until we got to a paved passageway, which was crammed with boutiques and eateries. People sat at outdoor bistro tables, eating and chatting and sipping coffee as if they were part of a quaint tourist scene in a movie. Awnings and umbrellas covered the area, making it even cozier. "I've never seen anything like this. So, these are laneways?"

"What do you think?"

"It's charming. I wouldn't have imagined all this was hiding back here in this narrow alleyway." Guess not all hidden things were horrible. I glanced into some of the shops as we strolled along. A few curious pigeons neck-waddled over to us and then fluttered on ahead.

"Here's The Chocolat Shoppe. Let's go." With a comical flourish, Marcus swung open the door. When I took in the intoxicating smells of chocolate I thanked God He'd decided to create the cacao bean. What a great idea.

The chic little shop had such a unique atmosphere—subdued lighting, shades of bronze trimmed in gold. The rich elegance enhanced the merchandise and made me salivate, which was exactly their intent.

Soon we were at the front counter and my eyes beheld a lush array of gourmet chocolates. I had to hold myself back from acting like a child and pressing my nose against the curved glass case as I stared at all the goodies—chocolate jewels. "So many, and they're so beautifully presented. They look like eatable treasures."

"Thank you," said the young woman behind the counter, clearly pleased with my reaction to their confections.

"Select as many as you like," Marcus said. "I'm buying."

I looked at him, wanting to frown at his crazy generosity, but couldn't when I saw his obvious joy. "But you bought my dinner last night."

"Please let me do this. I want to."

"All right." I gazed into the case. "Let's see. I'll take one of the rose creams, and one of the lavender truffles," I said to the woman. "Oh, and one of the raspberry mousse-filled ones too."

"That's all?" Marcus asked. "That'll just get you started on your chocolate high."

"I want to save room for lunch. What are you having?"

"Hot chocolate."

"Ohhh."

When the woman gave us our treats on crystal trays, we sat down to swoon. Or at least I did. I ate the chocolates with excruciating slowness, not wanting to rush the delicate process of rapture. "I've always loved chocolate, like any other woman, but I've never had anything like this." I licked my lips. "My taste buds are having a giddy moment."

"Good." Marcus grinned. "Want a sip of my cocoa?"

I'd been eyeing his beverage. "Maybe just a teeny bit."

He handed it over, and I took a luxurious sip. And then another. "Oh, my. A concoction straight from heaven." I handed his glass mug back to him before I tipped it up and drank it down. "I'm curious about something."

"Hmm?"

"How come I haven't heard any 'G'days' since I've been here? I was kind of looking forward to it. Is it just a myth that everybody says it? You know, kind of like how some of the people here think Texans are all cowboys?"

"It is an Aussie term, but it's not as popular in the city as it is in the bush." Marcus pointed to his upper lip. "You have a little chocolate moustache."

"Thanks." I daubed at my mouth. "I noticed you've picked up some of the culture and lingo here. So, do you sort of consider yourself an Aussie now?"

"No. I'm an American, but I'd like to fit in while I'm here. It would be nice to fit in somewhere during my lifetime."

"I do understand what you mean."

"Oh? Tell me." He took another sip from his mug.

"At least growing up, that's the same way I felt around my mother...wanting to fit in. My father passed away when I was little. I have a few fond memories of him. After the age of seven or so, I had a series of nannies, since my mother didn't want to be bothered with me. So, I grew up trying too hard at everything, always trying to seek her approval. All I really wanted was to be with her, instead of spending my time with a woman who was paid to take care of me." I wiped some invisible crumbs off the table, wishing I could flick the problems and years away.

"I'll bet that makes finding your sister even more important. It would give you a place to belong." His attention shifted briefly to a family who was sitting on the other side of the shop. They were laughing together, obviously enjoying one another's company.

"Yes, exactly." Marcus did understand me. "A place to belong. Like in your storybook *When Pigs Fly*. I loved that book. It was just what I needed to hear at the time. Maybe the story was more for me than Julie, although she loved it too. It made us cry when Bernie found his home at last . . . a place where he could belong."

"Made me cry too." Marcus smiled. "That's when I know it will touch somebody else."

How sweet. "Not many guys can say something like that with confidence."

"Well, as you already know, I'm not like most guys."

No indeed. I still could hardly believe the man who sat before me was *the* Miles Hooper. A storyteller who'd impacted my daughter's life, and my life as well. His whimsical tales were always woven with sad elements, but they were also full of heart and humor and a life lesson that was profound without being preachy. I hadn't told Julie yet, about Marcus being Miles, but I would tell her in time.

"I think it's sad you don't write anymore. People will miss your stories. All the children growing up now will never know the wonder of Miles Hooper."

"Thanks, but that's all behind me now. And my old books are still in print, so readers can enjoy those. That is, if kids today find them interesting. Every new generation has different needs and likes."

I took a sip of ice water but gazed at him over the rim of my glass. "But your books are classics. They will always be loved. They're like Pooh Bear, and I've never met anyone who didn't love Pooh."

"That's nice, Lily. I still get sizable royalties from those books. That and the trust fund keep me going."

I moved my glass tray to the side. "But what will you do with your life? The rest of it? You're still fairly young."

"Fairly young?" He grinned.

"Sorry. You know what I mean."

"I don't know." Marcus gripped the edge of the table. "To be honest, I feel that what I'm doing right now is the most important thing I've done since I've been here. This is paramount."

"Eating chocolate?"

"No, helping you to find your sister."

"I know." I made a floppy hand gesture that must have come off as juvenile. "I was just teasing you, which is something I don't do often. So, you really did know who Roo was from Winnie-the-Pooh. You know, when we first met?"

"Yes, I knew. I was just kidding around. Milne is one of my favorite authors. In fact, roo is another word for kangaroo here."

"I didn't know that. Interesting. But . . . why did you?"

"Why did I what, Love?"

I warmed inside and out. What was it about that single word that could shake a person senseless? Or maybe it was the person more than the word? "Why did you kid around so much when we first met? You seem different now." For some reason, I had to know.

"You mean, why didn't I act more normal?" he asked.

"Maybe, although I've never been certain what normal means. But it's like you were trying to charm me and drive me away at the same time."

"Very perceptive." Marcus wagged his finger at me.

"I had to become perceptive for survival. I have a teenage daughter."

"I thought you and your daughter had a perfect relationship."

"It's terrific, but not perfect." I shook my finger back at him. "But you're changing the subject."

Marcus put up his hands like I was about to shoot him.

I wadded up my paper napkin. "So, you admit it then? That you were trying to attract and repel me like some confused magnet."

"No. Maybe. The answer is yes, okay? Crazy, right?" he asked.

I pelted my wadded-up napkin at him. "Yeah, it is crazy." Then I shook my head. "Looks like you're just as messed up as I am."

CHAPTER
twelve

"I'm not going to reply to that one." He looked at me and calmed his mirth. "Okay. All right. I'll explain it. Why I wanted both to attract and repel you. There are parts of me that I keep hidden even from myself." He raised his chin as if his answer had been too deep and mysterious for further explanation.

"Well, that's the bargain-basement reply. Now give me an answer that's worth something."

Marcus flinched. "Ouch."

I grinned.

"Okay." He tapped his finger against his upper lip. "Well, it could be that I acted the way I did yesterday because I find it easier in the long run. I am a quirky man. Not always, but sometimes. And if I give you the full dose right away, like too many shots of espresso, and you don't flee, then I know things have a chance. I mean, what if I came off perfectly normal to begin with?" He wiggled his eyebrows. "And you were interested, but then I shocked you later by suddenly doing something off-the-wall? I guess I like to lay my cards out all at once. Keeps things simple and honest, in a messed-up way."

I waved my hand absently as I thought about it. "That's kind of warped, but I think I actually understood what you're saying, which is a little scary."

Marcus grinned. "Satisfied?"

"For now." I took a bite of the rose cream. I'd saved the best for last. "Oh, my. If chocolate could be a place, then this rose cream is the palace of Versailles." I closed my eyes to heighten the sensation of taste. Ah, yes. I sighed and opened my eyes. "What does your hot cocoa make you think of?"

"Hmm, let's see." He took another sip. "Like all the best days of . . . winter."

"Nice simile." In more ways than one. I licked my fingers. "There will surely be rose creams at the banquet in heaven. Have you ever had one of these particular chocolates?"

"No, can't say that I have."

"Here's the last bite." Without overthinking my actions, I reached out to him and set the piece of cream-filled chocolate in his mouth.

His eyelids closed as he chewed. "Oh, you're right. That is very good." When he opened his eyes again he stared at me. "I have lunch planned for you, and I think you'll really love the place. And then an entire afternoon of activities."

"I'm sure it'll be fun. But I guess we just had dessert before lunch."

"Sometimes it feels right . . . doesn't it?"

"Yes." I nodded. "Sometimes it just feels right."

Marcus drank down the last of his beverage and with dramatic flair said, "Come, woman. Your City Circle Tram awaits."

We left The Chocolat Shoppe and headed off in a different direction from where we'd come. When we'd made it to one of the bigger intersections, Marcus punched the button on the pole to get the traffic light to change.

It still amazed me to watch the clusters of humanity, seemingly countless nationalities—many of them young people—from all over the world, living out their lives in the city and adding to the unique and fascinating culture of Melbourne. "So, do you use the tram to get around the city? You don't have a car?"

"Some people have cars, but I don't . . ." Marcus paused. "Not since . . . well, you know."

How could I have forgotten? His sister, the accident. "I understand." I was sorry I'd mentioned his lack of a car, sorry to have taken a little of the shine from his smile.

We crossed the street together as the City Circle Tram rumbled by us. The streetcar was a quaint trolley, painted maroon and green with yellow and gold trim. It reminded me of the streetcars I'd seen as a child when Nanny Kate had taken me to Galveston on field trips—sort of a Norman Rockwell painting on wheels. "Why don't you tell me something touristy about the tram." Perhaps I could take Marcus's mind off his burden, since I was the one who'd reminded him of the accident.

"Well, the tram is used by about three million passengers a year. How's that?"

"Wow. That's a lot." The tram pulled to a stop a block ahead of us. "It looks crowded."

"Maybe we can catch it," Marcus said, "if we run." He took my hand and together we raced along the sidewalk toward the trolley.

We weren't going to make it. I could feel it. But it was so much fun running with Marcus I didn't care if we made it or not. Sure enough, just as we got close, the tram eased away from its stop. Instead of groaning we laughed. Out of breath, I lowered my hands to my knees.

"Guess we didn't make it. There'll be another one along in a few minutes. No worries."

I glanced at the people in the back of the tram.

A woman wearing a white dress and a jean jacket stood staring at me. She held up her palm to the window of the tram, not taking her eyes off me.

I gasped. It was as if I'd made it onto the tram and I was looking back at myself. "It's Camille," I said, holding out my palm to her. "Camille," I screamed.

"What? You saw her?" Marcus asked.

I took off running after the tram, even though it was impossible to catch up. "Camille!" The woman didn't remove her palm from the window. She stared at me, and I at her, until she became only a blur.

But on I ran. It was as if all the angst and loneliness of my youth, all the longing to be a family, the thrill of seeing Camille's face, propelled my legs forward. Even though the race was futile.

People paused along the sidewalk. Cars slowed next to me. In spite of the breeze rushing in my ears I could hear Marcus. He was right behind me, running too.

But then the toe of my shoe hit something unmovable. I stumbled. My body sailed downward. I thrust out my hands, and they slapped the sidewalk. My right knee caught the bulk of the impact, and I let out a scream. The pain surged through me as if my flesh had been lit by fire. My body curled up into a ball.

Marcus was by my side in a heartbeat, kneeling next to me. "Where are you injured? Lily? Talk to me."

Chapter
thirteen

I pointed to my right knee and let out a moan. Falling down. I'm so good at it. Story of my life.

Marcus lifted the torn material, which revealed a bloody mess. "Let's get you off the sidewalk." He scooped me in his arms and set me down on a bench. "I'm going to take you to a hospital."

"No, I'll be all right. It's not that serious. The pain will ease in a minute." I looked down at my knee. "See? It's more of a scrape than a cut."

Marcus leaned forward and clutched the edge of the bench. When he looked back at me, he'd turned almost as white as the dress I'd seen on the woman in the tram.

"Are you okay?" I asked him.

He seemed to breathe for the first time. "It's my job to keep you safe here. I've failed you."

Then I knew—he was reliving his sister's accident. Why had I run?

I stood as wobbly as a newborn lamb, but I forced my legs to ignore the pain shooting through my knee. "I'm going to be ship-shape. See?" My stomach lurched as I absorbed the pain.

Marcus studied me, his expression awash with what looked like defeat. "I'm supposed to be helping you, not—"

"I'm going to be fine." I sat back down and gently turned Marcus's face toward me. "All I need is to go to the hotel and clean up this wound. It was my fault for chasing that tram. Who would do such a silly thing? Well, no one would who has any good sense."

I tried to chuckle, but it came out lame, as Julie would call it. "I should have remembered that if Camille is well enough to ride the tram, then she would be playing her flute along the promenade this evening. But it all happened so fast I just reacted. It was a shock to see her, and on the very tram I was going to board." In fact, what if we'd arrived at the stop a little earlier? What if I'd finished up my chocolates a few seconds sooner? I stopped my mind games, since they would only make me miserable.

"So, it really was her?" Marcus asked.

I could barely hear him above the noise of the traffic. "Yes, I believe so. You were right. She looks like me. She really does." Camille was no phantom after all. God really had made two of us. I'd seen her face. My identical twin—Camille Violet Daniels. How wonderful and strange to look into my own eyes. What would Mother say? Would she be happy?

But why hadn't my sister at least made an attempt to get off the tram? Her expression wasn't of shock and desperation and joy like mine. It was something else, and yet I didn't know what that something else was exactly.

"I'll make sure you're right where you need to be this evening." Marcus rested his arm behind me on the bench. "Surely Camille will be there on the promenade."

"I hope so." I leaned back against the comfort of his arm.

"But first, let's get you cleaned up."

"All right." Marcus had gotten some of his color back, and I no longer felt woozy, so it seemed safe to head back to the hotel. But something uneasy stayed in my spirit, something connected to Camille's expression.

As we rose to leave, I looked back down the line where the tram had disappeared and then glanced across the avenue, between the speeding buses and honking cars. There on the other side of the street stood a woman dressed in white. It was the same woman from the tram—my twin—and she stood staring at me like a lost child. But how had she gotten off the tram? "Camille?"

I turned to Marcus to tell him, but he'd already taken in the situation. "I'll walk you over to her. She must have gotten off the tram and walked back."

"Miss? Camille?" I hollered to her. "Please wait for me. I'm coming over."

Marcus waited for a break in the traffic—maddening as it was—and then he helped me hop-hobble across the street to what I hoped would be my twin sister, the other mustard seed, who had only been a dream until this moment.

CHAPTER
fourteen

This was it. The moment. What I'd come for. It was her. It had to be Camille—my dear sister. Once on the other side, Marcus and I stepped up on the sidewalk. I approached the woman as if she were a wisp of a mist.

"You got off the tram," I said. "Thank you. I am so—"

"I told them it was an emergency, so they—" Her voice faded into a swirl of air. Except for the differences in our accents, Camille's voice was like mine. It had a creamy quality like a spoonful of pudding.

"Are you Camille Violet Daniels?"

"Yes."

I tried to take in more air, but my faster breaths only made me lightheaded. *Calm yourself, Lily.*

"You're thinner than I imagined. And you have longer hair." Camille clutched herself around her waist.

"So, you know who I am?" I wanted to memorize everything about her. My feverish study landed on her eyes. They had that same gray hue with flecks of green and brown. And the same probing, melancholy gaze as if perpetually searching for something. Perhaps she'd found it—perhaps we both had. So lovely. Camille was beautiful. Did that mean I was beautiful too? "Forgive me for staring. This is pretty wild to see you for the first time."

But then Camille was staring too. "Like looking into a mirror. Yeah," she said in a breathy voice. Her gaze intensified as it brimmed with cautious scrutiny.

"Yes." I chuckled, eager to hug her, but I took my cues from her more quiet approach and stayed back.

"So, you're my identical twin sister, Lily." Camille's remark came out more to herself than to me.

"Yes, I am. Lily Winter. I married, but I'm a widow now." I released another joyful chuckle. "I can't tell you how happy I am to find you. I thought it might not happen, and yet God saw fit to let us have a reunion." But concern wiggled between us. Why didn't Camille seem as elated as I was?

Camille turned her head and coughed. "It was from the note I sent your mother, wasn't it?"

"Yes. I would have come right away, six months ago when you sent the note, but Mother just now told me. I never knew about you until recently." I tried not to grind my teeth at the thought of Mother holding back such news.

"Yes, that sounds about right." Camille's tone held a slight edge. "But then I never expected anyone to come. I'm sorry you fell just now and hurt yourself, trying to find me."

"It's okay. I'm just so thrilled to meet you."

Camille stuck out her hand.

I took her hand in mine and gave it a jovial shake. Her skin felt cool and her muscles shivery. "Do you mind it if I give you a hug?"

"Of course not."

At first I wasn't sure if she meant a yes or no. I paused but when she took a step closer to me I took her in my arms for a good bear hug. The kind Julie always loved. She smelled of mint. Nice. But Camille didn't return the embrace. Her arms merely moved from her waist to her side. My spirit felt a little crushed. *Oh, dear God, what's wrong?* Why didn't my sister seem happy over our reunion? I released Camille and pulled back to study her. "I realize this is kind of sudden. Maybe I should have called you first. I didn't have your number. I wasn't sure—"

"I didn't send my phone number or address for a reason," she said.

"Oh, I see." But I didn't understand at all. The passersby gaped at us. A woman's purse bumped me. "You know, maybe it would be easier if we went inside. Somewhere cozy so we can talk."

I suddenly remembered Marcus, whom I'd forgotten to introduce. I glanced around and found him. He'd backed away from us—I assume to give us some privacy, but there was little to be had on the sidewalk. I gestured to Marcus to come over to meet my sister. Maybe he could add some warmth to our reunion. "Camille, this is my new Aussie friend, Marcus Averill. He's been helping me . . . to find you. I don't know what I would have done without him."

"Hi." Camille smiled, but didn't reach out her hand to him.

"Good to meet you," Marcus said to her. "I know Lily is excited to finally meet you."

"That's nice." Camille turned back to me. "I guess what I have to say can be said right here." She tugged on her ear, just the way I used to do when I was a kid.

"Okay." I had a feeling her next words were going to devastate me, so I wanted to run and hide. "Yes?"

"I have a message for your mother and for you," Camille said.

Even amidst the noise on the street and the hustle-bustle of people, the air seemed to crackle with nervous energy and ire. The world stopped its spinning as it waited—as I waited—for Camille's reply. For a sign of any kind that she might welcome me into her life.

Camille coughed again. This time with more fervor.

"Are you okay?"

"No. I've never been okay. That's the problem."

"I don't know what you mean." I tried to keep the rising panic out of my voice.

"I didn't send my phone number and address because part of me didn't want to have anything to do with your mother or father or with any of you. But I couldn't seem to sever things completely.

Another part of me wanted you to know what I've been through. I felt I deserved that small courtesy."

"Of course. I will—"

"You can tell Mr. and Mrs. Gray that they were heartless to give me away simply because I was sickly. What kind of a mother does that to her child at one year old?"

"I had no idea that's what happened." Father had actually agreed with Mother? To do something so merciless? I clutched my throat, desperate for her to understand me. "Mother told me you were taken away from her, but I had no idea what really happened."

Camille burbled out a laugh laced with bitterness. "So, this is the lie they told themselves and everyone around them."

"I doubt she's told anyone about you until now, except, of course, when you were first born. She would have had to tell some people then. Honestly, with such a horrible scenario Mother would be ashamed I'm sure. I hope she would be ashamed anyway. And I don't know about Father. He's been dead since I was nine."

"Oh."

"So much has happened. So many years . . ." I reached out to Camille, but seeing that she was already backing away, I dropped my hand. "Please, it's so noisy out here. Couldn't we talk somewhere quiet? Like a café?" My head went light and buzzy.

When Camille didn't reply, I said, "I agree. What our parents did to you was truly heartless. You've obviously been through some rough times because of them. Believe me, I know. Mother has been unkind to me more times than—"

"Please stop." Camille put up her hands. "You cannot possibly understand. After Mrs. Gray gave me away, I was adopted by Naomi and Terrell Daniels. My adoptive mother was a good woman, a decent mother, but she died when I was ten. My father swore it was an accident with some sleeping pills, but I know what really happened. She took her own life. She couldn't handle his abusive ways. After her death I had to grow up fast. My father lost his job and then started to drink. That made him become even more abusive. One night I barely survived the beating. So, please don't tell me you understand. It's deeply insulting to me."

Marcus stirred next to me but said nothing.

"It was a bad choice of words on my part. Please forgive me. I just want to get to know you. I want to have a relationship with—"

"But why?" Camille raised her hands and splayed her fingers in the air. "You're just going back home in a few days. We'll never see each other again. You have your life. I have mine, what little bit I've scraped together for myself. You were the chosen one, Lily. The child who was born with good health and put up on the shelf to be admired . . . treasured. I am the broken doll that was put in a cardboard box and given away.

"Now, almost forty years later," Camille went on to say, "you expect me to forget everything and make merry as if nothing happened. As if you can wipe away the past with a few pretty words. You've come to take a piece of my heart, but you might as well be asking for a slice of the moon." She covered her mouth with a handkerchief and coughed. "That's my message to you and your mother. I've been practicing it for a very long time."

"Oh, I see. Well . . ." Even though Camille and I spoke the same language, and all the words were at my disposal, I stammered, feeling bewildered and spent.

Before I could find the right words, Camille said, "Now, if you'll excuse me, Lily Winter, I'm going to finish living my life." And then Camille turned away from me and hurried down the sidewalk. Like a rock thrown into the sea, she was absorbed by the undulating crowd.

I turned to Marcus. "I don't want it to end this way. It just can't. What should I do?" I took hold of his arm, nearly tearing his sleeve.

"Lily, I'm so sorry," he said.

"I can't let her go. I'm going to run after her."

"You can't run anywhere with that wounded knee, but I can." Marcus took off after Camille, but I limped behind him. When some of the people walked on by and the crowd opened up, I got a better view of Camille and Marcus. He'd caught up with her, and they were talking. I stopped, watching intently. Marcus looked as if he was trying to convince her of something. Camille nodded slowly. She no longer appeared to be in a flight mode. Maybe Marcus could save the day, salvage the moment.

After a few moments, which seemed like time without end, he walked back toward me. With a smile on his handsome face.

Camille looked back at me. She didn't smile, but she gave me a nod and then strode on her way.

I limped up to Marcus. "What happened?" Please let it be good news.

CHAPTER
fifteen

"She's willing to meet with you," Marcus said to me.

"Really? How did you do it? What did you say?" I latched onto the sleeve of his jacket and didn't let go.

He glanced away, paused, and then looked at me. "I told your sister that there was a car accident a year ago that killed my sister, and it was my fault. And that I would give anything to see her again. Just one chance to say I was sorry and to tell her how much I love her. Please give Lily this one chance . . . the chance I'll never get."

A hundred emotions erupted inside me, and I could do nothing but let them out. I gave Marcus the hug that Camille would not accept. "Thank you." As if he were still connected to my sister, I didn't want to let go of him.

He wrapped his arms around me, creating a little cocoon from the noise and the crowds and the fresh remembrance of watching Camille walk away from me in an attitude of hurt and anger. "I realize I'm making a blubbering fool of myself out here on the sidewalk, but I don't care," I said into his jacket.

"It's all right." He rubbed my back and made soft noises that consoled me as I continued to bury my face in the curve of his arm. *Camille, why did you run? We need each other. How can you not see what I see?* A car honked and then screeched to a halt in the street, jarring me from my little womb of daydreams. I eased away from Marcus and asked, "Where am I supposed to meet her?"

"Tonight. She's going to play her flute. She'll be in her usual spot."

"That's wonderful. Thank you again and again." I shook my head. "But I don't know what went wrong earlier."

"I think she's scared. Maybe your sister had planned to tell you off and then be rid of you, but now that she's met you in person it wasn't so easy. She's scared to get involved . . . to care about you."

"Do you think that's really it?"

"It's just a guess," he said. "How's your knee?"

"I sort of forgot about it." I offered him a lukewarm smile.

"You might remember your knee again when we start walking. You still need to get it cleaned up and bandaged."

"We'd better go back for now." I knew we'd miss our fun outing, but for me the joy had ended when Camille walked away.

"Here, lean on me." Marcus held out his arm to me. "And if you don't, then I'm going to pick you up in front of this whole crowd and carry you back. Okay?"

It wasn't a request, so I quickly took Marcus's arm and put some of my weight on him.

When we'd made it back to the lobby of my hotel, I said, "I suddenly feel the full load of what just happened with my sister and the news about my parents, and to be honest, I'm worn out." Someone at the front desk looked over at me with concern. Since I didn't want to draw attention to myself, I lowered my voice. "I think I'd like to clean up and rest."

"Do you want to talk about it? Would that help?"

"I will sometime, but right now I just want to be in bed. I want to be unconscious from this day." I didn't even want to dream, fearing it wouldn't be a happy one.

"All right then. I understand. It must have been quite a blow today. I know it wasn't what you'd expected."

"Maybe I was hoping for one of those family reunions like you see on TV." I let out a chuckle. "Nothing ever really works out like we plan . . . does it?"

"No. But sometimes things turn out much better."

"Yes, that's true. Easy to forget that on a day like this."

Before Marcus turned to go, I asked, "How about dinner? Would that be okay?" I couldn't believe I suggested a date, but that was exactly what I'd done. And if Marcus said no I would go to my room and cry like a baby. I was that wound up emotionally from my encounter with Camille. And I was that fond of him.

"But tonight is special," Marcus said. "You don't want me to tag along. You should wait and eat after you hear Camille play. Your sister might be able to eat with you."

"Now that's thoughtful," I said.

"Don't get me wrong. I would love to take you out, but your sister seems skittish, and with me there you won't be able to really talk, and it sounds like you both have a great deal of road to cover. This evening needs to be about twins bonding for the first time, not a date with me, even though I'd love to be selfish and say yes. But I'd just clog up the works. Am I right?"

"When you word it like that I see your point." If my heart were a flower it would have withered just then.

Marcus raised his chin. "But you will miss me, no doubt."

"Yes. You will be missed." The same teasing and cocky attitude that had been so irritating when I'd first met Marcus no longer felt that way. It was funny and endearing. I would have smiled brighter, but my injured knee felt like it had been fed through a meat grinder.

"Do you need help in the lift?" he asked.

"The lift?"

"Sorry. The elevator." Marcus grinned. "Can you make it upstairs okay?"

"I can. Thanks."

Marcus seemed to be stalling. Perhaps he didn't want to go, just as I didn't really want him to go. "Are you sure you know the spot where your sister will be playing this evening?"

"I'm sure."

"Don't forget your sweater or you'll be cold."

"You mean my jumper?" I smiled.

"Your jumper." Marcus cleared his throat. "Well then, I guess I'll go. You need your rest."

"Yes. I do."

"Good. That's good." But instead of backing away he stepped closer to me. "This has been quite a day."

"It has." I perked up again. "Crazy. Memorable. Terrifying. Hopeful."

Marcus hovered near me. He smelled like coffee. Loved that scent.

I thought he might dip a little lower and a little closer and kiss me, but at the last second he pulled away. "I know you'll want to keep your calendar freer now because of your sister, but if you don't schedule anything tomorrow night, I would love to take you to one of the finer dining places here. Something very special."

"Okay. I would love that," I said just above a whisper.

"I'll pick you up tomorrow evening at six then, since Houstonians eat at a civilized hour."

I grinned. "I'm already looking forward to it." I watched him pause again and then walk toward the hotel's glass doors.

Just as he neared the exit, he turned around and looked at me one more time. He gave me a playful wink.

He'd caught me staring at him, but I didn't care. A tingling sensation trickled through me with that look of his, and I knew then that the never-been-worn, little black dress would no longer be in search of an evening . . .

CHAPTER
sixteen

I woke up to a noise so loud it frightened me. It was me—snoring. Must have come off as feminine as a tobacco-spitting lumberjack. Then I looked at the clock on the nightstand in my hotel room. Seven p.m. No! I'd planned on a short nap, not hibernation. I'd slept through lunch and almost dinner. And if I wasn't careful I'd miss meeting my sister. I was hopeless.

Speed dressing, I threw on some fresh clothes and limped-raced—my knee still smarting with every step—out of the hotel and along the promenade. When I arrived at the spot where I knew my sister would perform, a crowd had already gathered. I slowed my pace and then, as amicably as possible, I nudged my way through a cluster of people.

There she was, my sister, standing by the river, dressed in white, and playing her silver flute. Camille looked like a fairy straight from *A Midsummer Night's Dream.* Marcus had been right. People stood still, mesmerized by her music. Even though she had a downcast expression, her face appeared luminous and ivory and as delicately carved as a cameo. She held a faraway gaze as her ebony hair, shimmery like a raven's wings, danced around her face in the breeze. The sound floating from her flute was pure Celtic magic, and like the curling waters close by, the music slowly wound its way around our hearts.

This is my sister.

I wanted to shout it out, but of course I merely listened with a grateful heart. To find my sister made me feel as if I was more in sync with life, and yet how could that be? The thought seemed a little dramatic, and yet I knew it to be true. My life would be forever changed by my discovery, and I was glad for it.

How could Mother have done such a thing—keep one twin and give away the other? And what about Father? He was equally guilty, and yet I'd barely thought of his role in the affair. Mothers always seemed to take the brunt of the blame when it came to the neglect of a child. What had been their excuse for such behavior? *Lord, please help me not to hate my parents.*

When Camille came to the close of her melody she stood perfectly still, as if the music needed a moment of awe before she moved on. After several seconds, people broke into applause. Others dropped money into a bowl.

Camille looked up and noticed me but didn't return my smile.

When the crowd realized she was finished playing, they strolled on down the promenade.

I walked up to Camille as she took her flute apart and then gingerly set the three pieces into her case.

"That was amazing. I've never heard anything so beautiful."

"Thanks."

"I play the piano, but no one wants to hear it." Except Julie.

"Oh?" Camille gaped at me. "Sorry. This identical twin thing takes some getting used to."

"I know what you mean. We could have caused quite a ruckus growing up . . . switching our names and fooling everyone. Although I've never been one to tease people. I'm usually a pretty serious person overall." Oh, dear. I was turning into a motormouth. I prayed she wouldn't bolt again.

Camille didn't reply but picked up the cash in the bowl and stuffed it into her purse. Then she turned and looked out over the river.

I went to stand next to her and gazed toward the water along with her. Quiet was better anyway. This moment called for feeling not yammering.

Camille finally spoke. "I guess you think I'm a bad seed, don't you?"

"Not at all. How do you mean?"

"Well, you came all the way from the US to find me, injured yourself in the process, and then I basically told you to go jump in the river."

God, give me the right words. "It wasn't easy to hear what you had to say, I admit. But you've been through some terrible traumas in your life. Things I cannot understand."

Camille set her instrument case down by her feet. "But I ruined what you'd hoped to be a happy reunion. It's just that there's been this buildup of suffering for a long time and no one to blame. No one to yell at. And here you came. It's like you were this tiny tremor that set off an earthquake."

I breathed again, glad that we were really talking. "I'm sorry I said all the wrong things. It's just that I was so excited to see you."

"Yeah, I could tell." She smiled, just a little smile but it lit her face.

"Do you think there's any way we could start over? Maybe I could do better the second time around."

"All right. I should give you that, since you came all this way."

"I don't have much family left, so finding you was very important to me."

"You said you were a widow?" Camille asked.

"Yes, my husband passed away a year ago. I have a daughter named Julie, but she's in college now. She's the joy of my life." I pulled my hair back in a scrunchie, since it was whipping my face. "So, did you ever marry?"

"No, but I have a boyfriend . . . Jerald Waldgrave. He claims he's going to propose to me soon, but soon never seems to come." Camille straightened her dress.

A deeper meaning trolled just below the surface of Camille's admission, but I let it go. I instead began picking at my fingers.

Camille looked at my hands. "How long have you done that to your hands?"

"Ever since I was a kid, whenever I got anxious." I glanced at her hands. "Do you pick?"

"No, but I have TMJ from stress. Guess it all has to come out somewhere." She paused and then said, "Let me ask you something. What was Father like? I mean, the man who would have been my father?"

What could be said about him in just a few words? "He was a good man, but I think he suffered from depression some. He never seemed to want to play with me much or be a part of my life. I think he loved me, but I'm not sure he really liked me much. As I mentioned, he died when I was nine. To be honest I think it was Mother who made him depressed." That part reminded me of Camille's youth. "They didn't have a very happy marriage. But then every life she's touched has been made less happy by being near her."

"Including yours?"

I nodded. "Including mine. It's as if she's been living under a cloud of misery, and she wants to make sure everyone else's life is too. I never really understood it until today . . . maybe until that moment . . . when you told me the truth. It's not just a cloud of misery, but of guilt, over what she did . . . what they did."

Camille gathered a ribbon from her dress and wound the fabric around her finger until the tip turned an angry red. "So, you think she's sorry for what she did to me?"

"I can't know her mind for sure. We've never been close, but I see it now. It all makes sense. Perhaps this sin has slowly been eating away at her all these years."

Camille looked up at the sky. "I'd like to say it makes me glad to hear it. That she deserves every bit of misery that comes her way. But I can't. I know it would hurt God's ears to hear it, so I won't say it. But it's tempting."

"Aren't you freezing out here without a jacket?"

"I'm a little cold, but I'm used to it."

"Mother did a terrible thing, Camille, and she needs to confess her sins to God. But she's an agnostic, so that's a tragedy. *And* she needs a friend she can talk to about it, but she doesn't really have friends. But recently she hired one." I shivered and snuggled down into my jacket, thinking how absurd and hopeless it all sounded.

"What? Really? You can do that? Hire a friend?"

"Apparently. Mother's never been very interested in talking to me or making me a friend. In fact, when I went to visit her and she told me about you . . . we hadn't seen each other in a decade."

Camille gave me a heavy pause. "Really? Your relationship was that bad?"

"It was and still is. So, I can't say that I was ever put on a shelf and treasured. More like just put on a shelf and left to gather dust. But I'd like to make things right somehow. I want to . . ." Tears came then. I was about to embarrass myself, but I couldn't help it. "Isn't there anything I can do to help you? I mean, to ease the pain of this terrible thing Mother did to you? She—" My voice caught in my throat. "I'm sorry to be so emotional."

"You're all right. I used to cry like that. All the time, actually."

"You did?" I dug out several tissues from my purse, blew my nose, and cleaned up my face. "Do you mind if I ask how you got over the tendency to get weepy?"

Camille gazed out over the city. "They say that sometimes the orphan babies in China are left to themselves with little care of any kind. They cry for help until they cannot cry anymore. The tears and weary pleas for comfort and food are replaced by vacant stares. Their little spirits are broken—utterly. Those who've seen it say it's eerie . . . unnatural . . . that kind of silence. I think of those sweet babies when I play my music. I guess I'm playing for them and for the lost little girl inside me who never got to grow up."

CHAPTER
seventeen

I closed my eyes briefly, letting the full sensation of that great sadness work its way through me. The chasm between us grew deeper. I had known coldness in my youth, but I couldn't fathom the level of my sister's pain. Would I ever understand her suffering or know that young girl who was left alone with a villain? "I don't know what to say. 'Sorry' will never be enough."

Camille clasped her hands behind her back and faced me again. "In answer to your question, I can't see how there is anything you can do to make up for what happened. What was done cannot ever be undone."

"But what about a relationship? I want to know you. I would love my Julie to know you. Wouldn't life be better somehow for both of us if we could have the sisterhood that we were denied? It's too late to undo the past, but we could make something good, you and me, out of the time we have left."

"You're so passionate," Camille said.

"I am? I've never thought of myself that way."

"Oh, but you are. You're glowing with it. I forgot what it looked like." Then she added, "But hate is a kind of passion."

"Yes, it is."

Camille picked up her instrument case. "I admit, I did hate you both on days when things got unbearable for me. I hated your mother for tossing me away because I was sickly, and I hated you for being the one who got to stay. Who was good and perfect enough to be loved. That was the other thing, you see. I wrestled with that hatred and with the guilt that invariably comes with it. And yet I'd been innocent in all of this. So, some other part of me felt I had a right to those dark feelings. Sometimes it seemed to be all I had left."

She clutched the case to her. "And that moral dilemma made me crazy for a while. I was institutionalized for it. Eventually, the hatred dissolved into depression. So, I've been taking meds for it. That's probably why I weigh more than you do. It's one of the side effects of the drug. But I've been slowly tapering off the drugs for a while now."

Since the moment Mother had told me about Camille I hadn't imagined such scenarios. I wasn't sure what to do, what to say. My words were useless and empty. Tears came in trickles and then turned into quiet sobs. I no longer cared what people thought as they passed me on the street. I saw my mother and my father's sin, and it reeked of selfishness and cruelty.

So, I wept. Again. "I'm so sorry. I can't seem to stop crying. I'm just—"

"Oh, dear. We'd better get you inside. People are starting to gawk at us. Pretty soon they'll stop to ask if I've hit you or something. And you're turning blue in this sudden chill."

"I'll stop crying. I promise." Camille seemed uncomfortable with my emotions, but lately my tears had approached melodramatic proportions. I accepted a wad of tissues from her.

"If you don't stop weeping you're going to wind up with a vicious headache. At least that's what used to happen to me."

"I get them too." I cleaned my face again and gave her a smile of recovery.

"That's better. All right. I guess I shouldn't tell you any more about my life for a few minutes so you can recover. Otherwise, you'll end up in the nuthouse like me." She released a chuckle. "Are you ready for tea?"

I nodded. "I'd love something to eat too if that's okay."

"Well, what you call dinner in America is called tea here. Or roughly the same thing."

"Oh? Then I'd love tea."

"Come on." She waved me on to go with her. "I'll show you a non-touristy place where the food is great and cheap."

"Thanks." Dinner with Camille was just what I'd hoped for. I followed her along the promenade and then off the beaten path into a cubbyhole of an eatery that was barely visible from the walkway. The place, The Gondola Café, looked stark and simple. Photos of American celebrities plastered the walls, and music from the sixties and seventies blared out of the wall speakers. Plain metal tables filled the room, which were overflowing with locals and tourists. Not much for décor, but Camille had promised me the food was terrific. When we went to place our order, a burly man with a rose tattoo and a widow's peak barreled through a pair of swinging doors and looked back and forth at us from behind the counter.

He laughed, which set his jowls to jiggling. The man said, "Ya don't see identicals very oft. Say, one of you plays the flute out there, right?" He pointed his thumb toward the promenade.

"That's me." Camille smiled.

"An angel. That's what you play like."

"Thank you."

"You're very welcome, Love. Well, what'll it be? You'll have to speak up. There're a lot of yahoos in here this evening. Yeah."

"Let's have the meat pie with gravy," Camille said to me. "Sounds fattening, but you won't regret it."

I hesitated.

"Come on, give it a burl."

I didn't know what that meant, but I told the man in a loud voice above the crowd, "I'll have the meat pie with gravy."

"Make it two," Camille said.

The man hollered back to the kitchen. "Two dog's eyes." He gave us a toothy grin. "Be out in a jiff."

Dog's eyes? Must be a colloquialism, but I wasn't sure I wanted to know any more details concerning my order. I let it rest as we settled ourselves down at one of the last open tables. "I'm amazed all these people aren't outside."

"The tables are probably full out there." Camille pulled off her scarf, which was loosely wrapped around her neck, and set it on the table. She looked intently at me, something we both had been doing to each other.

"It's hard for us to stop staring at each other I guess."

She lifted the tiny vase of roses to her nose and took a whiff.

"I'm curious about a lot of things," I said. "You know, the fact that we're twins."

"I'm pretty curious too. Remember, I've known about you all my life, so I've had time to wonder about all kinds of things."

We both leaned toward each other at the same time. "You go first," I said.

"Well, I have slightly crooked teeth on the bottom row and a mole on my left arm right by my elbow."

I showed her my mole in the same spot and my somewhat crooked teeth on the bottom. Then I grinned.

"Okay," she continued. "I can't use a map, but I don't know why. I get the hiccups after one sip of soda, and I always close my eyes during the scary part of movies."

I waved my hand across the table. "Same all the way across the board, except I try not to watch scary movies. Right after I heard about you, I looked up some things online. Did you know we have the same brain wave patterns? Not identical, but close."

"Yes, I read that too." Camille titled her head at me, studying me. "Maybe that's why since I've met you, even in this short time . . . I almost know what you're going to say. At least what you're saying doesn't surprise me as much as it should. Do you know what I mean?"

"I do. Scary, but fun, right?" I brightened but tried not to overwhelm her with my excitement.

"Sort of, yes." Camille shifted in her chair. "Now for the more serious stuff. Usually, adoptions are closed, which would have made this harder . . . this little reunion. But I knew early on that I'd been adopted, and that it was the open kind. Naomi told me who my birth mother was and why I was given away. She wanted me to know the truth. I appreciated that about her, being straight with me, even though it wasn't easy on me to hear it or easy on her to tell me. But the open adoption never made sense, since there was almost no communication. But the older I get the more tempting it is to ask questions . . . the really hard ones. Maybe someday when you and your mother are on better terms you can ask her some of my questions. Then you can email me."

"Are you sure you don't want to ask Mother yourself?" I picked at my paper napkin, plucking it like feathers. At least I wasn't plucking at my fingers.

"I don't think I'd better do that. I'd end up screaming at your mother, and she'd order me out of the house. It'd be quite a scene. I don't know how I could be civil to her. So, I don't see the point in flying to America to be angrier than I've already been. Besides, that flight costs a small fortune. How did you manage it? Do you have lots of money?"

"I have money from my husband's life insurance after he died and from my job as a secretary, but I'm not rich. I'm trying to help Julie through college, so the money isn't flowing as well as it did before she left. But coming here was a priority. It was something I felt I had to do . . . to find you." I wanted to reach out to her, to touch her hand, but it was still too soon.

"Nothing would have changed if you hadn't come, though. We would have gone on with our lives just the same. Yeah."

"But if I'd stayed at home and done nothing it would have . . . I mean, I couldn't just let you go. Once I knew you existed, it changed everything. Even my daughter, Julie, was excited for us to meet. She always dreamed of having an aunt and cousins. I mean, you are Julie's Aunt Camille."

"Julie's aunt." She seemed to mull it over. "That does have a nice sound to it. But you let your mother go just like I let all of you go. You didn't visit her for a whole decade. How is that different than our separation?"

"Good point, but my mother didn't want to see me. I wanted to connect, but she made it nearly impossible. I don't like forcing my way in when I'm not wanted."

Camille chuckled. "You could have fooled me about that earlier today."

"I guess I was kind of pushy."

Our food came then—a small round pie with tomato sauce on top. "Wow, I've had chicken pot pie but nothing like this."

"Hope you like it. This meat pie is rabbit with mushrooms."

Rabbit? I paused. "Oh?" They cooked such unique meats in Aussieland. Not just the usual chicken, fish, pork, and beef fare, but little Roos and lambkins and Easter bunnies. I tried not to wince, since I didn't want to hurt Camille's feelings. Instead, I dug in, blew on my forkful, and eased it into my mouth. "Ohhh, this is good." I took another decadent bite. I pointed to her left hand with my fork. "So, you're a left-hander like I am. I think it's pretty uncommon for both twins to be left-handed. I guess that make us . . . exceptional."

Camille smiled then—a good smile—and it pleased me to see it.

The Beatles' tune "Eleanor Rigby" started wafting out of the speakers. "You know, come to think of it, I've heard a lot of pop music since I've been here. And they talk about US news on TV a lot more than I'd expected. What's up with that?"

"Aussies have a real fondness for America, but sometimes you wouldn't think so when they start arguing about politics and such." Camille took a bite of her meat pie.

"How do you mean?"

"Well, let me just say that Melbourne is a rather secular city."

"Isn't it hard on your faith?"

She took a sip of her water. "I attend St. Paul's Cathedral, but I haven't joined the church yet. My life always seems to be moving on. I'm like this piece of driftwood, never quite finding that distant shore. That was yet another reason I was hoping my boyfriend would propose. I thought it would help me to settle down. You may not know this, but even though I live in Melbourne, I'm still an American citizen. Actually, I've lived all over . . . here and there."

"Really? Tell me about it."

Camille ran her fingernail across her hand, leaving a white mark on her skin. "After Mum died, my stupid-as-a-bunyip father dragged me around from country to country, including the US. I guess he kept me around to cook for him. He was not only an alcoholic and abusive, but he was a wanderer. Never could stay put. And so even though I loathed him, I guess I became a wanderer too. Then because of a friend's positive experience and encouragement I wound up here in Melbourne. So, I guess my accent and clothes and cultural leanings are all muddled." She gave her head a little shake. "I'm a mishmash of everything and nothing."

"Well, you're not nothing to me." I offered her a decisive nod.

"Your boyfriend must really care about you," Camille said, clearly changing the subject. "He was adamant today that I needed to give you a chance to speak your mind."

"I'm awfully glad he talked to you, but Marcus is not my boyfriend. We've only just met."

Camille cocked her head at me. "I think he likes you . . . a lot."

"What makes you say that?"

"The way he looks at you."

I pulled back a little, clueless but curiously happy about her announcement. "How do you mean?"

She shrugged. "You know what I mean. The *look*."

I crossed my arms. "I want details. I want—"

"Okay, okay. Marcus looks at you like, I don't know, like he's a diamond in the dark, but you're the only halogen light in the world to bring out the fire."

I burst out laughing. "Ridiculous. How in the world did you come up with that?"

She crossed her arms, mimicking me. "Just an observation. I wish my boyfriend would look at me that way."

"Oh?"

Camille studied me carefully. "Be honest now. You didn't know he cared?"

"Okay. I knew a little." I scraped up some of the gravy with my spoon, took a big high-caloric bite, and moaned over all the flavors and richness. "This is really good."

"So, what do you plan to do with Marcus when you leave?" Camille asked. "Just dump him?"

"Well, dumping implies that we have something serious going on. If there is anything happening it would be at an early stage."

Camille fingered the rose in the tiny vase. "Like a seedling?"

"No, like the seed."

She grinned. "You're kind of funny, Lily Winter."

"Thanks. I guess."

But I honestly didn't know what would happen to Marcus, to us, if things progressed. Now Camille was making me squirm. Time to change the topic. "So, are you and your boyfriend serious about marriage? If you don't mind me asking?"

"I'm serious, but I guess he isn't." She turned up her nose like she had a nasty taste in her mouth. "No proposal yet, and as I think I mentioned to you . . . we've been dating for a year."

"Will I get to meet him?"

"Mabes."

"What's mabes?"

"It's just something I say sometimes. Short for maybe. People like to abbreviate words here."

"I've heard about that."

"If it's okay . . . I don't want to talk about Jerald anymore."

"Okay." I didn't want to talk about Marcus either. New subject. "So, let me ask you this . . . if Mother wanted you to come for a visit and she paid your way, would you consider it? I think she needs to see you before she dies."

"Dies?" Camille set her fork down. "Is she dying?"

"No, not that I know of, but she's older now. Sometimes it only takes a little fall or an illness, to . . . well, you know."

"Going back would be difficult. I always promised myself that I would never return to see what could have been. To know my other life." Camille's shoulders sagged, but there was the slightest resignation in her tone.

Perhaps I'd softened her toward the idea of coming for a visit. "I'd like to lie to you and say things are fine. But there's been enough lying over the years . . . and secrets. I guess I was hoping we could all have a fresh start or at least give it a try."

"You've become more of an optimist than I am," Camille said.

"Well, did Mrs. Gray ever mention that she wanted to see me?"

"Not yet, but the fact that Mother finally told me about you means something significant. I hope you'll consider it. You could even go back with me when I return, and together we could—"

Camille put up her hands. "No more, Lily. I don't want to argue with you about this. I'm having a nice time, so let's just drop it."

"All right." I backed down. The last thing I wanted to do was drive Camille away again. I wanted so much to make this work, to no longer be severed from my flesh and blood. I suddenly thought of my front yard back home and the river birch tree planted there— the one that started with two trunks. When one died, I cut it off, but the other trunk never fully recovered. The tree never grew quite straight or healthy without the other appendage—never the way it was meant to be. "So, can we have lunch tomorrow?"

"Maybe."

Keep it light, Lily. I had only three bites of meat pie left, so I slowed my gobbling to make the evening last longer. "So, when you were little did you have trouble going to sleep?"

"Always."

I grinned. "Me too."

"Well, I couldn't sleep until I went through my little ritual."

"What was that?"

Camille made a stacking gesture. "I piled all my stuffed animals around me on my bed and made a fortress, a safe place to be with my little furry friends who would follow me into my dream world. Then once they were all lined up and in place, I feel asleep."

"I can't believe it. Me too." I nearly screamed the words. I'd always heard that twins were so alike in nature and so close in mindset it almost mimicked a sixth sense. If Camille gave me the chance to get to know her, it would be fascinating to see the genetic cord that might reveal itself in time. But time was something there would be little of. I'd need to make the most of every moment.

"So, you really like your meat pie? You didn't mind eating Thumper?"

I blinked. "You're kind of funny, Camille Violet Daniels."

"I think you bring it out in me. Listen, I got to thinking . . . I can't meet you for lunch tomorrow, but I can do tea again. I wish I could offer more, but I'm busy with other obligations . . . job . . . Jerald."

Oh dear. Tea meant dinnertime, and I'd promised Marcus we'd go out. Surely he would understand, though. Camille was the reason I'd come to Melbourne. I liked Marcus, more by the day, but Camille would have to be my priority.

When we'd finished our food and headed out into the brisk wind, Camille said, "Well, good night, Lily. It was good. Better than I'd expected."

"See you tomorrow. Same time, same place."

"Sure. See you tomorrow." Camille turned and walked away in the opposite direction. When she'd vanished around a corner I realized I still hadn't gotten her phone number or address. In other words, if she chose not to play her flute or meet me tomorrow evening I would have lost track of her again. What had I been thinking? I was so thrilled to get to know her I'd forgotten how volatile it all could be, like the winds of Melbourne. I'd just have to trust her word.

With that new thought nagging at me, I zipped up my coat against the biting wind and returned to my hotel. When I whooshed into the lobby, to my great surprise, Marcus was there waiting for me. He leaped from the couch when he saw me.

CHAPTER
eighteen

"What are you doing here?" I walked over to him, happy to see his smile.

"I came in after tea. I wanted to see how it went with your sister."

Okay, so was this guy trying to melt my heart? "Thanks." I wanted to give Marcus a hug, since I excelled at hugs. It felt right as rain on flowers to do so, and yet I held back. Maybe Camille's question had influenced me—what would I do with Marcus when it was time to go home?

"So, how did it go? And how's your knee?"

"My knee aches, but I'll be fine. I'm on the mend. And it went well with Camille. At first she was aloof, but that was understandable. She's been hurt in ways I cringe to imagine. But after a while she warmed up to me. I think the more time we spend together, the better." Now, for the hard part. "In fact, the only time Camille could be with me tomorrow was for dinner, or tea." I grinned. "So, do you mind if we move our plans? I know—"

"I don't mind at all."

"Oh?" I waited a second or two for Marcus to pick another evening for our date, but his pause went longer than expected. "Marcus? What is it?"

"You know, I did have some time to think while I waited for you, and I couldn't be happier that you found your sister. It's what we hoped and prayed for. And now you're getting to know her. I feel honored that I was a part of this endeavor."

Endeavor? His little speech made me scared. "What are you trying to say?"

"I'm saying that I was happy to help you, but now I'll just be getting in your way. You need to be thinking about Camille right now. Family. That's what's important. Because you won't get to be with her much longer."

"Well, I still have two and a half weeks here, and it's true, I do want to make Camille a priority. But it's not a problem for us to continue to see each other. You sound like you want me to go." Like it's over. I held my hand over my mouth so he couldn't see my chin quiver.

"No, not at all." Marcus took a step closer to me but refrained from touching me. "Of course I don't want you to go, but I'm trying to be realistic. I'm trying to think ahead for both of us. Even if our friendship continues to grow into more, well, it seems a little unfeasible, don't you think, because of where we've chosen to live? How would it work? It wouldn't be like living across town or even across the state of Texas to date. We'll be on opposite sides of the planet. Maybe we need to talk about that."

Marcus was breaking things off without giving it a chance— without giving us a chance? I felt pain, a sharp pain in my chest, since the tie he'd just severed had already been attached to my heart. A sudden indignation pushed away any rational replies, and I blurted out, "You're right. You should go." I nodded with vigor and crossed my arms. "Yes, you should go. Now."

Marcus winced.

"Why do you look wounded? You've stated your case, and it's a good one. I've had similar questions, so I know how you feel. I don't see how any more talk will help or change our circumstances. You're right. We have no chance at all. It's an impossible situation with us being on opposite sides of the world."

Marcus stared at me. "Okay."

My stomach turned sour, and the ache was much worse than my fear of flying.

"Well then, I guess I'll say good night." Marcus paused, and when I didn't uncross my arms or soften my pursed lips he slowly turned to go.

"Goodbye." My voice cracked, but I stood straight. "You are such a Leroy," I murmured without censoring myself.

He whipped back around, facing me. "What did you say?"

"I said, 'You're such a Leroy.' You know, from the book *What the Buffalo Left Behind*."

"Yeah, I'm kind of familiar, since I wrote it. So, what do you mean? Are you calling me a coward?"

"Yes, I am. I loved that buffalo character. But before Leroy found his courage he spent way too much time thinking with his head and not his heart. So much so, he forgot how to live. What happened to all your courage, Marcus? All that bagpipe bravado you had when you first sat down next to me on that park bench? I know you said you were trying to repel me and attract me at the same time. I get that part, but why were you trying to attract me at all if you weren't willing to follow through if something happened? If I'm not mistaken here . . . something happened."

I cringed at my boldness, but I felt compelled to continue, since I wasn't ever going to see him again anyway. I would make my case. "I repeat. You're just like Leroy . . . only without all the hide and burly brown fur . . . and hooves and stuff." My speech went the way of silliness, but I held my ground and raised my chin.

Marcus grinned at me.

I frowned.

He grinned bigger.

"What are you looking at? I demand to know what you're thinking, if you don't mind. Please?" I mouthed.

"I was just waiting," he said. "With the way you have your cheeks puffed up like that, I assumed you had more to say."

"I guess I do. Listen, you made me care about you. There's something going on here, between us. Something that's worth pursuing. But if you pull a Leroy, then it's going to keep you from living . . . from knowing about us. What could have been. Maybe. Don't you think?"

Marcus just stood there. *Say something! I'm dying here.* I wasn't going to humiliate myself further. "Excuse me, but I'm totally drained, and my knee suddenly feels like it's been tenderized with a meat hammer. I'm going to bed." I strode away from him. Tears burned my eyes. But before I'd made it to the elevator button I heard someone striding up behind me. *Please let it be him.*

Marcus touched my shoulder, and I stopped my striding. He turned me around and held me by my shoulders. He didn't search my eyes or wait for a nod, he just took my face into his palms and kissed me. And what a kiss. It was the Pulitzer Prize of kisses. The Taj Mahal. It was the summit experience—that crazy-flapping, victorious flag at the peak of Mount Everest. It was the kind of kiss one should remember always, should place in a shadowbox—if that were possible—to dream and sigh over in one's old age. Mmm. I reached up and curled my arms around his neck and made sure he understood how glad I was to see him come back to me. When we eased apart I said to him, "I guess this means something. Right?"

"Yes. It means you can stop calling me Leroy."

I threw my head back, laughing. "But what about the whole opposite-sides-of-the-planet thing?"

"We'll take it one day at a time, Love."

I tugged on the lapels of his jacket. "I can't believe we've only known each other for two days."

"Well, some people only need two minutes."

"I suppose so."

"But what about Camille?" he asked. "I want to spend as much time with you as possible, but I also don't want you to have regrets by losing your focus."

"I will find time for both of you. I promise."

"Good." He nodded. "That's a very good promise and one I will hold you to."

I hooked my finger into the pocket of his jacket and gave it a tug. "Were you really walking away for good just now? You know, forever and ever?"

"What you didn't know was that I wouldn't have made it to the street before I would have marched back in here to tell you what a buffoon I was for making such a speech."

"I'm sorry I called you a Leroy. It was cruel."

"Yes, it was cruel. I may never recover." He grinned. "But that's okay . . . since the moment I laid eyes on you I thought you were a Zelda."

"No, not Zelda. Anyone but her." I raised my brow in pretend outrage. "She's a bald ostrich."

"Well, you're Zelda without the skinny neck and feathers and big webbed feet."

"Guess I deserved that."

"Yes." Marcus kissed the tip of my nose. "But Zelda also has a heart of gold."

CHAPTER
nineteen

In spite of my throbbing knee, in spite of the concerns that my sister might not show for our next outing, and in spite of my latest encounter with Marcus, sleep came as softly to me as a baby's touch. In fact, I welcomed sleep with open arms and fell into dreaming of Marcus's kiss—our shadowbox kiss.

The next day my more-than-a-friend—Marcus—took me on a whirl of activities around the city. That is, as many as my recovering knee could stand: Federation Square, an art museum, a train ride to the zoo. The zoo featured the most adorable kangaroos and an animal called a wombat, which looked just like a pillow with eyes. We munched on bubblegum-flavored fairy floss, which was really just the Aussie version of cotton candy. And then for lunch we went to an indigenous-themed restaurant, which was decorated with Aboriginal works of art. They had a couple of items on the menu—eel and emu—that I assumed I'd hate but didn't. I could not have been more impressed with all there was to see and do inside and outside the city. Like Marcus, I now had a sweet spot for Melbourne.

After we parted for the evening, I headed to the place by the river where my sister performed. She wasn't there. I glanced all around, thinking I'd made a mistake with the spot or the time, but I knew I hadn't. Maybe she was merely running late. In an effort to keep my worry-meter from pinging off the charts I strolled down the promenade, hoping to run into her.

After a few minutes of walking, I spotted Camille. Relief flooded me. But something wasn't right. She not only wasn't performing, but she stood arguing with a man in front of the Crown Complex, next to one of the monolith-type structures that adorned the front. Was that the boyfriend she'd mentioned? I held back, not wanting to interrupt or even hear their argument, but the man's sharp words pierced the air.

"How could I have convinced myself that I loved you," the man said. "Tell me."

Camille reached out to him. "I know you're upset about being fired again, but you shouldn't take it out—"

He slapped her hand away. "How dare you bring that up. You know what? Before I go, I'm going to teach you a lesson." The man—red-faced and muscles taut—yanked the instrument case from Camille's hand.

"Give it to me. You know it's all I have left."

The man hurled Camille's flute into the river below.

"No!" Her voice shriveled into a whimper as the case splashed into the water. She swung at him.

He caught her hand and spewed curses at her. Then he stormed off without even glancing back.

Camille leaned over the railing, almost as if she were going to throw up, but coughed instead.

At that same instant, a massive flame belched out of the top of one of the black towers. And then a mushroom cloud of gas, still burning, released into the air, reminding me of the clouds of fire when Dorothy dared approach the Wizard of Oz. Somewhere on the other side, tourists squealed, apparently stunned with astonishment and delight at the show.

I reared back. *Goodness me.* Such an inferno. Even at that great distance, the heat prickled my flesh. Another black tower let loose with a plume of fire and then another and another until the whole row of pinnacles was ablaze. Camille paid no attention to the spectacle. She must have gotten used to the heat and fiery display.

Camille, dear Camille. I'm so sorry. Should I comfort her, or would it frighten her to know I'd seen their argument? I couldn't fake that kind of thing. I couldn't look like I was just appearing and hadn't seen the drama. My face would betray me right away, and I knew I couldn't live with the lie. *Oh, dear God in heaven, tell me what to do.*

I stood paralyzed, not wanting to move forward or go back. All the while, people were milling by, but giving her a wide berth. I finally decided to take a chance. Camille might bolt when she saw me, but she was my sister after all, and she needed me. I had to do something.

I walked up to her. "Camille? May I help?"

CHAPTER
twenty

Camille looked at me, her face full of fear. "Lily?"

She let me take her into my arms and rub her back just as I'd always done for Julie when she was distressed about something. "You don't have to tell me what happened."

"I have no one else to tell." She pulled away. "Jerald left me. After a year of dating. Of promises. Little whispers of such love and devotion. Now it's over . . . just like that. Yeah. It's over. He said I will never see him again."

"I'm so sorry." I ran my hands down her arms and held her hands, which shivered at my touch. "So, you loved this man?"

"Don't look at me that way. I know what you're thinking. That Jerald was a bad man. Yes, he did a terrible thing to me just now, destroying my flute, my music and part of my livelihood. But he was angry because I'd mentioned that he'd gotten fired. It was his weak spot, and I knew it."

I squeezed her hands, but I was certain I didn't look convinced. How could I be? Camille spoke the wild talk of a woman whose love had blinded her from all common sense.

Camille wiggled her hands out of my grasp. "I'm telling you the truth. He wasn't always like this. He's kind of a rough guy, and he could really throw a wobbly, but he's had trouble holding down a job, and it's made him feel like nothing. Like less of a man. I guess it sounds like an excuse, but he really was damaged emotionally by all the rejection."

"Most of us are damaged in some way, but we don't destroy other people's property in the process or destroy their livelihood. He could have just walked away." I didn't know the man, but I thought a good flogging would be in order. If Jerald could behave that way openly on the streets, I cringed to think how he might have abused Camille behind closed doors.

"Honestly, I don't know how Jerald will live now, without me, but I'm sure something will turn up."

Camille hadn't heard a word I'd said. "You mean you were paying his way?" *Oh, dear, please say you weren't.*

"Worse than that." She gazed out over the river. "I loaned Jerald some money, which he gambled away on the pokies. He was so . . ." Her voice trailed away in a hoarse murmur.

How could my sister put up with such abuse, especially after what she'd already been through with her adoptive father? Humans were so frail, so vulnerable.

"That was my only flute, and I can't afford another one."

"Do you think you can get any of the money back from him? You know, so you can buy another one?"

Camille released a bitter laugh. "No, I've seen the last of Jerald. That I know for sure."

I wanted to ask her how she'd gotten herself bound to such a worthless and iniquitous man. I wanted to know if she saw the pattern she was creating from her past. That she was choosing anguish out of some unhealthy desires. Perhaps she'd come to think of herself as deserving unhappiness and pain. I remained silent on the subject—for now. "Do you need any money? I could get some through one of the ATMs."

Camille shook her head. "I won't do that to you. Fortunately, I still have my daytime job. I work at a small grocery store. I can get by. And eventually I'll be able to buy another flute."

If sadness could melt a heart, then mine had become a little pool. Not just for my sister's loss, but for what she couldn't see. She didn't seem to recognize the strong connection between her choices and her unhappiness. "I wish I could do something. I feel useless."

"You could buy me a cuppa. Or maybe a cappuccino with extra foam." She tried on a weak smile. "We have the best in the world here."

"Let's do it. It'll keep me awake half the night, but then so will what happened to you today."

"I'm sorry about that. But for now, let's have that coffee. We can eat later." Camille reached over to me and zipped up my jacket. "You always look like you're shivering."

"I'm used to lots of heat in Houston, so yeah, I'm freezing."

"Spring is almost here, Lily."

I hoped that was true in a number of ways.

When we were cozy with our cappuccinos in one of the local coffee shops, I hovered my spoon over the cup, not wanting to mess up the creamy heart design on the top of the foam. "I hate to stir or take a sip. It's so pretty. And I like the fact that they give it to us in porcelain cups, not to-go mugs."

"That's because we take our coffee seriously here, and you shouldn't drink cappuccino out of paper cups unless you absolutely have to."

I took a sip, letting myself slurp it. "Oh, wow." I slapped the table. "Best cappuccino I've ever had." I licked at and then daubed at the foamy mustache with my napkin.

"See? The best." Camille suddenly coughed, which turned into quite a bout. She took several quick sips of her coffee. Her shoulders relaxed, but her cup made a clattery landing on the saucer when she set it down.

"You okay?"

"Not really." Camille stared into her cup.

"I don't mean to pry, but what exactly are your health issues? I noticed your cough when we first met on the street."

"I've never known what was wrong. The doctors don't know either. It seems I've always been ailing with something, just like when I was little. I guess I never outgrew that sickly nature."

"Do you think it could be—"

"Listen, Lily, I need to ask you something."

Sounded serious. I took a deep sip of my coffee. "Okay. Anything at all."

"As you already know, I expected Jerald to propose. He won't now. Obviously. But with that loss goes some of my hope for making a family here. As old as I am and with my health issues I wasn't expecting to ever have a baby. But I'd hoped to adopt a little girl someday, although I don't know when that will be. Maybe it's just a pipe dream too. But now without Jerald, I have no one. Nothing. I'm like a ship bobbling around, lost at sea."

"You don't have any friends?"

"I did, but my best friend, Samantha, moved to America a few months ago. I thought we'd stay close. I hoped so anyway, but it didn't work. We emailed and texted for a while, but now I never hear from her. It was just too much I guess. She moved on, made new friends there."

"That's unfortunate."

"Yes. It is. And now comes my question. Well, I guess it isn't a question. It's an announcement." Camille looked at me then, really looked at me, her jaw set with determination. "I've decided . . . when you go back to America . . . I'm going with you."

Chapter
twenty-one

I opened my mouth, but nothing came out.

Camille grinned. "Guess I shocked you a good one."

I laughed. "You did. I'm happy, of course. I just didn't expect you to say it, because you were so opposed to the idea when I brought it up before."

"Well, everything changed for me today." She dropped her shoulders as if in sad surrender. "My whole life."

"I can't think of anything that would make me happier than to take you back with me. Julie will be thrilled too."

Camille rested back in her chair. "It wouldn't be forever."

"You may stay with me for as long as you like. I have a house and two extra bedrooms. It's kind of old, but it's a comfy place. It's home."

Camille placed her palm on the window glass next to us just as she had when I first saw her on the tram. She said softly, "From what I gather . . . Mrs. Gray isn't all that big on seeing me."

"But Mother did tell me about you. She opened that door, and it makes me think she would be willing to open other doors. Deep down, I'm sure she wants to see you again."

"But why should I be the one to shove open the door, Lily?" she asked. "Mrs. Gray is the one who should be clamoring to see me, begging my forgiveness."

"I admit, it's all pretty screwed up. We're a very dysfunctional family. But you coming home will jar things back. Make things right. I just know it. Kind of like, well, you know, when you shake a pecan tree and all the nuts come down."

"Yeah, well that doesn't help me to feel warm and fuzzy." She grimaced.

"Sorry, bad simile."

"Are you really that much more of an optimist than I am?"

"No."

We laughed.

I drank down the rest of my cappuccino, wiped off my foamy mustache, and then gave myself a moment to rejoice. Camille was right—spring was on its way. I ordered another cappuccino to celebrate. I had more than I'd ever hoped for—a twin sister who wanted to be my sister and who wanted to come home, even if only for a visit.

"When would we be going back?" Camille asked.

"In about two and a half weeks."

"That should give me time to close down some of my life here. I admit that even though I feel a measure of despair right now, I also feel something else. Something I didn't expect to feel. Relief that I don't have to look into those green eyes of Jerald's anymore and feel . . . edgy."

"Relief is good." I reached out to her with my right palm.

At the same exact moment, Camille stretched out her left hand, and we met palm to palm.

We stared at each other and then put our hands down and laughed.

"Creepy, isn't it . . . the way we think alike . . . move alike?" she asked.

"It is . . . wonderfully strange."

"I'd so glad you came to Australia, Lily."

"Me too," I said. "I suppose we need to make a plan now."

"Well, while we make our plans I can show you Parliament. That is, if we hurry. Then we can eat."

"I would love that. I haven't seen it yet."

"It's not far from here."

⋙⋘

After a short taxi ride, we both stood inside Queen's Hall in Parliament House. I looked around, taking in the stately hall. It took my breath away. The ivory room had a grand air and seemed to embrace the sky with its high ceilings and Greek columns. The great hall, steeped in history, celebrated Australia's ties to England with a magnificent statue of Queen Victoria in all her regalia. Just beautiful.

I linked arms with my sister. I would not let anything spoil our lovely day, and I refused to ponder the one assaulting word that could topple our tower of joy.

Mother.

CHAPTER
twenty-two

Over the next few days, Camille was so exhausted from working long hours at the grocery store that she insisted I go out with Marcus on a date. It was the special evening he'd been patiently waiting for—and one that I'd spent plenty of time daydreaming about.

Back in my hotel room, I slipped on the little black dress that I'd brought from home and had yet to wear. I adjusted the cap sleeves off my shoulders and curled my hair on top of my head with a silvery clip—a style I'd only worn for fancy affairs, which, come to think of it, rarely arrived. Feeling on a roll with my primping, I put on a rhinestone necklace and earrings and stared at myself in a long mirror. Hmm. Not too shabby for an empty-nester mother who's thirty-nine. But had I gilded the lily a bit too much? I tilted my chin. *No, I think not.* I laughed.

I made my way to the elevator, pushed the button, and just as the doors opened in the lobby, Marcus found me. His hand struck his heart as a wide grin consumed his face.

Okay. I get it. Marcus thinks I clean up well. He didn't look too bad himself in his gray pinstripe suit and tie.

Marcus walked up to me, took me by the hand ever so lightly, and twirled me as if we were in the middle of a dance. "You are devastating, Love."

"But it's just a dress that I picked out for—"

Marcus touched his finger to my lips to quiet my protests. "Please don't start running yourself down. You are devastating, Lily

Winter. Maybe I should make you write it on the chalkboard a hundred times."

I chuckled. "You look devastating too." Was that Armani? I had no idea, but it looked expensive and tailored.

"Thanks." He offered his arm. "Ready for an evening to text home about?"

"I am."

Marcus escorted me along the promenade by the Yarra River and into a restaurant called The Garden Pool.

The ambiance was all about the simple but chic beauty of a Japanese garden. Hundreds of candles lit the room, and violin music floated in around us. After I'd carried on about the décor like a bumpkin, the maître d' seated us in a prime spot by a waterfall that flowed demurely into an ornamental pool. "Beautiful."

He nodded his approval as he gazed at me.

How romantic. I hadn't known such attention in my life, but I welcomed it with open arms. Deep down where my guilt always festered, I knew it wasn't fair to compare Marcus to my deceased husband, and yet in my humanness, I did it anyway. Except for the affair, Richard hadn't been unkind to me, but he'd never made me feel special. And then, after his infidelity, I never recovered from the feeling that I wasn't much of anything to look at or had any qualities that my husband or any man would find interesting or attractive. I lived inside a mindset of just making due, and it had always been enough—until now.

Mist came to my eyes even before the waitress arrived with the menus. I'd never make it through the evening at this rate without having to blow my nose in the ladies' room a dozen times.

Marcus slid his hand across the table and took my hand in his.

His hand felt warm, sturdy, just right. And the connection, his touch, made me prickly. Not in a barbed cactus way, but in an over-the-moon, can-this-really-be-happening-to-me way. *Calm down, Lily.*

"Are you okay?" he asked quietly.

"These are happy tears, I assure you. To be honest, Marcus, I'm not all that used to the attention. It's making me wonderfully uncomfortable."

"Good." He leaned back and straightened his tie. "I hope before the evening is over I've found some ways to make you even more wonderfully uncomfortable."

There was that look again—guess it was the one Camille had told me about. The one that I had noticed but couldn't quite acknowledge.

With those words, and Marcus's delightful gaze, I flushed like I'd swallowed a whole chili pepper. While Marcus talked to the waiter, I daubed at my forehead with my napkin.

After a special welcome from the manager, linen napkins were whisked in the air and placed ever so gingerly on our laps. We were then handed two large brown leather menus to peruse. Oh, how I loved being pampered.

Glancing over the options I tried to keep from blinking at the prices. Very few items were listed, and they were all sooo expensive. It was a good thing Marcus had money, since the meal would cost him a fortune. When we'd made our order of steaks with pumpkin and greens, we settled into the quiet splendor of the place.

"This restaurant is wonderful, but it's also empty. I wonder why. Is it the prices?"

"No." Marcus leaned over to me. "It's empty because we have the place to ourselves."

"Really?" I got a little worried. "Just how rich are you?"

Marcus laughed. "Only a little. Don't be overly impressed. I'm friends with the manager, and he feels he owes me this kindness. Although I'm not sure why."

I looked around and whispered, "What did you do for him, if you don't mind me asking?"

"Something I would have done anyway." Marcus paused, but when I looked as though I really wanted to know the answer he said, "I was here eating, and one of his customers choked. I did the Heimlich maneuver on him, and it worked."

"You saved a man's life here?"

"Well, anyone would have done the same thing. I just happen to have been in the right place at the right time to be helpful."

"You're being way too modest."

Marcus chuckled. "I doubt that."

"But thank you for this wonderful evening. No one has ever done anything so grand for me. Not even close. Thank you."

"You're welcome, Lily Winter. There's no one else I wanted to do it for." He tapped his fist against his heart. "You are a flower most rare."

I grinned. "Well, actually there are two of us flowers."

"Ahh, yes, there are two flowers, but no one is exactly like Lily Winter. Not even Camille."

"So, am I a flower with thorns?"

"No, you're the one I want to wear on my lapel . . . near my heart."

I smiled at that. And here I'd been worried that Marcus had fallen a little bit in love with Camille and her music. Marcus did indeed have a way with words, though, being a writer by trade. It was his business to know how to say pretty things. Or, that is, it used to be his business before the accident. I would like to ask him if saving someone's life eased the guilt of losing his sister, but that had to be the worst possible kind of chitchat for a romantic evening. So I moved on to another topic. "I wasn't sure whether to tell you or not, since it's a private thing, but Camille said it was okay to share it."

"Sounds pretty heavy."

"Some of it is, and some of it isn't. Camille has agreed to come back home with me. Not permanently, but for a long visit."

"Now that's amazing news." Marcus leaned toward me. "How in the world did you get her to agree to that?"

"She and I have been slowly bonding, but the main reason she changed her mind was because of her boyfriend. He left her. They'd been in a relationship for a year, and she'd hoped he would propose. But he didn't. There can be no reconciliation, nor would she want it. I know I certainly wouldn't want her to go back to him even if he begged. He was a louse, and that's being very kind in my assessment."

"I'm sorry to hear that your sister has suffered even more abuse."

I took a sip of my Pellegrino. "Why is that? Why is it that women who are abused as children sometimes find themselves in a similar situation, even when they have a choice?"

"I guess it's hard to leave a road you're familiar with, even when it's rough. You'll be a real encouragement to Camille. I'm sure you'll help her to see that she's worthy of someone better."

"I hope so."

"I'm curious," Marcus said. "From everything you've told me about your mother, how do you think she'll handle Camille coming back to see her after all these years?"

"I have no idea. It could blow up in our faces, and Mother could order us out of the house. Or Mother might feel some remorse for giving Camille away all those years ago. But that could only happen with a miracle. Most likely it'll be somewhere in the middle, as most of life is. Mother will be glad to see her, but she won't say the right words. Not quite. I'm not sure she knows how. They seem to be locked up inside her, unable to get out. Then we'll all three settle into a general dysfunctional malaise. But I have to try. It's the right thing to do. And my daughter will love Camille. It'll be great for Julie to have an aunt." I gave my hands a waving gesture. "But I promise I won't spend the whole evening talking about my sister. You can tell I'm a little wired."

"I'm distressed with whatever you're distressed with . . . happy about whatever you're happy about."

Sweet man. "So, what did you do with your day?"

Marcus reached into an inner pocket of his suit jacket and pulled out a small box. "I did a little volunteer work over at St. Paul's."

"Oh?" I smiled but barely heard him because of the distraction of the black box sitting in front of me. Surely not. It was waaay too soon for a proposal. Couldn't be. Was it? My heartbeat did some funky ka-bangs. "For me?"

Marcus leaned forward and whispered, "Well, I'm certainly not going to give it to the waitress."

"I'm glad for that. I don't think the woman's been off of her training wheels that long." I grinned and picked up the box, but my fingers trembled so much that I fumbled with it, nearly making it flip out of my hand. *Calm yourself, Lily.* Without any more internal drumrolls I cracked open the box. Nestled in the velvet folds sat three silver charms. "Ohhh. How lovely."

My stomach untied its knots. I could breathe again. There was no proposal—just the sweetest gift imaginable. "For my bracelet. I love them." I lifted out three small charms. "A piano, a guitar, and a flute. You're not only thoughtful to have given me a gift . . . but a good listener to know our passions."

"It's to celebrate the three of you and your music, but also I'm hoping it'll encourage you to go back to the piano."

"I think it's just the thing to do it." I held the gift to my heart. "I'll put them on my bracelet as soon as I get back to my hotel. Thank you, Marcus. But what are we celebrating?"

He lifted his glass. "To a woman named Lily Winter who traveled all the way to Australia and who happened to sit down on my favorite bench. I'm so glad she did."

"I will never forget that spot."

"Nor I. I thought you were going to throttle me when I first sat down."

I chuckled. "I'm glad I didn't."

❧❦❧

Our quiet dinner for two went on to become the magnum opus of romantic dates. When the last mouthwatering bite had been consumed, we left and took a stroll by the river, not far from the botanic gardens. The evening was warmer than usual, and the wind had calmed, so for once I didn't feel I needed a coat. But then maybe I was getting used to the climate.

Marcus offered his arm, and I circled mine through his. When we came to a place that wasn't cluttered with tourists, we stopped and settled on a bench. He patted the spot by him, and without hesitation, I scooted up right next to him. He placed his arm behind me as if we'd being doing that routine for a lifetime. Goodness me. What a difference a few days could make. I could no longer even imagine why I disliked Marcus at first. I had been gazing through the filmy glass of my weary and potholed perceptions. But then I'd changed too. I guess the lily had finally started to bloom.

"I'm beginning to count the days left . . . you know, before you leave. And it's too soon," Marcus said in a gravelly voice so full of emotion that it made me look up at him. "Way too soon." He loosened his tie. "Are you sure you really need that job of yours?"

"It would be wonderful to stay a few more weeks. But as you know, I'm on a leave of absence. I'm not independently wealthy, so eventually I do need to go back to my job, as much as I dislike it."

"What do you want to do? Something relating to music?" he asked.

"No, but maybe something creative. I'm not sure. Guess I still haven't grown up yet."

"That's okay, since not growing up is a prerequisite for being creative."

"I suppose that's true. But it's hard to quit, since everything in oil-related services pays so well. Even a secretary's job. I stay there for Julie's sake, actually. You know, to make sure I have enough money for us."

Marcus caught my gaze. "But Julie's gone now."

"True, but I want to help her with college. Who knows . . . maybe it is time to make a few changes."

"Changes." Marcus leaned down. "Yes, you might be—" His words ran out as he hovered by my lips. His breath, warm and tickly on my cheek.

I lifted my chin and met him halfway to enjoy some confection that was far sweeter than the apple dumpling we'd had for dessert. I'd been waiting all evening for that kiss—maybe my whole life. My spirit took flight, and it reminded me of when I was a girl, and Nanny Kate had let me fly my first kite. The sun on my face, the tug and rush of the kite taking off and soaring in the breeze high above me. It was a moment not to be forgotten—just like this one. When we reeled in our delight, I said, "Wasn't that the nicest thing?"

"I thought so too . . . very nice."

"But what were you about to say earlier about changes?"

"I don't know. When I'm around you I lose my train of thought." Marcus twirled a curl of my hair around his finger. "I just know these next two weeks will go by much too quickly. Even now the minutes are ticking at a maddening rate, making me crazy, making me wish I could reach out and stop the hands of the clock. Or at least slow it down. Make every moment last."

I felt that desperation like Marcus. I felt the confusion too. Our relationship was far enough along that we knew something wonderful was happening, but what would we do now? *Lord, give me wisdom.*

❧❧❧

Marcus wrapped his hand over mine. "I may be forced to come visit you in Houston."

"I would like that . . . very much."

"I've been so moved by your determination to reconcile with your family that I've wondered if I can't do the same with mine. You know, somehow make things right, even though my parents don't appear all that receptive."

"That's such a good idea, Marcus." I gave his hand a caress.

"Of course, it could be a disaster, just as you said about taking Camille home." He grinned. "But I admire your desire to try."

A sudden chill whipped up from the river, making me shiver.

"Let's get you back to the hotel." Marcus warmed up my hands. Then he warmed up my lips one more time, but like the gentleman he was, he escorted me back to my hotel as promised. I went up to my room with a strange joy, a mixture of so many emotions I couldn't categorize them in my usual emotional filing system. They were new ones, the kind you keep close to touch and study and know, not out of reach, hidden away in a bottom drawer or filed away like office data that was rarely used. Guess I'd been a secretary a bit too long. Even my metaphors were clerical.

❧∂◞❧

Over the two weeks before my departure I spent lots of time with Marcus, and of course Camille joined us whenever she could get off work. By bus, we traveled on the Great Ocean Road to see the Twelve Apostles, which turned out to be spectacular—limestone sentinels jutting up from a sparkling turquoise ocean. We saw miles of eucalyptus woods, and if one looked closely, hugging the branches and gaping down at us were koala bears looking just like stuffed animals. I snapped a bezillion photos to show Julie.

As the time got closer for my departure Marcus threw in a few more adventures. We toured an old gold-rush town, where we journeyed below ground to see the way life had been for the miners long ago. We explored Melbourne's aquarium and the famous flea market, and stood happily terrified as we swayed on top of the tallest building in the Southern Hemisphere.

Then leaving the most enchanting experience for last, we drove two hours from Melbourne to see the famous parade of the fairy penguins. I nearly froze to death, but the three of us bundled in blankets at sunset and watched hundreds of the tiny creatures march out of the waves toward the dunes on Phillip Island—toward home.

I remember thinking yes, my time had also come to take my little family home. But with that joy came a sorrow. Saying goodbye to Marcus.

Each time we went out I sensed a silent countdown. Marcus and I no longer spoke of it, since it was easier not to mention it, but each day had become a small goodbye as we waited for the big one. The one that would surely make me cry a river.

❦

And then the day came—that day—it fell on an ordinary Monday.

The taxicab driver put the last of our suitcases into his trunk. Camille said her goodbyes to Marcus, gave him a hug, and slipped inside the cab.

It was my turn now—the moment of the big farewell.

CHAPTER
twenty-three

Marcus pulled me to him in an embrace, the kind that overflowed with unspoken sentiment. "I should be driving you to the airport. That is, if I had a car and I wasn't concerned about driving on the other side of the road, and well, not getting you and your sister there in one piece."

Dear Marcus. Would he ever recover? I smiled at him. "This is the best way. There'll be fewer people here when I embarrass myself crying."

He chuckled. "Oh, Lily. I'll miss all of you, even your tears." He gathered my hair in his hands and brought it around to frame my face. "I wish you'd had more time here. There was still a world to share with you. You only got to see a tiny fraction of Australia. You didn't even see the Outback or Sydney or . . ." His voiced faded in the breeze.

Was he only longing to play the affectionate tour guide with his adoring fan, or were other more profound emotions hiding in his words—the kind that could last a lifetime? I pulled away to look into his eyes. No doubt, great affection radiated in his countenance, but was there love? Since no real declarations had been made, I said, "I just want you to know that if something happens, and you change your mind about coming to Houston, I won't hold it against you. I promise I won't shriek at you on the phone or riddle you with guilt or bawl like a baby. Well, I might do that last one." I chuckled. "But I promise you I'll be brave."

Marcus took me by the shoulders and caught my misty gaze. "Then I must never give you a reason to be brave."

"I'm serious." My chin quivered.

He kissed my chin and my mouth and then whispered into my hair, "I'm serious too."

I breathed him in one last time. Some scent that was fresh and clean, but his touch would be even more memorable—like solid earth covered in a soft green moss. The touch of the man who'd changed my life.

The cabdriver cleared his throat.

Marcus cocked his head at the man. "Hey, mate, give us a minute here. Haven't you ever had to say goodbye?"

The cabby grinned and shook his head. "It's your dollar."

"Guess it's time to go." I stroked my finger along the contours of Marcus's cheek, memorizing every angle of that emotive, whiskery face of his. I tucked away the moment, wanting to imagine it all the way home, hoping to imagine it always.

Marcus took hold of my finger and kissed it.

"I don't want us to miss our flight. Okay, you've got my numbers and home address, so if you do come—"

"When I come," he corrected me.

"For when you come back home to your America."

"That's better. It does have a nice warm ring to it, doesn't it?"

"It does." More tears threatened. No matter how we spun the phrases and promises, the moment felt like the closing of a beautiful play—a drama worthy of a standing ovation—but a performance in which the hero and heroine are torn apart for good. I scrunched up my face to keep more tears from streaming down, but they did anyway, against my will.

Marcus kissed my cheeks where the tears fell.

"I've got to stop crying." I swiped the tears away and chuckled. "Honestly, I've got to go." I wanted to scream out that I'd changed my mind and I would stay in Melbourne, but we both knew that was ridiculous. All was set in stone, and my main concern had to be Camille, my new family.

I slipped a letter into his pocket. "For later when I'm gone."

"For me?"

"For you. Well, goodbye, Marcus."

He patted his pocket where I'd put the letter. "See you soon . . . Love."

I grinned. Then I turned away from him and scooted into the taxi next to Camille.

When I looked at Marcus again, the sun had lit his smile. And such a smile—such an inspiration to know that even after all he'd been through with his family that his smile could still come out looking like a sunrise. I wish I'd written more in the letter. It was too short, and not nearly sweet enough. But I'd wanted him to know that my time in Melbourne had been some of the best weeks of my life. Beyond the joy of finding my dear Camille, there had been such dazzling sites shared with Marcus, the exotic foods and unique culture and diverse peoples, and the quieter, holy moments, like evensong. It would all be missed. Every last moment of it.

Just as the taxi pulled away Marcus picked up his bagpipes and began to play an Irish tune. I had no idea what the melody was, but it sounded sweet and sad, and it would be forever branded on my heart. What a send-off—majestic, beguiling, and so very Marcus. Guess I'd need tiny silver bagpipes to put on my charm bracelet.

I strained to watch Marcus for as long as I could, until the cabdriver turned the corner, and then he was out of sight. That's when I rested my head on Camille's shoulder and the rest of my tears began to flow.

Even though Camille didn't seem to know what to do with my pitiful state, she held to me tightly.

The words to a beloved Irish blessing came to me then—one Nanny Kate had me memorize as a child—but its bittersweet refrain brought with it as much sorrow as it did consolation.

"May the road rise to meet you,
May the wind be always at your back.
May the sun shine warm upon your face,
The rains fall soft upon your fields.
And until we meet again,
May God hold you in the palm of His hand."

Yes, until we meet again. O Lord, please do keep Marcus in the palm of Your hand, but remember our affections and do let us meet again. Let this be the beginning to our lives together and not the end.

PART TWO

the homecoming

CHAPTER
twenty-four

Camille handed me a wad of tissues. "Guess I should have brought another box."

I chuckled. "I'll be okay now. It hurt a little more than I thought it would . . . this prying my heartstrings loose."

Camille looked out the cab window.

As we rode along, various scenes played out before us—a child swinging between two parents, a camera flashing among friends, someone running late for something that must have been important. Life went on, even when hearts were breaking.

"Imagine being with your guy for a year and then saying goodbye," Camille said, still staring out the window.

Surely she wasn't still pining after that horrible man. "I'm sorry for the way he hurt you, but somewhere deep down . . . aren't you relieved that he's gone?"

"But I still miss some things about Jerald." Camille shrugged. "As crazy as it seems to you."

"I didn't know the man. Hard to judge fully." It was easier to give her a little leeway on the subject since we were heading far away from him.

"Do you love Mrs. Gray even though she's made you miserable?" Camille asked.

"Yes, but isn't that different?"

She looked at me. "How?"

"I didn't choose Mother for my mother. It was just the way it happened. I'm trying to make the best of the mom God gave me. You could choose a finer man, one who deserves you."

"I suppose. I should choose somebody like Marcus?"

"Yeah, somebody like Marcus. But *not* Marcus." I grinned.

Camille chuckled and gave me a dainty punch on the arm.

Could it be that Camille was envious of my relationship? Guess I wouldn't know until I asked, but that query wouldn't come today. "We did miss a lot of fun growing up."

"We could have played such tricks on our boyfriends," Camille said, "as we switched back and forth. Loads of mischief. I can just imagine it."

The cabdriver gave us a grin into his rearview mirror.

"I suppose so. Although I didn't have that many beaus to tease."

Camille slipped a cough drop into her mouth. "Hmm. I wonder which one of us was born first."

"I have no idea. What made you think of that?"

"I just thought that whichever one of us was born a few minutes earlier would probably end up acting like a big sister."

"Well, I think in our case we need to be each other's big sis." I gave her sleeve a tug. "You know, watch each other's backs."

"It's a deal." We hooked pinkies and shook. Then we laughed.

All the various stages of check-in at the airport went smoothly enough, and the long flight to Houston, with a layover in LA, was not nearly so stomach-twisting as the one going over. Not because it felt less bumpy, but because I was a more seasoned flyer, and I had a sister to enjoy. But during the tossing and turning hours, trying to get some shut-eye, my mind became occupied with plenty of other matters—such as how Mother was going to react when she saw Camille, and the other way around. Hard to fathom.

And then there were the endless little reveries about Marcus, wondering if his promise to visit me would get pushed off so many times that he'd no longer remember why he was coming at all. Or if the intensity of joy we felt now would get watered down in the never-ending flow of daily struggles. Only God knew the answer, but I would need to leave that last question far behind like the vapor trail in the wake of our jet.

After we landed at Intercontinental Airport in Houston and picked up our bags, we stopped in the garage for my car.

"Don't you have a friend to pick you up at the airport?" Camille asked. "It must get expensive to keep your car in the garage."

"I didn't want to bother my friends. To be honest, I don't have a lot of close friends. You know, the kind you can call up at 3:00 in the morning to go to the hospital?"

Camille raised an eyebrow as she heaved our suitcases into my trunk. "Or even any friends to take you to the airport at a reasonable hour of the day?"

"No, not really."

"You sound like me. If I had left Australia for good, there weren't really that many friends to say goodbye to. I can be a loner at times. Not sure why. That's a part of me I'm still exploring."

"Maybe that's the one thing we have in common with Mother. That she's had to pay a woman to be her friend." I turned on the engine and then looked at her for a straight answer. "So, *did* you leave Australia for good?"

"I don't know, but we'll see how it goes here. It would be a leap for me, but I don't feel I have all that much to go back to now."

I pulled out of the parking garage, and before long we were whirling down the Beltway toward my house in Northwest Houston.

"So, this is Houston . . . where I started my life. The palm trees are pretty, and the crepe myrtle and oleander, but it's more humid than Melbourne. That's for sure. I noticed the sauna as soon as we left the building." She gave her blouse a few fluttering tugs to let in some air and then lowered the window. "You've got mozzies too." She shooed out a buzzing mosquito.

"You might want to switch to natural fibers until it cools down some. Cotton will breathe better in this warmth and humidity." I grinned. "But you'll get used to it, just like I was beginning to get used to the cold in Melbourne. But as I'm sure you know, while you all were heading into spring there, Houstonians are moving into fall now. It'll be a little cooler soon and drier."

"I think I should start saying that too . . . you all with that Texas accent you have."

"Well, to say it like a real Texan you have to jam the words together."

"Y'all. And I could buy some cowgirl boots while I'm here too."

I chuckled. "They would look good on you, especially with your white dress and jean jacket."

"Well, whatever would look good on me will look good on you. By the way, is it true that everybody in Texas carries a weapon like the gunslingers in the old West?"

"Only in your imagination."

Camille grinned. "Didn't think so, but I thought I'd ask." She stretched and yawned. "Sorry to conk out on you, but I need a cat-nap. I was too restless to sleep much on the plane."

"Go right ahead. With this rush hour traffic you should get a thirty-minute nap."

Camille rested her head back and within a short time she was happily snoring away. Loudly, just like I did, enough to frighten small animals.

I glanced over at her, still amazed that she had actually come home with me. So few things in life worked out that way—like you want them to—but God had ordained that I should have my sister back. And I couldn't have been more thankful.

But invariably when I had most of my ducks in a row, and the aviary brood was reasonably happy, I couldn't celebrate. I had to chase down those last ornery ducks. In this case it was Marcus and that gaping hole he left in my heart.

Everything I looked at made me think of him. Truth was I already missed him with a vengeance. How could it have happened? If life were a mystery, then love was beyond understanding. It was a puzzle with half of the pieces missing. Some of the pieces got vacuumed up. Others got forever lost under the couch. But the box, oh the picture on the box. What delight God had made when He created love between a man and a woman. Oh, no, there was that word.

Love.

While Camille was still deep in slumber my thoughts ran amok. The little-big word *love* played in my head without supervision. Apparently my thoughts needed supervision. No one could fall in love in three weeks. My emotions had merely spent too much time on the treadmill of jet lag.

"So, when do you think is the right time for me to spring myself on your mother?" Camille said suddenly in a groggy voice.

I startled. "I don't know. Maybe we could go over to her house tomorrow after we've had a good night's sleep."

Camille picked up a lock of my long hair and studied it. "You don't cover your gray, do you?"

"No. Not yet anyway."

"Hmm. I have to, but then I have more gray hair than you." Camille scooted up in the seat. "All right, we'll wait until tomorrow to see Mrs. Gray, but if you think I'll get a good night's sleep on the eve of when I finally have a chance to give my biological mother a piece of my mind, you're dreaming."

I winced. "The way you worded that just now . . . well, it doesn't sound like the comment of someone who wants to reconcile."

Camille adjusted the cool-air vent so that it blew right on her. "You are such a dreamer, Lily. I wish I were. You'll have to teach me. I used to be when I was younger, but I guess life crushed it out of me."

"No one's ever said that before . . . that I was a dreamer." Sounded nice.

"Well, you are."

She rubbed her neck. "Besides, true reconciliation includes discussion. Maybe even a heated debate or two. Otherwise it's anemic and worthless. It isn't real, and it won't hold up. It'll only be made of paper if we don't get down to it." She looked at me. "Lily, don't ever forget, our mother ruined my life."

She said the words—*our mother*—and it was such a unique thing to hear, I grinned.

"And just what is so funny?" Camille asked.

"It's the first time you called Mrs. Gray *our* mother."

"Well, I slipped." She stared out the window. "I should have used the word *biological*. She's that and nothing more. But I mean it. I'm not going in there to kowtow to that woman. I'm going to stand my ground. To find out some things. To open some secret boxes hidden in the attic so to speak. I want to know what happened. All of it in her words. And I want an apology from her lips. If it causes an all-out war, so be it. Wars do end."

I sighed, thinking of my ducks—one more darted out of line and maybe even headed for a busy street. "Yes, wars do end, Camille, but not without casualties."

CHAPTER
twenty-five

That night, after I got all tucked into my pillow-top bed, wearing a fresh pair of jammies and knowing that my identical twin sister slept in the next room and that my own sweet Julie was excited about coming to join our happy reunion, I should have been near comatose with contented slumber.

But I wasn't.

Even though most folks would have called my Australian journey a roaring success, I couldn't sleep. I hated conflict, and I knew we were headed for a verbal bloodbath in the morning with Mother. Not to mention the fact that I cared for a man I had no business caring for because he lived on the other side of the globe.

But eventually, the sandmen gave it their best shot, and I floated off for a while. I woke to blaring sunlight and to Camille jumping on my bed.

"Are you going to sleep all day?" she asked.

I opened one eye. "Are you actually bouncing on the bed like a five-year-old?"

"Yeah." She danced a jig with movements that were so deliberately understated it looked hilarious.

I laughed. "I like your Hello Kitty nightgown." It was good to see Camille in such a happy mood and with a burst of energy. Maybe just getting away from her past was giving her a new lease on life. I hadn't heard her cough in a while either. I stared at her. "You're absolutely glowing."

"Maybe it's my new peach blush." She bounced a little more. "But it's ten, and I want to meet this ogre woman named Mrs. Gray."

Oh, yeah. We were going over to Mother's house today. I lifted my head and groaned. "Did you say ten? Really?" I glanced at the clock. Ten. "Guess I needed the sleep. But why am I still tired and you're not?" I let my head slap back down on the pillow like a dead cod.

"I made myself some eggs. Hope that was okay. I've been exploring too. I like your house. Quaint and homey like I thought it would be. Yeah." She peered down at me. Her hair had been gathered in a clip, which made the ends of her locks look like feathers.

"Thanks. I'm glad you felt you could make yourself at home." I yawned. "Give me a sec. I'll feel human again if I can just shower and have some coffee."

"Do you want me to make you some eggs and toast while you shower and get ready? It's all I could find in the fridge." She rocked her head back and forth, making her dark feathers quiver.

"Sure, that would be nice. And then we'll drive over to Mother's house."

"Is it very far away?"

"Not terribly far, but then everything is spread out in Houston. It's not like Melbourne, where you can take a tram or train to most things. You need a car here to get around."

"Oh." Camille lowered herself on the bed and sat cross-legged next to me.

I hadn't made that physical maneuver with my legs since I was nineteen.

"Well, I can always use your car." She picked at the woolly flowers on my chenille bedspread. "That is, if I need a car. Don't you have any public transportation?"

"Some, but it's not the same as in Melbourne. You'll see how we're too spread out for it to work as well as it does there."

"Oh." Camille mimicked playing a flute.

"You're welcome to my car when I'm not at work. But you'll have to be careful. We drive on the wrong side of the road here, depending on your perspective."

"Oh, right. Forgot about that. Lots of changes here."

"You've got a little something dark just above your lip."

Camille swiped it off. "Probably my Vegemite. I brought some of it with me to put on my toast. Can't seem to do without it."

"What's that?"

"It's sort of a yeasty brown spread that Aussies are addicted to."

"Eww. Sounds ghastly."

"I admit it's an acquired taste, but I'm telling you, Vegemite is as popular there as the bush ballad 'Waltzing Matilda' and the one-finger wave."

"Oh?" Just as I was about to ask a question about the song, Camille sprang off the bed and then darted off into another room. I raised my head off the pillow. Funny thing—I was a lot like Camille, and yet I sensed our differences keenly. Once she was out of the grasp of despair, she became a fairy, while I stayed locked in another story playing the fairy godmother role. Maybe I *was* born first.

I tried to spring out of bed like Camille, but my leg got into such a charley horse that by the time I'd stomped it out, springing was the last thing on my mind. I groaned, rolled my eyes, and headed to the shower.

Camille's butter-and-cream-laden scrambled eggs turned out to be good, but the toast she'd smeared with Vegemite tasted more curious than delicious. Guess it really was an acquired taste as Camille had said. Oh, well. A million calories later, I drove my sister over to Mother's home. I pulled up to the house and parked. It looked the same. Big. Austere. Maybe a bit dog-eared. Something I hadn't noticed before.

"Oh, wow. This is her house?" Camille asked.

"This is it."

"So, this is where you grew up? For real?"

"I think we moved here when I was six or seven. I can't remember."

Camille looked down at her jean skirt and white blouse and grimaced. "I guess I didn't really think of your mother being that rich."

"Rich in money . . . poor in spirit."

"So, you were used to elegant surroundings and having everything."

"Appearances can be deceptive. I was used to this house, yes, but some would say the interior is austere, not beautiful. You'll see soon enough what I mean. And even though my needs were met physically, they weren't met emotionally. Most of my nannies were nice, but not like a real mother. And as far as faith, I had to find God on my own. Or I should say He found me, just like He found you. My mother hated any displays of religious devotion, especially Christian. She seemed to think it conveyed a weak constitution. And in spite of all that, I would have forced my way in with Julie at least on Christmases if Mother hadn't taken such a harsh stance—that when I left as a young woman, my company in the Gray house was no longer needed nor wanted."

"Are you sure you weren't raised by Cruella de Vil?" Camille asked.

I chuckled. "I would have given up all the money we had for a pile of hugs. Or if Mother had been the one to take me to church. Or maybe even some shared laughter around the dinner table."

"But what about your father?"

"Remember, he died when I was young. Well, about the same age as when you lost your mother. So, it was just Mother and me for a long time."

"It really isn't what I imagined for you all those years."

"Please know, Camille, when I tell you pieces of my story, I'm not trying to discount what you went through growing up. I think your father is a monster, and I can't even imagine how you survived what you went through. But life in the Gray household became like, well, like a gray twilight with little hope of dawn."

"I'm sorry, Lily. I don't mean to diminish what you went through either. If we'd been kept together, we would have helped each other. Together we could have made spring."

"Yes, that's true. Maybe we can now . . . even if she never gives us her blessing. We're in control of our joy together as sisters. Whatever she may do or say."

"I agree." Camille leaned over and gave me a hug. "I guess we'd better go in."

I took in some oxygen. It didn't help one bit, so I looked up to the heavens.

We headed up to the front walkway and then the door. "Remember I told you that Mother hired a friend?"

"Yes. So, she'll be here now?" Camille straightened. "Does she stay all the time?"

"She'll probably be here, but I don't think she lives in the house. The woman, Dragan Humphreys, doubles as a housekeeper, butler-type person."

"Dragan? What a name. Sounds like something from a gothic horror novel. So, the woman who answers the door won't be Mrs. Gray."

"No."

"Okay. I'm ready." Camille turned her smug demeanor down a notch.

I rang the bell, praying for the best, hoping we didn't find the worst.

Before we could take the dialogue any further, the door unlocked and opened.

CHAPTER
twenty-six

Dragan Humphreys stood before us, a wall of consternation and bafflement.

I dove right in. "Hi, Dragan. This is my sister, Camille, from Australia, and we're here to see Mother."

Dragan looked at us both, back and forth, obviously traumatized about the identical twin thing. In fact, her expression tottered on the edge of such anxiety that I found it quite satisfying. *God, forgive me.* I even wished I could have flashed a photo of it to put on some social networking site. That is, if I was ever on any social networking sites. "Is Mother in?"

"She's always in," Dragan stuttered, "but I'll need to check if she's able to see you."

"Is Mother ill?" I moved a little closer to the open door.

"She's not ill, but I still need to check with her." She raised her nostrils at us. No doubt Dragan enjoyed throwing her weight around like a sumo wrestler. She was certainly as attractive as one. *Oh, dear. Oh, dear. Oh, dear.* If God was going to be rooting for me, I guess I'd need to clean up the muddy playing field of my thought-life.

"Oh, she'll see us," Camille said. "I've come all the way around the world for a visit with Mrs. Gray, and she *will* see me."

"I'll still need to check." Dragan's eyes took on the half-lidded eyes of a snake, but along with her cold decree she opened the door wider for us to come in.

We stepped inside. Dragan seemed almost the same as she did weeks before, except her muumuu and flip-flops seemed dirtier, and the off-gassing from her body was even more toxic with liquor fumes.

"Please wait here."

My sister looked around as Dragan shambled off to request some kind of sanction on our visit. How ridiculous. I picked over another ugly assortment of mind droppings.

Meanwhile, Camille traipsed around the entry hall, smirking at the statues and generally turning up the intensity on her sass. But I wasn't going to point my finger at my sister for bad behavior, since my mother had the corner on that market.

Camille pointed to an embroidered design within an elaborately gilded frame. "What is that?"

"It's the Gray family coat of arms. Mother is proud of her Irish heritage and marrying into a well-known Irish clan, even if she didn't love the family all that much."

She clasped her hands behind her and stared at the coat of arms with interest.

"Maybe that's why you're attracted to Celtic music. It's the Irish blood coursing through your veins."

"It's that dreamer in you coming out." Camille simpered at me and then looked back at the coat of arms. "I admit, the armor and colors look majestic, but what do the words on the banner at the top of the crest mean? I thought—"

Dragan returned, interrupting us and looking glad for it. She wore the same droll serpentine expression she had when she answered the door. At least the woman was consistent. "She'll see you in the study," she said. "You both can show yourselves in." Then to my relief the woman walked off to haunt some other part of the house.

Camille rolled her eyes. "She'll see you in the study," she whispered to me, repeating Dragan's words. "Do people really say stuff like that?"

"Apparently *she* does." I grinned. The sound of our footsteps against the cold, unforgiving marble got angrier as we made our way toward Mother. I opened the door to the study, and we walked into her domain of hardbound books, ancient but expensive furnishings, and dust, which floated in the air nervously as if afraid to settle on anything.

Mother sat stiff in her high-back chair just the way she had the infamous day of my return to her life and my subsequent departure, but this time my chin was a little higher and my spirit lighter.

"Mrs. Gray?" Camille's voice and body had gone as rigid as Mother's back.

"Come in," Mother said with the air of a queen. She leaned forward on her throne. All she lacked was a scepter.

When we could all get a good look at each other, Mother said, "Sit down." Her general tone hadn't changed, although I did catch a look of surprise and some scrutiny when her gaze landed on Camille.

I obeyed by sitting in one of the chairs across from Mother, but Camille only looked at the other empty chair and then back at Mother. "I'd rather stand. Thanks."

"I wondered if you'd come to see me," Mother said.

"I'm here," Camille said, "although it doesn't feel like much of a reunion. But I came because of this brave woman, my sister, who spent some of her life savings to go halfway around the world to find me and who helped pay my way here. But I also came because my boyfriend broke things off, and I felt there wasn't much reason to stay in Australia."

Oh, wow, Camille, don't serve all the bitter herbs at once.

"Well, you're certainly not shy about sharing your mind." Mother smoothed the doily on the arm of her chair. "What happened to your parents? Wouldn't they want you to stay nearby in Australia?"

"My mother died when I was ten, and so then my father raised me. He never wanted me, so I left when I was eighteen. We've never talked since, and I have no idea where he is now. I've been traveling around and landed in Melbourne."

Mother flinched at that admission, but then quickly her granite countenance returned.

Camille ignored her and faced the oversized window looking into the solarium. "Your cyclamen are dying. The sun is too intense where you've placed them. The leaves are burning up. They'll be dead within a week," she said with what seemed like equal measures of authority and impassiveness.

Mother raised a skeptical brow. "And I suppose you're an authority on flowers."

"You mean angiosperms? A bit. I have a degree in botany," Camille said.

Wonder of wonders. Why hadn't Camille told me? She was full of surprises.

"Humph. Well, I had no idea." Mother softened a bit. "You both grew up to look so much the same. Just—"

"Why wouldn't we be the same?" Camille asked. "We're identical twins."

"Don't interrupt me, child," Mother said.

Camille shrugged. "I'm no longer a child. And I'm certainly not your child. A choice you made."

"You don't know the facts," Mother said. "I'm sure your mother never told you all the story. She wouldn't want you to—"

"Be careful of the tone you use when talking about my mother. Naomi raised me when you were too inconvenienced." The bite in Camille's voice was unmistakable.

I leaned forward in my chair. "Camille, it's not helping to raise your voice. We need to—"

Camille swung back around and glared at me. "We need to what? Cower in the shadows like scared little rabbits? What good did that do all these years? I refuse to be sucked into whatever dysfunction is going on here. We're going to talk this out now." She turned her head and coughed.

"I told Lily the truth." Mother smacked the armrest with her hands, making furious little puffs of dust. "You were taken away from me by my mother."

"Well, I'm very curious how that came to be," Camille said, "since your name is also on the adoption papers."

"I will tell you, but only if you sit down." Mother pointed to the chair. "I can't take all this looming about." She took a sip of water from the glass sitting on the end table, but as she set it back down her hand trembled.

"No." Camille looked around the room, cracking her knuckles one by one. "I'm not in the mood to sit."

I gave my sister an imploring expression. "Mother still deserves some respect."

Something shimmered across my sister's expression as if she was going to rev up for an argument, but then she relented and sat in the chair next to me.

Mother cleared her throat. "When you both were born, Lily was well, and Camille, you had one illness after the other. You were sick all the time with a never-ending trail of ailments. And one of those times, when you were feverish with a cold and bronchitis, your grandmother, my mother, was holding you. She caught the fever you had and nearly died. After that she never fully recovered her health. Nor do I think . . . did she ever forgive you."

"But I was a baby," Camille said. "How could a grandmother—"

"Because . . ." Mother raised her finger for silence. "She was a hard woman. Much harder than I am, I can assure you. Now please allow me to finish my story. Back then we had no money to speak of, because your father couldn't hold down a job. My mother, who was wealthy, refused to help us with the expenses surrounding your doctor bills and hospital stays, claiming that it was her son-in-law's responsibility to take care of his family, not hers."

Mother ground her nails into the armrest. "My mother ruled over our lives back then like a tyrant, and I was so young I didn't know how to stand up to her. Anyway, she convinced us adoption was the only way for us to survive financially. She threatened us, saying she would disinherit us if we didn't comply with her wishes. She orchestrated the whole affair of finding you a mother, but I insisted it be an open adoption so I could see you from time to time. And I requested that you be allowed to keep your first and middle names. My mother agreed to those two demands and so did the couple who came forward to—"

Camille's cough turned deeper as if choking.

I rose to help her, but she stayed me with her hand.

"Here, girl, pour yourself some water," Mother said.

My sister complied and then sat back down with a defiant plop.

I wasn't sure how long I could swallow my anger toward Mother and her insensitivity toward Camille. I felt a craving to pick at my fingers but instead dug my fingernails into my palms.

"As I was saying," Mother went on, "a couple came forward who agreed to adopt you, even though they knew about your sickly constitution. I stayed in touch with your adoptive mother, Naomi, for a while, to make sure they treated you well. From all appearances you were in good hands. But then your parents moved around so often, I lost track of you. In the end, I thought it was best to let you go. To let this family take care of you."

An eerie silence settled over Camille, and then she said, "In a way, this is much worse than I imagined. I was traded in for an inheritance like a person cashes in chips at a casino."

"Oh, such a gift for drama, just like Lily," Mother said. "You are identical to your sister. For your information, I didn't care that much for the money, but your father was keen on it, since he couldn't hold down a decent job if his life depended on it."

Camille shook her head as she rose. "So many excuses, so little love." She walked over to a bookshelf, pulled out a volume, and opened it. "You could have said no to your mother. Pure and simple."

"Bah. No one said no to her." Mother took another sip from her water glass. "And it did seem like the most humane way to handle the situation."

Camille slammed the book shut. "But I was your flesh and blood, not some mongrel dog to dump at the pound!"

"There is more to the story if you can be silent for a moment." Mother tried to set her water glass on the end table, but it slipped slightly and nearly toppled. She righted the glass, and then her face contorted into a glare as she looked at the portrait of our father on the wall. "Maternity was forced onto me by my husband, you see. I had told him right from the beginning I never wanted to have children. I didn't have enough motherly instincts for it . . . but you know how men can be when they want their way about things. So, Camille, be grateful you had Naomi. And Lily, be glad you had some good nannies over the years, especially Nanny Kate. Well, of course none of that came to be until after my mother passed away and we were able to afford it, but my point is there are things to be thankful for in all of this."

"More excuses. Nothing more." Camille slipped the book back on the shelf, walked over to the solarium, and placed her palm on the glass the way she'd done the day on the tram. "I feel sorry for Lily, to have had you for a mother . . . someone who didn't care about her own children. You didn't have to follow in your mother's footsteps, you know. You could have been different. You could have been a great mother, but you chose not to be. It's as simple and as heartless as that."

"Watch what you're saying, girl. I did give you life," Mother said. "I deserve to be—"

"No. You're wrong." Camille said softly. "*God* gave me life." This time she didn't turn around.

"Oh, let's not go down that road," Mother said. "Leave God out of it."

I couldn't restrain my indignation any longer. "That's been your problem, Mother. You have left God out of everything, including the decisions you made long ago and even now. You've come up with explanations today for what happened all those years ago . . . money problems, illness, lack of natural longings to mother, pressure, whatever. But your reasoning is like a serious crack in a priceless vase. With your excuses you've reduced the precious blessing of motherhood into a piece of garage sale rubbish."

I stood, looking at Mother without turning away. "What Camille didn't tell you was that she was physically abused by the man you handed her over to. One time she almost died from one of those beatings. Does that rouse any motherly instincts in you?"

"How could I have known that someone who acted like a good father would turn out to be a hooligan?" Mother asked. "How could that possibly—"

"He was far more than a mere hoon, Mrs. Gray," Camille said from the window. "He belonged in prison."

"Yes, that's true." I turned back to Mother. "My point is . . . you and Father could have found a way to keep this family together. When I think of my own daughter, Julie, there isn't anything that could have taken her away from me. Not illness or poverty. Or threats from you or anyone. I would have fought for her until I had no breath left in my body." My hands tightened into fists until they went numb.

Mother grinned. "So, the Land Down Under has given you some real backbone, I see."

"No," I said, "it was always there. I inherited it from you."

The room got quiet while Mother mulled over a reply that surprised even me.

I wasn't sure if my last comment was a compliment or a criticism.

Someone tapped on the semi-closed door, making me jump.

I frowned at the interruption. "Please not now, Dragan," I muttered.

"Hellooo," a man's voice could be heard from behind the study door. "Some woman named Dragon said I should let myself in."

I knew that voice, but it wasn't possible. "Marcus, is that you?"

CHAPTER
twenty-seven

"Lily?" The door swung open, and there stood Marcus, as handsome and sunny and cheeky as ever. Even though it had only been a short time since I'd seen him last, oh how I had missed that blue-eyed twinkle.

"Marcus." I strode over to him, and he took me into his arms. "What are you doing here?" I folded into his embrace, a place that felt good and right and safe. Even his green silk shirt felt inviting. He'd brought Australia with him, and every memory made there.

"I'm here because of the weather," he said.

I chuckled. "What does that mean?"

Marcus pulled away and held me by my shoulders. "The weather got too cold without you. Couldn't stand it for one more minute."

I laughed a laugh brimming with delight. I felt like a child on Christmas morning.

My mother cleared her throat. "So, who are you?"

Her voice shook me back to reality.

As Marcus walked toward Mother, he nodded to my sister. "Good to see you."

"Hi, Marcus. What a happy surprise," Camille said.

Marcus gave my sister a wave. "Thanks." Then he bowed slightly to Mother. "You must be Mrs. Gray. I can see where the twins get their beauty."

Mother laughed, but it was more blustery than buoyant. "Who are you, besides being a liar?"

"I am Marcus Averill from Melbourne. And I have been called many things in my life, but never a liar." He reached out his hand so decisively that Mother reached out and allowed him to give her hand a small shake.

"Mother, Marcus and I became good friends while I was there."

He raised an eyebrow at me. "We are a bit more than good friends, Lily, dear." He turned back to Mother.

Mother shifted in her chair, examining Marcus as if he were a specimen in a jar. "Are you here on business?"

Marcus looked back at her with a curious glint. "No, I'm here for Lily. She took Australia by storm, you see, and the continent has not quite recovered. At least I haven't."

"Bah." Mother flubbered out a mouthful of air. "Are you really saying that you came all the way here from Australia for Lily?"

"Yes, Mrs. Gray," Marcus said, "that is exactly what I'm saying."

Mother donned a dubious expression. "Why in the world?"

I wanted to groan at Mother's insensitive response, but Marcus simply replied, "Because when Lily left me we needed more time to explore our feelings for each other. By coming here . . . I'm giving us that time."

"Mother, aren't you going to invite Marcus to sit down?"

"No worries." Marcus put up his hands. "I see that I've intruded, so I'll be on my way back to the Silver Bayou Inn. Lily, I'm hoping to see you later today for dinner. We have each other's cell phone numbers." Then he turned to my mother. "It was good to meet you, Mrs. Gray." He gave Camille a friendly wave, and then after a wink directed at me, he quickly made his departure.

All I could think to do next was escape from Mother's stuffy old mansion and spend the rest of the day with Marcus and Camille. I couldn't believe that he'd come so quickly—that he cared that much. My whole body felt like one enormous grin.

"Well, I'm zonked," Camille suddenly said. "I'd like to go back to your house, Lily." She turned to Mother. "Mrs. Gray, it's been . . . well, enlightening."

Mother made a snuffling noise I hadn't heard before. Did she have the beginnings of a cold? "Well, you've come all this way," she said. "You might as well visit me once more before you go back to Melbourne."

"It depends on how I feel," Camille said, sounding more weary than usual.

"So, you never recovered your health in all these years?" Mother asked.

"No, I never did. But I'm alive and grateful." Camille pulled a small package out of her pocket. "I almost forgot. I brought you a lamington. I wanted you to have something sweet from Melbourne. Thought you might like it." She set the little Aussie cake down on the coffee table.

"Lamington?" Mother said, gaping at the little sponge cake. "I don't usually indulge in such nonsense, but maybe this one time."

"Well, hoo-roo," Camille said.

"What did you call me?" Mother asked.

Camille grinned. "It means goodbye."

"Oh. Goodbye then." Mother leaned forward and watched Camille walk out the door with more curiosity than I would have imagined. She even reached for the cube-shaped cake and placed it on her lap.

But Camille never glanced back to see the inquisitive expression on Mother's face.

"Goodbye, Mother." A "thank you" for finding her daughter would have been appreciated, but it certainly wasn't expected. I walked out of the study and shut the door. Dragan had vanished like a dust devil in a rain shower. We were more than happy to let ourselves out.

"Well, what did you think of Mother?" I asked Camille when we were settled in my car. "It's a lot to take in, I know."

Camille laced her fingers together on her lap. "I do feel sorry for you. To have grown up that way. It really must have been difficult. She is a hard woman with some serious issues. And I agree that somehow, even though she doesn't admit to any guilt over what happened, the past has made her bitter and miserable. She needs a good cleansing of the soul."

I turned on the engine. "Maybe now that you're here, it will be the impetus she needs to take a good look at the past, to see the truth. Maybe light can come to this dark gray forest after all."

Camille's shoulders drooped. "It would take a miracle."

"She did ask us to visit again. I was surprised about that."

"I don't know, Lily. You want this so badly... all this reconciliation and restoration. But I'm just glad to have a sister. It might be too much trouble to make Mrs. Gray come around. And too much pain." Camille rubbed her stomach. "Speaking of pain, I don't feel that well. I need to go to bed when we get home. Must be traveler's malaise."

I reached over and felt her forehead. "No fever. That's good. We'll get you right to bed with some chicken soup."

"Thanks."

I grinned. "Since Julie's gone it's nice to have someone to pamper. But I'm sorry you don't feel well. I'll get you fixed up. No worries."

Camille smiled at my attempt to sound like an Aussie.

"I'm not worried. In fact, I'm beginning to wonder how I managed without a sister all these years." Her eyes and voice softened into earnestness. "Say, you know that day on the tram when you showed up, running after me?"

"How could I ever forget it?" I grinned.

"Well, I'd just prayed . . . an hour before . . . that if my life wasn't going in the right direction, that God would rescue me from myself. That He would provide me a way out of the life I'd created. And then there you were."

"I'm glad I was there. I've needed you my whole life and never even knew it."

She chuckled.

I gave her hand a squeeze and then said, "Say, I didn't know you had a degree in botany."

"There's still a lot you don't know about me. But I'm sure I will tell all . . . in good time."

I guess Camille didn't know all my secrets either, but hopefully we'd have lots of moments in the future to pick through the old trunks of our pasts.

After I drove Camille back to my house and got her all snug in bed and sipping on a mug of chicken soup, she patted my hand and singsonged, "Okay, Mommy, you've done your best."

I grinned at her reference to me as mom. "Do you need anything else?"

"Yes, I do. I want you to go visit Marcus. He's probably at his hotel, watching reruns of some awful reality TV show and bored out of his mind, counting the minutes until he can have dinner with you tonight."

"It still amazes me that he followed behind us so quickly."

"Handle him with care," Camille said. "It must be very serious on his part if he couldn't do without you for a few hours."

"I missed him too."

"Well then, I expect to be a maid of honor soon."

"Whoa." I laughed. "I think we're getting a little ahead of ourselves here, but thanks for your confidence."

"One more thing." Camille went somber on me. "Maybe I'm becoming a worrywart like you, but—"

"Hey—"

"Now, now." She held up her hands. "I don't mean that in a bad way, but I hope you don't ruin your chances with Marcus."

"Why would I do that?"

"I don't know." Camille shrugged. "If I say it out loud it might sound silly, but okay . . . well, when an eagle loses a feather on one side of its wings, it drops a feather on the other side. Sort of a balancing act. It just happens. One of the mysteries of nature."

"Obviously, you must have a deeper meaning here."

"I hope since I lost Jerald that you won't somehow lose Marcus." She gave her head a little shake. "I told you it would sound silly. I'm just afraid you might do something, even if it's subconsciously, that might make Marcus go away . . . you know, in an effort to make me feel less lonely or—"

"Please don't think that. I'm plenty selfish enough that I wouldn't break things off with Marcus to make you feel better about Jerald. We're fine. I promise."

"Good honest answer. I'm glad to hear it. So, in that case, go, Lily." Camille shooed me. "Go put him out of his misery, and go have a good time. You always look like you're in need of a fun day."

"Are you sure you're not just trying to get rid of me so you can polish off the last of the cookie dough ice cream in the freezer?"

"What? You've got cookie dough?"

"The good kind." I smiled. "It's yours if you want it."

"Okay, thanks. But go."

I went to the bedroom door and turned back. "You have my number if you need me. I'll have my cell phone right with me, so—"

"Gooo, Lily."

I chuckled. "Okaaay. I'm going."

I thought I'd surprise Marcus by dropping by his hotel, although surprises had never been my thing. But I gave myself a nudge and did it anyway.

The Silver Bayou Inn turned out to be a lovely boutique hotel located in the heart of Houston. After I parked and made my way inside, I excitedly pushed in the numbers to Marcus's cell number to tell him of my unannounced visit. I glanced around the lobby, and my breath caught at the sight of Marcus sitting with a woman. To be more exact—a beautiful red-haired woman with big Texas hair and enough curves to make an overstuffed couch envious.

The woman leaned her head toward Marcus as they stared at a book. The picture of them together, looking so intimate—hair touching hair—pierced me through. It didn't look like Camille would have to worry about Marcus being at the hotel in any kind of misery, waiting for me. He looked far from woeful.

So, who was this woman, and what were they looking at? Had he already found someone else in the short hours I was away? Was he a man a little too much like my husband? I hadn't known Marcus long after all. In fact, we had what some people would call a whirlwind romance—a phrase I never would have imagined attaching to my life. But there it was.

Feeling suddenly embarrassed about being there and a little lightheaded, I walked and then sprinted toward the main double doors of the hotel. Just when I thought I might make a clean escape I took one more glance back at them, which made my foot catch on the base of a potted palm. I landed, sprawled out on the slick ceramic-tiled floor like a flattened turtle. For a second I remained that way—in one of the most unladylike poses imaginable.

Then as if things couldn't get worse, in the seconds I raised my head to gain my equilibrium, I looked up to see Marcus and the red-haired woman gazing down at me like I was an alien who'd just landed in the hotel lobby.

CHAPTER
twenty-eight

"Lily, what in the world happened?" Marcus scooped me up faster than I could say *bombshell*. "Are you all right, Love?"

"I will be in a minute or two." Humiliation had never been so ripe for the plucking. I tried the act of breathing again. My lungs appeared to be functional.

"We both glanced up as you were taking your tumble," Marcus said. "Did you sprain anything?" He didn't let go of his firm hold on me.

"No, I don't think so." I dusted off my blue silk dress, the one I'd worn to impress Marcus. To make him think I was the most beautiful woman in the world. Hmm. I was obviously delusional. My dress now had a tear. And so did my pride.

The woman said, "You must be *the* Lily." She gave her big hair a shake. "What a delight to meet you. I'm Pamela Sky."

Pamela shook my hand so hard I thought my arm might jerk right off like a loose limb on a Mr. Potato Head toy.

"I was just asking Marcus here to let me come visit you," Pamela said. "I'm so glad you're here. What a surprise."

I'll say. Had I once again fallen down the rabbit hole like Alice? "But why would you want to meet me?"

Pamela looked incredulous. "Because I wanted to thank you for what you did."

"I haven't told Lily yet," Marcus said to Pamela. "I wanted to surprise her at tea tonight."

"Surprise me?" Did I need any more surprises for the day?

Pamela slapped her hands together. "Have I spoiled your happy time? Oh, I'm so sorry, Marcus."

"It's fine. Why don't we all sit down?" Marcus escorted me over to the corner of the lobby with Pamela in tow.

When Marcus and I were situated in a posh love seat with Pamela across from us, he said, "Go ahead, Pam."

"Me? Okay." The woman named Pamela held up the book that she and Marcus had been staring at together when I arrived. "This is it. A sketchbook. Because of you, Lily, Marcus has decided to go back to writing and illustrating for kids again. It's wonderful, and you're the miracle that brought Marcus back. Or I should say Miles Hooper."

Oh, my. "Yes, you're right. It is wonderful. That is what I had hoped for. Prayed for." I licked my lips, knowing I was about to ask something stupid. "But do you mind if I ask who you are?"

Marcus and Pamela laughed.

"I'm sorry. I said my name but not how I'm involved," Pamela said.

"Ms. Sky is my agent," Marcus said.

"Ohhh." I chuckled, feeling drenched in relief. "I guess I should have figured that out." If I'd had a sparkler I would have run through the hotel twirling it and shouting.

Pamela waved me off. "Not at all. That was my fault. I'm just so excited to have Marcus back for a client . . . or I should say Miles Hooper . . . that I forgot to add the 'agent' part."

"But how did I help make any of this happen?" I searched Marcus looking for an answer.

"Surely you know," he said to me. "Because you were relentless in trying to bring your family back together. It's inspiring. So much so, that I've dedicated my new book to you."

His words made my face heat up, enough to rival a sizzling summer day in Houston. "Thank you. I would never have expected that." I leaned over and kissed his cheek. It felt so good to do that. Better than a piano concerto or hot fudge on ice cream or even a trip around the world.

"Look at you two. You make the sweetest couple." Pamela turned the sketchbook around and showed me one of Marcus's drawings.

A family of kangaroos played on a hilltop in a state of merry reunion, and the most adorable joey peeked out of its mother's pouch. "The drawing is amazing. Such rich color and detail and . . . warmth. Kids will love it. So do I."

"It'll be his best work ever, but the setting will be Australia." Pamela was effervescing all over the place. "This is going to be a book about families coming together. That there really is no place else on earth like home."

"It sounds like a much-needed story for kids . . . for everyone. What's the title?"

Marcus kissed my hand. "The title is *Love Will Bring Me Home.*"

CHAPTER
twenty-nine

I hummed to myself in the grocery store, and I sang along with the tunes on the car radio. I was officially in a good mood, and nothing was going to squelch it. Not Mother. Not anyone.

I glanced in the rearview mirror. A pleasant glow covered me like a fuzzy towel after a warm bubble bath. Marcus was obviously a man who kept his promises, and my silly fears had been proven so wrong they'd been ridiculous. To celebrate, I opened a fresh pack of gum and popped a stick in my mouth for a cheery chew.

Hope seemed to be in everything, even in Mother's mixed response to our reunion. Autumn was around the corner, and the air had turned a little drier and made the breeze a little cooler. Nice. The mums would start peeking their pretty little heads out soon. And, of course, the fact that Marcus was coming to dinner added to my overall giddiness. My Julie being in college, I'd still have two of my favorite people under the same roof.

I parked the car, grabbed my bags of groceries, and scurried into the house to check on Camille. Hopefully she felt rested and well enough to enjoy a big spaghetti supper. But when I'd put away the groceries and made it to the guest bedroom, the room was empty. "I'm home," I yoo-hooed and then listened.

A cough erupted from the bathroom.

The door was shut. "Sis?" I walked down the hallway and tapped lightly on the door. "You okay?"

After a pause, Camille emerged. Her face looked pale and damp and drenched in fear, like she'd awakened from a nightmare.

"What is it?" I rubbed her back as she headed to her bedroom.

She shivered beneath her thin nightgown. Camille sat on the side of the bed and slumped over. Then after taking in several slow breaths, she crawled under the covers and rested back on the pillow.

I tucked her in with the quilt. "Was it Mother?" I asked softly. "Was she too much for you today? I thought maybe we should have rested up more for the onslaught. I mean, she can be—"

"It wasn't your mother. I mean, you're right. She was no picnic to deal with, but it's not why I'm feeling the way I do. It's something else." She slipped her hands on top of the quilt and started to pick at her fingers.

I rested my hand over hers. "Please, don't *you* start with that habit."

"Better than my TMJ."

"What is it?" I sat down next to her on the bed. "Do you want to talk about it? You can tell me anything. I hope you know that."

"I do." She laid her arm across her forehead. "I might as well talk about it. There'll be no hiding it soon anyway."

"No hiding what?"

"Lily, you're so innocent. Can't you guess?"

"Not really."

She covered her face with the quilt. "The glow. The wild mood swings. The woozy stomach." Her words came out muffled from under the quilt, but I'd heard them well enough to know what she meant.

I chuckled at the absurdity of it. "Do you mean you're pregnant?"

Camille made no more sounds from under the covers.

I swallowed my gum. *Lord, have mercy.*

CHAPTER
thirty

I peeled the quilt back from Camille's face. There was no teasing or joy in her expression. "Really? How do you know?"

"I brought one of the home pregnancy tests along with me. Since I'd missed three periods I thought there was a chance. I've missed periods before, though, so at first I didn't think much about it. But lately I started having other signs. I've been woozy on and off, but I'd never really been sick at my stomach . . . until today. Now I know for sure. A few minutes ago the test came out positive."

"Oh, wow." I felt like I'd just fallen off a cliff, and I saw no bottom.

"Just guessing I think I'm probably just over three months along, although I don't seem to be showing much. I just thought I'd put on some weight lately."

"I assume it's Jerald's baby." The words were out before I'd even thought about them.

"Of course it's his." Camille slapped her palms on the quilt. "How could you ask such a thing?"

"I'm sorry." I fluttered my hands. "I realize how unkind that came off. I didn't mean it. I'm just so stunned that I didn't know what to say." In fact, my head still buzzed with the shock.

"It's not what you think, Lily."

"What do you mean?" I wasn't sure what I thought, except that it was the last thing I'd ever imagined in the middle of our home-coming.

"You're thinking I gave my consent to Jerald, but I didn't."

I stiffened. "Do you mean he raped you?"

"I really thought God would come through for me on this one, since what I did wasn't really . . ."

"Wasn't really what?" I asked the words as lovingly as possible, but my mind screamed for the answers.

"Let me just start from the beginning." Camille scooted up in the bed and rested against the headboard. "As you know already, we'd dated a year. I'd said no to him about sex. I wanted to wait until we were married. But he got tired of waiting, and so one evening while we were watching TV on my couch, well, things got out of hand. He knew I desperately wanted to marry and have a family before I was too old. He promised to marry me. He even whispered his love to me right there, to show me how serious he was. I still told him no and tried to push him off, but he overpowered me." Camille didn't cry, but her words were full of tears.

"He raped you." I ground my fist into the bedding. "What a fiend." I stood then, enraged at her boyfriend. "Too bad we're not back in Melbourne. I would have pushed him into the Yarra River. Did you call the police? Why didn't you give him the boot then?"

She took my hand, and I settled back down on the bed.

"I didn't call the police," she said, "and I didn't give him the boot."

"Why in the world not?"

"Because somehow things got muddled in my head as they usually do . . . and in the end, I blamed myself."

"Why?" The word seemed to echo around the room, but I said it again, this time more softly. "Why, Camille?"

"Isn't that what women like me do?" Camille asked. "They always blame themselves?"

"What do you mean . . . women like you?"

"I don't know. My father, the way he treated me . . . well, I felt so worthless for so long that I . . ." She looked at me. "He never sexually abused me, but he did hurt me in other ways. I got used to the rough treatment and the cruel words. Eventually, it felt like I deserved it. That I was inferior to other girls. That no matter how hard I tried I would never rise above what he thought of me. The names he called me, well, I can't even repeat them. He made me feel dirty. Maybe that's why I'm always wearing the color white. I want back the innocence and self-esteem and youth that my father stole from me."

"Oh, Camille, it was never how things were supposed to be. I apologize for your father, for Jerald, and for my mother."

"Sweet Lily." Camille smoothed the quilt with her hand.

"But don't you want to see justice? Put Jerald behind bars where criminals belong? I would."

"But you're not the one having a baby. You might feel differently in my shoes. It changes my priorities. It changes everything. I don't want a courtroom scene or a legal battle of any kind, and that's what it would turn into if I told the police it was rape."

A sparrow flew over to the window and landed by the glass, fluttering its wings, looking so contented and innocent that it broke the spell of our despair for a moment. *I know, Lord, if You watch over the sparrows You are certainly watching over us right now, in these rough circumstances.*

Hard to believe there were people in the world who had no remorse, no shame in crushing innocence. To know Jerald walked the earth a free man while he needed to be in jail for what he did to my sister made me ill. What if Jerald were to do it again—to his next girlfriend? "But that's how thugs like Jerald get away with such wickedness," I said in a tender voice, "to not press charges."

Camille looked back at me, no longer full of energy as I had seen her that morning. "I know that, and it would be satisfying to see justice. But I want life to start fresh for my baby. I don't want to have us embroiled in more ugliness."

I sighed. "I do see your point . . . sort of."

"I'm just glad that Jerald is out of our lives for good. I'm grateful to be far away from his clutches. Being away from the control he had over my life. I can now see so many things clearly. I'd been blinded to his polluted spirit. Making excuses for him. You'll never hear me take up for him again." Camille worked her finger along the patterns of the quilt as if it were a maze. "But a little of my defensiveness might have been connected to Marcus."

"How so? You mean, because of the comparison?"

"You don't really notice how tarnished a penny has become until you set it next to a brand-new shiny one. You see, you had someone fine and wonderful falling for you, and I had someone horrible who only pretended to love me. A man who was capable of rape. Does the comparison get much worse? I mean, I wanted Jerald to be good like Marcus. I guess some of the time I pretended he was good, since I wanted it so badly."

"I'm sorry that my joy added to your unhappiness."

Camille smiled. "You're the only person I know who could apologize for joy. But I love you for that. The kindness. There's so little of it left in the world, that when you see it, experience it, the beauty of it stands alone."

"That means a lot to me . . . to hear you say it."

Camille placed her hand in mine. "Promise me something, Lily."

"Sure. What is it?"

"I want to be accountable to you as my child grows up. I can see that it's been easy for me to fall into the clutches of dysfunction because of my background, but no more. I don't want to use that as an excuse to raise my child in dysfunction because that is what I've known. I want the generational oppression to stop now. Promise me you'll tell me in the future if you see me sliding off into the muck again. Okay?"

Seemed like in the course of minutes, with the news of her child, Camille had grown up. "Okay, as long as you'll do the same for me."

Camille nodded. "Done."

I went over to the bureau and pulled out an album. "I have some photos I want to show you."

"Do you have any pictures of us together? You know, that first year? Never mind. What was I thinking? You wouldn't, since you didn't know about me."

"I'm sorry. We should ask Mother about that when we go over there again." Although that didn't have a promising feel to it. "These are photos of Julie mostly, when she was a baby."

"I want to see them, of course." She waved me to bring the album over to the bed. When we'd both gotten cozy under the covers with the album, Camille cracked open the book to the first page. She grinned and pointed to the photo with Julie still inside me. "Look at you, pregnant."

"I was nine months there. Ready to bust. Even my belly button bulged." I scooted closer to Camille.

"You're as big as a house." She tapped the photo. "A two-story with a triple-stall garage and awnings."

"Hey." I gave her a sisterly push and laughed. "But I know it's true."

"Guess I'll look just the same. I don't really mind." She moved her hand to the next photo—one of Julie as a newborn at the hospital. "Ohh, your daughter is so tiny here but as cute as a rosebud." She tapped her finger on a picture of the whole family, the one where we were building a birdhouse. "So, this was your husband, Richard. Tall, attractive. Looks like he has a sunny disposition. The perfect family." She leaned closer. "But . . ."

"What is it?"

"Something in your expression. Something's missing. Only one side of your mouth is turned up, like the person taking the picture has sweet-talked you into a smile. It didn't come from your soul."

Camille could see. She knew. "Well, no marriage is perfect."

"I've heard that." She didn't look convinced but went back to the photo. "Looks like your family was making a birdhouse together. Sweet idea. I hope to do those sorts of hobbies with my child."

Little did Camille know that our birdhouse never sheltered any birds. After we'd made it and put it in the garden I sealed it with a mesh screen to keep the birds from making a nest inside. I didn't want them to foul it up with their artistic doodles. But even with my extra measures, a swarm of wasps came and made a mess anyway. So like my life with Richard—in spite of the fact that I'd fortified our marriage against adultery—I had failed. Some woman named Vontella had shown up and had fouled it up anyway. I would tell Camille the rest of my marital story, but today was not the right time for that tale.

"But even without the perfect marriage, it must have been great to be a team . . . makes life easier. Mmm. And all that help with dirty diapers." Camille looked up at me. "You know, the scariest part of my situation is that I'm going to be a single mom."

I took her hand and placed it against my cheek. "You're not alone. You have me. And you have God."

"That's good. I'm going to need you both. I wonder if God will help us with the dirty diapers."

I chuckled, which made her laugh. She would need lots of that kind of therapy as the months ticked by.

Camille took on a more subdued look. "And I know this too . . . because of my age and because of my weakened condition health-wise, the doctors will call it a high-risk pregnancy. And because of the circumstances some people might try to encourage me to have an abortion. But I want you to know that nothing could convince me to take that course. I know what it's like to be unloved and to be unsafe, and I want my baby to know safety and love, while she's growing up but also while she's inside me."

I leaned over and kissed her forehead.

"I'll rest as much as I can too. That will help us both." Camille smiled and turned the page of the album. "I'll play the flute for her. Julie will play her guitar, and you'll play the piano. She'll be born with a song in her heart. That's it. I'll name her Melody. How about that?"

I smiled. "Lovely name. But what if it's a boy? Or twin boys?"

She gasped and then grinned. "You're right. It might be twin boys for all I know. Well, if they have big ears and they're as homely as Jerald, that'll be okay too. Two things for sure . . . they'll be loved, and they'll never be separated."

"I'm sure they won't." Suddenly remembering the dinner I needed to fix, I rose off the bed. "If you don't need me, I'd better get supper going. Marcus is coming."

"Tonight? Over here? Oh, I'm sorry I forgot to ask you about Marcus."

"Well, you've been a little bit preoccupied with your own situation."

"But did it go well when you surprised Marcus at the hotel?" Camille asked.

"Yes. Lots to tell you. I'll give you the full report after supper . . . after tea, that is."

She grinned. "Listen, I can stay in my room and rest or look at family albums if you guys want to be alone."

"No, not at all. You're my family. If you feel up to it and you want to eat with us, I'd love for you to be at the table."

"All right. I'll try." Camille scooted back under the covers.

I drew the quilt up around her as I had always done for Julie. "Lils?"

"Hmm?"

"The baby will be okay, don't you think?"

I wiped the damp curls from her face. "Yes, and she'll be beautiful like you."

Camille smiled. "And she'll look a little like you too."

"I suppose so." What an interesting thought.

"So, when am I going to meet my niece, Julie?"

"In a few days. I texted her, and she's thrilled you're here." I walked to the doorway and turned around. "Well, I guess I'd better get dinner started or we'll be eating something ghastly from the freezer."

Camille grinned. "One more thing . . . let's keep the news of the baby between us. Our secret, just for now."

I put my finger to my lips. "Mum's the word."

She repeated my words as she rested back on the pillow.

I headed to the kitchen and scurried around, trying to put together some semblance of a dinner, but my mind kept going over Camille's words and her plight. Poor thing. To be abused by her father and then by her boyfriend, only to find out she was pregnant, seemed like too many hardships to endure. Too much to fathom. But this I knew—I would weather this latest storm with her all the way. Whatever it took, we would face it together.

Minutes later, I'd browned the hamburger, but decided to cheat the process by pouring in a jar of pasta sauce from the cupboard. There was no time to prepare anything from scratch, so hopefully no one would notice that I'd skipped a few steps. I turned down the flame and let the meat sauce simmer.

While I continued to fuss around the kitchen, my mind overflowed with so much new information I barely knew what to do with it all. It appeared that I might be helping to raise a newborn if my sister chose to stay. Seemed like a challenging but fun prospect, but someday soon I would have to go back to work. Like sand in an hourglass, my leave of absence would eventually run out. I couldn't live forever on my husband's life insurance money, and I needed to keep most of my savings for retirement. Unfortunately, though, the longer I stayed away from my secretarial job the less I felt inclined to go back. What to do about that? I had no idea. Guess it was a dilemma that would have to be hammered out on another day.

CHAPTER
thirty-one

In the midst of my mind ramblings and dinner preparations, the doorbell rang. Oh, dear. Surely, it wasn't Marcus. He'd be waaay too early. And I hadn't even had time to tidy the house. I looked at all the piles of bills and papers on the counter and moaned. Apparently I'd lost some of my organizational skills as a secretary too.

After traipsing to the small entry—hoping it wasn't someone selling something—I opened the door. *Marcus?* "You're early."

The look on Marcus's face was genuine penitence. "Look, I know you said tea was at six, but I came early to help you. And I'm using that as my official excuse to see you a bit longer."

"No worries." I opened the door. "Come in."

Marcus came inside and kissed me on both cheeks.

"An Aussie tradition, I suppose?"

"Yes, it is. And I'm glad for it."

I chuckled. Excellent tradition, and one we needed to adopt in the States.

"I realized you must be dog-tired from jet lag. I should have offered to take you out."

"Nonsense. I want to cook you a meal. I'm tired, but I promise you it's a good kind of tired."

Marcus raised a finger. "I'm very good at dicing vegetables, and I'm not afraid of onions."

"Good. That's what I need. A real man who's fearless in the kitchen. But are you sure you're not the one with some jet lag?"

"To be honest, I'm a little worn out, but it's something else, not jet lag."

Oh, no. "What is it?"

"I'll tell you my story while I slice tomatoes or plant oregano, or play a mandolin for you or whatever you need me to do."

I patted him on the shoulders. "I still can't believe you're here in the US. In my home. So surreal. I thought it would be weeks, and then I got a little worried . . . you know, that you might change your mind and not come at all."

"Of course I was going to come. But as it turned out, I just couldn't wait. You should have seen me when your cab drove away with you, and it turned the last corner. The moment your wave and smile vanished I became a sorry case. I thought I was having chest pain. Instead of making a useless trip to the hospital I got on a plane. It was heart trouble all right, but it wasn't anything a doctor could fix."

"I'm so glad you came." I touched his cheek. "And I'm so very glad it wasn't a heart attack."

"Me too." Marcus leaned in to my touch.

"I've got the meat sauce on for a simmer, so we can chat in the living room for a minute if you want to."

"Lead the way. I'd follow you anywhere."

Guess that was true. I sat on the sofa in the living room, while Marcus pored over all the family photos on the fireplace mantel, asking questions about each one, especially the one where I was a little kid, sporting a mammoth grin with no front teeth. "You were a cute kid."

"Thanks."

Marcus sat down next to me. "I like your house by the way. It suits you. Very comfy. In fact, I think I even caught one of your throw pillows trying to give me a hug just now."

I chuckled. "Thanks. That's sweet." We both got quiet and dreamy, and I knew we were going to lean into some happy smooching on the couch, but I also knew that supper would not make itself. I chose the disciplined road. "Eventually we need to make a salad. So, you're handy in the kitchen, eh?"

"I can slice and dice with my eyes closed."

"Good thing we have an emergency room nearby."

When we'd both settled in the kitchen cutting up bell peppers and cucumbers and red onions for the salad, I asked. "So, what is it you need to tell me?" I hoped it wasn't bad news. I wasn't sure how much more I could take after Camille's announcement.

Marcus glanced over at me. Then he stopped his work at the cutting board. "It's about my parents."

I turned off the faucet and dried my hands. "Really? Do they know you're here?"

"They do. I called them from the hotel. Amazingly, they want to see me."

"That's wonderful. Truly." I reached over and gave the cuff of Marcus's sleeve an affectionate tug.

"My father had a biopsy recently. It came out normal, but it scared him. Scared them both. They started thinking about their lives, what's really important. And I guess the prodigal son returning figured in their revelations."

"I couldn't be happier for you."

He went back to slicing the vegetables. "I mentioned you. I couldn't help but mention you."

Really? "Was that wise? I'd hate to rock the boat when you just got it righted again. And you're going to lose a finger with that knife if you don't stop staring at me."

He chuckled and looked back down at his work. "You won't rock any boats. They want to meet you."

"Are you sure?" I leaned over the pot to check the softening strands of pasta. The boiling water foamed up, giving my face a sauna bath. Too hot. I turned down the burner and stirred. "Maybe they were just being polite."

Marcus studied me. "I know my parents well enough to know when they're faking it."

"Did you mean to see them right away?" I thought of Camille and how she needed me, especially right now as she adjusted to her condition, physically and emotionally.

"Well, that's the thing I needed to ask you. I'll be driving up to Dallas to see my parents." Marcus stopped his work and faced me. "Will you go with me tomorrow?"

Tomorrow? The spoon dropped out of my hand and onto the floor. "But this will be a crucial meeting. One that could have tremendous consequences one way or the other. I don't want to take the chance to tip the scale in the wrong direction. They should see you first, without the pressure of a stranger in their midst. There will be a lot of heavy talk. Hard things might get said before the fun catching-up part. Don't you think?"

I picked the utensil off the floor and tossed it into the sink. "Or maybe I'm being a big fat squawking chicken, since I hate confrontation." I leaned over the sink and looked out the window at my mums. The tiny buds suddenly looked wilted, terrified that the last hours of summer would be the hottest. "Any way you look at it, though, it has conflict written all over it."

"It's a valid argument. But I'd still like to have you there with me. I know having you by my side will tip the scales, as you put it, only in my favor. For more than a decade they've been trying to get me settled down with a wife and family. I was always happy to marry and have kids, but I never found the right woman. Now, this would please them to see that—"

"But, Marcus." Fear niggled its way into my spirit. "As happy as I am for you and with you, I feel it might be a lie. I mean, we're just dating. Seriously dating, yes, but we've made no commitments. And if I show up it could easily appear like more." I opened the cupboard and stared inside. "I feel so discombobulated I don't even know what I'm searching for in this cabinet." What was I afraid of all of a sudden—commitment? "Marcus?" The word came out as a plea.

He came over to me then. Marcus closed the cabinet door and gently took me into his arms. "I'm sorry. I never want to discombobulate you. I know my request was full of self-interest and, well, self-preservation. Forgive me. I wasn't paying enough attention to you . . . at how uncomfortable this made you. And it was inappropriate of me to pressure you like that. You're right. It would be best if I do this alone." He gave me a warm snuggly hug. "You okay now?"

"I'm okay. When you hold me like this it would be easy to agree to most anything." I knew I would regret the words the second they were out of my mouth, but since Marcus had come all the way around the world for me, I said, "Well, what if you're careful to introduce me just as your girlfriend and nothing more."

"Lily." He pulled back. "Are you sure you aren't saying this because you're under the intoxicating influence of my embrace?"

I laughed. "Probably, but I will go. I want to be by your side." Even if it scares the giblets out of me.

"I promise there will be no hint of those dastardly words *fiancée* or *wedding*." He let me go. "At least not yet anyway."

I chuckled. "Okay."

"Unless, of course, you bring it up and you force the nuptial issue." He went back to his work at the counter. "Then I might have to reconsider."

"No. There'll be no arm twisting from me."

"Believe me, you wouldn't have to twist my arm at this point. My theory is . . . it might only take a kiss."

I shook my head at him, but a grin was not far behind. It grieved me that my sister had waited too long for a man to propose to her, and yet it felt like Marcus wanted to pop the question way too soon. Why did things have to be so complicated? So backward? "Mmm.

It might only take a kiss. That has a starry-eyed sound to it . . . like a line a writer might use."

"Owww." Marcus winced. "Ouch."

I grinned. "I'm not the only one around here who can tease."

He dropped his work again and strolled over to me. "Maybe it's more than a line. Maybe it's a romantic theory worthy of further study." He lowered his gaze to my lips.

One hand pushed him away while another pulled him to me. "Sounds delicious, but we're never going to get supper done at this rate."

He locked his eyes on me. "There's more to sustenance than mere food, woman."

"I forgot to ask you what you thought of my mother."

He tilted his head at me. "I think she has issues that can be resolved, but this isn't the best time to chat about your mother."

"I agree."

"Finally."

The embrace took a more meaningful turn then, and even though the sauce was spattering all over the stove, and the pasta pan was nearly boiling dry, we hovered toward each other.

Marcus whispered in my ear, "I think I'd like to test this theory of mine . . . that it might only take one good kiss to summon a proposal."

"Well, I can't guarantee anything," I whispered back, "but I'd certainly hate to be a hindrance to your research."

CHAPTER
thirty-two

Early the next morning on our road trip to Dallas—in Marcus's rental car and with me at the wheel—we had a chance to get to know each other on a deeper level. We covered our childhoods and our families. Our favorite things. Our fears and dreams. Our various friendships and romantic relationships when we were teenagers. My marriage. And, of course, Julie.

We went beyond the casual chitchat of first dates, and delved into more important issues, the ones couples talk about when they get more serious about each other. I liked almost everything I saw on Marcus's table when he got it all laid out, and he seemed to respond positively to all my answers and viewpoints. It was obvious we were not perfect people, but we both loved God and we were both smitten with each other.

Later, as we drove through the residential area of Dallas, Marcus gaped at me when I told him one of my crazy escapades as a child.

"So, let me get this straight," he said, "you nearly blew yourself up. How exactly did that happen?"

"Well, one of the neighborhood kids, Ziggy, found a box of gunpowder on a high shelf out in his garage. Obviously it was something we weren't supposed to be playing with, but he and I decided it might be fun to see if we could blow up some rotten vegetables we found out in the garden. We did indeed discover it was a blast . . ."

Marcus laughed.

"So, we tried it on bigger and bigger vegetables and fruits. I'm telling you it's a real rush to watch a watermelon go ka-boom."

He threw his head back, laughing. "I would love to have seen this."

I passed a truck that was going too slowly. "Well, the story takes a dark turn. After a while we got bored with exploding vegetation, so we just threw bits of the gunpowder into a small fire, watching it fire up and sparkle like fireworks."

"What? Where was your nanny in all this?"

"My nanny at the time, a woman named Matilda, was having cookies and coffee in the house where we were visiting, while Ziggy and I were hiding behind an empty horse barn with our gunpowder. They couldn't hear a thing. So, back to the dark turn. Little did we know that bits of gunpowder were seeping through my fingers each time I went from the box to the fire. That action made a rough fuse, which neither one of us noticed."

"Oh, Lily, you're kidding."

"No joke." I gripped the steering wheel, remembering the blast. The thunder of it, the jolt, and the smell of scorched hair. "After a while the fuse lit, and it blew up the whole box of gunpowder. The explosion sent me sort of jumping as well as flying over a fence. I wasn't permanently damaged, but for a while I had a ringing in my ears and some of my hair got scorched. It was a piece of my childhood that I will never forget, I can tell you that. And one my nanny will never forget either, since she got fired over it."

Marcus whistled. "It's a miracle you're alive and that you didn't get severely injured."

"True."

"There are a lot of miracles in this life, Lily."

"Also true."

"And one of them was when you decided to get on that plane to Australia."

Delight rushed through me, making me smile.

"By the way, we're almost there. Okay, now. Make a left on this street . . . Timberland Trails."

When I did, Marcus pointed to the right. "My parents' home is that one over there. The two story red brick with the green shutters and the American flag."

"It looks like a friendly house. Very Norman Rockwell–ish." It was a nice size, well-designed, and unpretentious. A home said a lot about the people inside. At least that had always been my theory. The only thing that seemed odd was the blinds—they were all closed tightly. I pulled up to the house and cut the engine. "So, are you ready for this?" Was I ready for this?

"As ready as I'll ever be." Marcus adjusted his tie and cleared his throat. "After a year, this is hard. I can't imagine going ten years like you did. How did you manage going back that first time?"

"The grace of God I guess." I picked up my purse, wondering if I had enough tissues. Just in case things got emotional.

"But the thing is, when you went back to see your mom after all those years, you hadn't been guilty of anything. You weren't even guilty of not going to visit her, since you told me she hadn't wanted your company. You were an innocent. I'm not."

"None of us are completely innocent. Not me, not your parents." I wanted to hold Marcus's hand, but I fiddled with the buttons on the console instead. "And you didn't mean to fall asleep at the wheel. You wouldn't have harmed a hair on your sister's head. You loved her. While it was tragic, what happened, it wasn't right for your parents to disown you."

"I suppose not. But I can see the temptation. It seemed easier to unleash all their anger on something . . . someone." Marcus adjusted his tie again.

"There needs to be forgiveness, though, and I hope it starts today." I handed Marcus the keys to his rental car.

He gestured to my door. "Stay put. I'm coming around to open your door."

I sat still while Marcus came around to my side, and like the genteel man he was, he opened my door, took my hand, and helped me out. As we walked up the sidewalk to the house I circled my arm through his, a place that now felt homey like a comfortable pair of slippers.

The blinds in one of the front windows moved as if someone had been watching. Guess they knew we'd arrived. I didn't mention it to Marcus or tell him how scared I was to meet his parents, especially under such difficult circumstances. He already knew, so there was no sense in belaboring the point. The anxiety on my part would only add to his own.

The closer we got to the front door the more Marcus's arm stiffened. I deliberately relaxed my own and patted his.

Seconds later we stood on the porch, staring at the tattered autumn wreath on the front door.

Marcus paused, reached over to the round bell, and gave it a decisive push.

Hmm. I suddenly hoped my dress was nice enough and not too low-cut. I'd spent half an hour agonizing over what to wear to give Marcus's parents just the right message, and yet now I questioned my choice. Too late for any changes now. I practiced my smile and a few words of greeting in my head. I tried not to tap my foot or fidget. I was glad, at least, that I had no need to worry about Camille while I was gone. She seemed more stable emotionally and physically, and she'd insisted I come along with Marcus. As I left her she was relaxing on the back deck, reading a novel.

After a moment or two of waiting, Marcus stepped on a few fallen acorns, which made an impatient crunching sound under his shoe. "I wonder if they changed their minds." Just as he reached out to ring the bell a second time, the door eased open.

I was surprised to see a woman who appeared more youthful than my mother. Mrs. Averill did, however, wear a pinched and tired look as if the only thing on her mind was to take a very long rest from life.

"Hi, Mom." Marcus smiled and inched forward.

"Hi. Both of you, please come in." His mother opened the door wider.

We both stepped inside the entryway. Mrs. Averill's face lit with what appeared to be gladness, and yet she didn't hug Marcus. Her eyes were lined in red, but it was impossible to know whether she'd been weeping from the excitement over their reunion or from the painful memories that would surely come from his visit. Maybe a little of both.

Marcus glanced around the entrance and beyond as if searching for something—someone. "The place still looks the same."

His mother heaved a sigh. "I guess your father felt there'd been enough change, so he wouldn't let me alter anything, even the old drapes . . ."

Marcus and his mother locked eyes, and in those moments something shifted. He thumped his fist into his palm as if he were starting a game of rock-paper-scissors.

It must have been a secret code from when he was a boy, because it instantly made his mother smile, changing the whole landscape of her face as well as the room.

"It's good to see you, Mom," he said. "I've missed you."

"I've missed you too," she said in an unsteady voice. She glanced my way. "Please introduce me, Son."

"Mom, this is Lily Winter."

We shook hands. "Nice to meet you, Mrs. Averill."

"Glad to meet you too." Mrs. Averill slid her hands along her flared skirt, smoothing it.

Marcus milled around the entry hall. "Where's Dad? Is he having a hard time with me coming home?"

Mrs. Averill straightened a figurine on the table. "Yes. A little."

"I'm just glad you both agreed to let me come home for a bit."

"Oh, well, it's not that bad." His mother waved him off. "You're going to make us sound like horrible parents in front of your friend, here."

"I don't mean to do that. But Dad was pretty clear when I left. So I thought—"

"I know, Son." His mother looked down, shifting the weight on her feet. "It wasn't my idea. It was your father's." Her lip quivered.

Marcus went over to his mother and put his arms around her. "I'm sorry for upsetting you. I should have let it go. Would it be all right for us to go into the living room and sit down?"

"Of course. Please make yourself at home, both of you." Mrs. Averill gestured toward the living room. "I have some coffee on. Would either of you like some?"

"No, thank you." I scrubbed my fingers along my arms, feeling a chill.

"None for me," Marcus said. "Thanks."

"Well, then." His mother backed away. "I'll go and see where your father is."

When she left the entry Marcus strolled into the living room. "Not exactly a joyous homecoming."

I followed him and sat on the couch. "But your mom *did* offer coffee. That was nice."

"Not quite the fattened calf, but it'll do."

It seemed clear to me now what God was up to—that He'd put us together to help each other through the same plight, the same familial turmoil. I wasn't sure how it would all work out, but life was no doubt made easier by the empathetic camaraderie of similar circumstances. What mystery there was in the Almighty and His ways.

Marcus sat down next to me and picked up a family photo, which sat on an end table. The photo included three people, Mr. and Mrs. Averill and a young girl. Must be Ellie, his sister. But why didn't the photo include Marcus?

His shoulders sagged some, but he said nothing as he set the photo down. While we were waiting on his mother, an older man who looked a lot like Marcus appeared in the doorway.

Marcus looked up. "Sir?"

For just one moment—an empty one jammed full of more raw emotion than humans were meant to endure—I could not guess how things would work out. I could almost hear Marcus's plea to heaven.

Mr. Averill stood there in his three-piece suit and tie while we waited for the first flicker of welcome. "Marcus?" His first word came out as a question.

"Dad." Marcus rose. "It's good to see you."

His father strode toward him, and when they met in the living room, he stuck out his hand. "Well, so you came home for a visit."

"Yeah. I did."

"You seem thin. Didn't they feed you in the Outback?" his father asked.

"Yes, there's plenty of food. I don't eat as much as I used to, but I've been getting along all right."

His father turned his attention to me. "And who's your friend? Are you an Aussie?"

"No. I'm from Houston." Best to keep things simple. Less of a target to shoot at.

After Marcus made the formal introductions, I quickly wiped my sweaty palm behind me on my dress and said, "It's nice to meet you, sir."

"Same here," Mr. Averill said to me, and then to Marcus, "I think your mother has made us a late lunch. Why don't we go in and sit down?"

We filed tidily into the dining room where the table was set with a linen tablecloth and napkins and a bowl of short-cut roses. The room looked lovely but unused. Mrs. Averill brought in a loaf of sliced bread and sat down.

When we were all seated, Mr. Averill said a word of grace, very short and very solemn, and then his wife passed the roast and mashed potatoes around the table. No one said anything, so as the seconds ticked by it was as if Marcus had lost the little bit of ground he'd gained.

"So," his father broke the silence, "what have you been doing with yourself in Australia all this time?"

"Staying busy." Marcus let his fork rest back on his plate and looked directly at his father until he had his full attention. "That's not the whole truth. I've not been that busy. I don't have a real job. I live off my royalties. I have seen some of the sights, but mostly I've lived like a vagabond. When I met Lily on a park bench in Melbourne, I even looked like one."

Oh, dear. Like Camille had done with Mother on her arrival, he was emptying his whole duffel bag at once. "Marcus is being modest," I said. "He's spent some of his time at St. Paul's Cathedral, doing volunteer work with the youth. They speak highly of him there. And I would call his clothes more casual than anything."

I waited for Mr. Averill to respond, but he just plowed into his mashed potatoes.

Timidly, a bug made its way across the hardwood floor. It stopped by my chair, and seemed to consider me before it vanished under the table. I wasn't big on bugs, but I kept my feet still, not wanting to crush the poor thing. I had a feeling there would be enough of that for one day.

Mr. Averill cleared his throat, and I jolted back to the conversation, or the lack of one. The sugar bowl came my way, but I passed it on, since I didn't want to add the clicking of glass to the tension in the room.

His father scooped several spoonfuls of sugar into his tea and stirred, clattering the utensil around on the glass. "Lily, what do you do?"

I took a sip of my iced tea, since my mouth had become an arid terrain. "I'm a secretary for an oil company."

"Good solid business, but do you ever aspire for more?" Mr. Averill asked. "You know, hoping to be more than someone's lackey?"

"Dad," Marcus said, "I hardly think that an executive secretary should be thought of as someone's lackey. It's a very—"

"Okay, so it wasn't the best choice of words." His father put up a hand. "New subject. So, how in the world did you two become friends? Lily, were you on vacation in Melbourne when you met Marcus?"

"Actually, I was there to find my twin sister, Camille."

"Was she lost?" A chuckle rippled beneath the surface of Mr. Averill's expression.

I bristled at his flippant attitude, but let it go. "It's a long story." And a story I had no intention of telling him, not with that jeer dancing on his lips. "But I ran into Marcus while I was there, and he volunteered to help me find her."

"Just like that?" Mr. Averill stabbed his fork into the roast beef. "He volunteered to help someone he didn't even know?"

The man made it sound as if Marcus was wanting in his character for reaching out to help me. "Yes, he did. At first, I hesitated, because he was a stranger and all, but—"

"Good girl." Mr. Averill pointed his fork at me.

I tried to keep my Irish ire from flaring. "*However,* at the time, I didn't know how foolish that decision would have been. With Marcus's help, we did find Camille, and she flew back with me to Houston. We're in the middle of a family reunion because of the help from your son."

"You give me too much credit," Marcus said. His expression pleaded, "Please don't spread my praise too thickly."

"Not at all. It's as true as can be." I smiled at him, not giving an inch, since I wasn't about to sit still and watch Mr. Averill pulverize his son. I could take Mother lambasting me, but for some reason witnessing the same thing happening to Marcus felt unbearable.

"Well, then, Son, you should be commended for being the redeemer of families." His father tore a roll apart and reached for the butter. "Rather ironic, wouldn't you say?"

"Charles," his mother said. "Please."

I fiddled with a loose thread on my dress. All I had to do was pull and one of my buttons would go clattering to the floor. So tempting. Perhaps it would be a small act of defiance on my part, but more importantly, it might redirect the flow of conversation. Before I could pull, Mrs. Averill spoke up again.

"Marcus? Have you called any of your old friends since you've been back? I know they'll want to touch base." Her tone came off as tremulous as a fluttering leaf in a hurricane.

Marcus stirred his fork around in his peas and then mashed them between the prongs. "I'm sure I can call some of them soon, but I just got back."

I tried to spread some butter on my bread, but it kept falling off in cold chunks. The meal was not getting off to a great start, and it had nothing to do with the food. Mr. Averill's formal, commanding attitude reminded me of my mother. Had our childhoods been more similar than I imagined?

"My agent drove down from Austin," Marcus added.

"Humph." His father curled his palms against the edge of the table and straightened his elbows like a prosecuting attorney might do on the railing in front of the jury. "What in the world does *she* want?"

Marcus leaned forward. "Pamela's excited because I've started to illustrate and write again. I'd been floundering all this time until I met Lily. She's inspired me to pursue my gift again." His voice held traces of boyish enthusiasm in spite of the cold reception.

But this didn't seem like the best time to bring up his career. I guess Marcus just wanted to dive right in and get it over with. But the waters around the table looked frigid enough to cause some serious frostbite.

Marcus's father folded his napkin, set it on the table, and then pressed a crease in the cloth with his finger. The few seconds of quiet before he spoke were like the moments inside the eye of a tornado. "Have you conveniently forgotten it was this so-called gift, this artistic obsession of yours, this selfish and all-consuming need for pleasing the public at all costs that kept you in a constant state of exhaustion . . . which killed your sister?"

CHAPTER
thirty-three

Marcus flushed red. "No, I have not forgotten. How could I? She was my precious baby sister. I will never forget her or what happened for as long as I live."

Mrs. Averill's knife clattered on the butter plate, making me jump.

If there were ever a good time to pick at my fingers it was now, but I chose to sit on my hands instead. The food no longer mattered anyway.

"Charles. It's not the right time to bring this up. We have a guest." Mrs. Averill raised her chin.

"Then tell me, when is the right time, Gerty?" Mr. Averill fell back in his chair. "You seem to have all the answers. Tell me."

"I don't know." Mrs. Averill curled a lock of hair behind her ear. "But I can't see how that tone of yours is going to accomplish anything."

Mr. Averill raised his hands. "Well, I have to get in my words now, just in case our son decides to flee the country again."

"Sir, with all due respect, you asked me to leave," Marcus said. "I didn't think it would matter what country I lived in as long as I was gone."

"Of course it matters. You running off like that was the coward's way out. You thought you'd punish us for what I said, even though you knew they were words said in the heat of an argument."

"Dad, I'm here to make amends in any way I can." Marcus's tone came off firm but respectful. "I want to once again say how sorry I am. But I don't understand something. You say I'm punishing you for doing the very thing you asked me to do. I want to make things right, but how can I? It feels as though you're making forgiveness unattainable."

His mother scooted her chair back quickly as if she wanted to flee the room. "Forgiveness seems unattainable, Marcus, because your father has made it so."

Mr. Averill slammed his fist down on the table. "Gerty, that's enough. I will not allow you to—"

"Please," Marcus said to his father. "Don't speak to Mom that way. You can take it out on me all you want, but not on Mom. I won't let you do that."

Mr. Averill raised his chin and then said in an ominously low voice, "Well, this is my house, and—"

"No more, Charles," Mrs. Averill said. "I have kept silent about this for too long. I've been trying to keep the peace, but this is an unhealthy kind of peace. It's not real. I will say this . . . I can understand your anger at Marcus for what he did. He wasn't using good sense that evening when he drove off with Ellie, but this rage has gone on too long."

Mrs. Averill's hands trembled as she put her napkin on the table. "I don't know. It's like you're thrashing around in a cage, angry at the whole world. You're mad at the girl at the grocery store checkout for not ringing you up fast enough. I never said anything, but you embarrassed me in front of one of my friends from church who was standing in line that day. The men who do our lawn are never speedy enough. Our dentist, our insurance agent, our pastor . . . you've written them all off for one reason or another. And your anger is destroying what's left of our family. These last few months should have been a time of mending fences, but for you, it was a season of burning bridges."

She stood and straightened her shoulders. "I love you, Charles, but this destructive behavior you have directed toward Marcus and me and God and the rest of the world has got to stop before it kills us all. That's not what Ellie would have wanted."

Mr. Averill huffed. "How do you know what Ellie wanted? She's not here to defend herself. She's dead. My girl is dead."

"Yes, Ellie, *our* daughter, is dead." Mrs. Averill pinched at a piece of the tablecloth. "But . . . Ellie loved our Lord, and I'm at peace with where she is. We'll never forget her, of course, and we'll never stop missing her until we can hold her again in the heavenly realms, but Charles, it's time to be free of this anger and live again."

"Seems like everyone wants to leave our daughter behind." Mr. Averill pressed his fingers against his eyes. "Ellie was the dearest, sweetest thing. Never asked much of anyone. She wasn't obsessed about fame or money. She was just Ellie."

"Ellie was sweet and dear to all of us," Mrs. Averill said, "but you're looking at her life through rose-colored glasses now that she's gone. That's very common to do that. But Ellie had plenty of teenage angst along with the sweetness. And you're looking at your son with no mercy whatsoever. No love. It's not right. This isn't what God wants for you or our family. And if I remember correctly you used to care about what God thought."

Marcus remained silent.

I could barely breathe.

Mr. Averill spread his fingers on the table and leaned forward. "Well, I'm not so freewheeling with my forgiveness. Not when it comes to my flesh and blood."

"But Marcus is your flesh and blood just like Ellie."

Mr. Averill frowned at his wife. "But Ellie wasn't a *murderer*."

"Charles, I love you. I do. But that is the last time I will listen to you make that abominable remark about *our* son. Ellie's death was an accident, and knowing my son the way I do I'm sure he's awakened every morning of his life remembering the scene in punishing detail. Marcus certainly doesn't need you to torture him. I'm sure he's tormented himself plenty this past year, enough to last a lifetime."

"What are you up to?" Mr. Averill crossed his arms. "You sound like you're going somewhere, which is—"

"I am, Charles." With great composure, Mrs. Averill said, "I'm leaving you."

CHAPTER
thirty-four

"You can't do that." Mr. Averill glowered at his wife.

"You no longer have any say in the matter." Her expression was one of tranquility, but it wasn't without despair.

"What? You already had this planned out?"

"I knew how this would go today. I prayed it would not, but there is such a thing as free will, and you've decided to go down this road . . . this path of bitterness. Well, it's a path I can no longer travel with you. You see, it's slowly killing me. My heart doctor says I cannot keep living under this kind of ongoing stress, or I will have a heart attack. Not just heart flutters and the racing heartbeat that sent me to the hospital several months ago, but the real thing. I want to save my health for you and for our son. I'd like to be alive in case God gives us the blessing of grandchildren. So, for now, I'm going."

"But where will you live?" Mr. Averill rose from his chair.

"I'm not going to Australia," she replied, "but I can understand why Marcus went that far. Maybe it's not far enough. But I'm going to live with my friend Susanna out in the country. She's invited me to stay. I'm not coming back until you've had counseling sessions with the pastor and you've proven that you mean to love this family again and not pour it full of hate."

"This is preposterous. Silly, even. I won't let you go." His eyes flashed with fury.

"Yes, I thought you might say something like that." Mrs. Averill's wrinkles seemed to deepen. "But my bags are already packed."

She turned away from her husband and looked at me. "I'm sorry you heard all this, Lily. It was very upsetting for me to have a stranger see this side of us, but what's done is done. I don't know how you two feel about each other, but if it turns out to be serious, Lily, I hope you won't hold this day against us as a family."

"No, not at all." I gave her my warmest smile.

"Good. We used to be a good and loving family, but we lost our way. Maybe that's what happened to your sister. I'm glad she's back home. Someday our son will be able to know home again, the way it used to be."

"I'm very sorry, Mrs. Averill." I had no idea what more I could say. I wanted to comfort the woman, and yet I could sense that Marcus's father wasn't going to tolerate much more chatter.

"Thank you for that, Lily. I hope we can meet again in happier times . . . someday." Mrs. Averill said to her son, "I love you. More than you know. I'm sorry this happened on your special day of homecoming. Please don't feel this is your fault. With God's help there will be better days."

"I love you, Mom," Marcus said. "And I'm sorry too."

Mrs. Averill focused on her husband again. "Charles, there are meals in the freezer for two weeks ahead. But after that, you'll be on your own. Marcus and Lily, please finish your lunch if you'd like. But if you'll excuse me."

Mr. Averill jolted toward his wife as if he were going to physically stop her from going, but she calmly looked at him. Something in her stare must have made him retreat, since he sat back down.

Marcus's mother picked up her plate with the uneaten food, took one look into the mirror on the dining room wall, and left the room.

Mr. Averill turned to his son. "I hope you're satisfied. Look what you've done now." He turned his fury on me. "And you, young lady, were no help to be here . . . encouraging my son the way you did, to take back up with that dreadful profession."

I rose, feeling sick at my stomach. "Perhaps Marcus and I should go now. I've intruded long enough."

"Yes, you have," Mr. Averill said.

Marcus rose and slapped his napkin down on the table. "You may speak to me in any way you choose, but you will not speak to Lily that way. She is innocent of any wrongdoing in spite of what you say. She is one of the finest people I have ever had the pleasure to know. I had hoped you would both get to know her as I do."

Mr. Averill grunted.

"And please stop being so hard on Mom," Marcus said. "She loves you. You need to think about what the doctor said about her health. It would be tragic to have another funeral." He refocused on me. "Lily, it's best we go . . . for now."

Mr. Averill remained in his chair and in his brooding silence as Marcus escorted me out of the dining room.

CHAPTER
thirty-five

Later, in the car, after a profound apology from Marcus—concerning his father's behavior and for bringing me along on such a doomed excursion—our drive on I-45 toward Houston became a quiet one. I had my own thoughts to plague me, wondering why it was that families got so far off the path that they could no longer find their way back. Marcus may have been thinking the same thing. I didn't know. Normally, I would have blamed myself somehow and cried a river until my head throbbed, but I could see that the situation was more complex than that. And my tears would not have helped.

Just as I considered a beefy conversation with the Almighty, lightning and thunder rolled in around us—not the emotional kind but the weather kind. The blackest clouds I'd ever seen trolled in behind our car as if chasing us, and then in one great blast, the storm unleashed several more lightning bolts—surely enough energy to power a city—making me let out a yelp and swerve the car so much that I nearly ran us off the freeway.

Marcus grabbed the dash.

I pulled over on the side of the road as I let out a happy holler that we were still alive.

My whoop sounded so ridiculous there was nothing to do but laugh. That part felt good. We needed the release. And Marcus needed to see that other people were fully capable of having car accidents.

Then the rain clouds let go in a big way as if the angels were pelting us with millions of water balloons. The wind, gusty and wild, seemed to be playing a game of tug-of-war with our car.

I scrunched up my shoulders. "Do you think there's a funnel cloud above us?"

Marcus pointed to the underpass. "Why don't we pull under that bridge until it calms down."

"Okay." I came to a stop beneath the underpass. The roar of the storm lessened—being muffled under the bridge—enough to let us relax for a moment. "That's better."

"I've wanted to talk to you this whole drive, but I felt we needed time to think," Marcus said. "Well, *I* needed to think. So, maybe this is a good time to talk."

I ground my thumbs into the steering wheel. "Guess I know what you're wanting to talk about."

"You don't know all of it." Marcus tugged on his hair like he might consider pulling some of it out. "As I mentioned earlier, I shouldn't have asked you to come along with me this first time with my parents. You should never have had to witness that . . . to be subjected to those insults. I'm especially sorry, since you've been through a lot with your mother recently."

"It's okay. I'm stronger than I used to be. And I was glad to have been by your side."

Marcus touched my cheek. "Please know, in case you're thinking about blaming yourself for any of this, which I know you have a tendency to do . . . not a bit of it was your fault. To be honest, though, I never imagined my mother would leave him. I hadn't spent much time thinking about her burden, grieving for Ellie while she tried to keep Dad from spiraling out of control. She seemed to be at her wit's end with him, and I can't blame her. He's no longer himself. My father wasn't this way when I was growing up. Well, on an occasion he had a temper, but he wasn't bitter like you saw him today. He was a good man, quiet strength. I'm sure he still is, under all those layers of grief."

"I'm sure he is. Grief is pretty horrible stuff. Emotions we don't really know how to deal with. We just fumble around with them."

"How true," Marcus said.

"In spite of the harsh words, I feel sorry for your father. He must be hurting something awful to say the things he did."

"Thank you for saying that. For not hating my father and for not running out of the house in the heat of the battle, which would have been tempting."

I smiled. "There was a moment or two at the table that fleeing would have been appealing."

Marcus reached over to the keys and shut off the engine. "That's better. There's something else I want to say. You know, I had such conflicting emotions while we were all arguing around the table. There we were in the midst of this war with my father and my mother's love being strained to the ends, and it could have made some people cynical about love for the rest of their lives. And yet all the while as I looked across the table at you I was thinking . . ."

"Oh?" My skin prickled.

"I was thinking . . . that I have never loved anyone more in my life than when I gazed at you today."

I chuckled. Giggled was more like it. "Do you mind saying it again?" I touched my arms. "I got goose bumps when you said it."

Marcus laughed. "I love you, Lily. I do. I know it's early on in our relationship, but I'm not going to try and hide it any longer. Or even wait until the storm passes from my life with my parents. And to think it all started between us from the moment I saw you on that park bench stuffing your mouth full of marshmallows and being all feisty and miserable because of your empty nest. It started there." He lifted my hand and placed it over his heart. "But it ended right here . . . in this spot."

I felt thunderstruck, and it had nothing to do with the storm raging above the overpass. I loved him too, but was the timing right to say these things?

"Lily, you've gotten awfully quiet. This would be a good time for you to say something. Anything at all." He clasped my hand in his.

"You are such a dear. But are you sure what you're experiencing isn't something else? Are you sure it's love?"

"What else could I be feeling?" Marcus asked.

"I don't know, maybe a grateful heart that you made it out of your parents' house alive today?"

He chuckled. "No, that's not what I'm feeling."

"Sorry. That wasn't funny."

"Well, it was a little funny."

I grinned. "It's just—"

"No, Love, there's no talking me out of this. I know exactly what I feel. I'm forty . . . certainly not a boy anymore, even though I've made a lot of mistakes. I'm a grown man, and I've dated plenty of women. I've seen some of the world. I know the underbelly of family life. It can be miserable at times, and yet I've still been able to fall in love."

"But why? Why do you love me? I can't believe I'm trying to talk a man out of loving me, but love always seemed precarious to me. Like the loveliest bloom on the trellis, always way out of reach."

"Listen to you. Where did you get such a sad notion of love?"

"Certainly not from my daughter. I'm not sure a mother could love a daughter more than I love my Julie, and I know she loves me. But romantic love, well, I've never fully understood it."

Marcus studied me then. "But didn't you and your husband fall in love once upon a time?"

"I loved him, yes. Well, since you already know so much about me . . . about my husband's transgression and all . . . I might as well tell you the rest. Richard claimed to love me, but I always wondered. My husband grew up in poverty, and when he saw my mother's house and wealth, well, I think he became much more enamored with me after that. At the time we dated, my mother was in poor health from time to time, so Richard may have gotten the idea that he would inherit her fortune soon after we were married. But as it turned out, Richard's health failed first, with his heart attack."

Thunder drummed around us, but the intensity had lessened. Perhaps the storm was moving on now. "It feels wrong to say these things about Richard," I went on to say, "since he's not here to defend himself. I never talk about this sort of thing with Julie. I want her to have only pleasant thoughts about her father. And for the most part, he was a good father. But as far as romantic love I just wasn't sure where he stood. At least after we were married. He made plenty of declarations beforehand." I paused, wondering how much more I should elaborate. "So, that's my sad tale of woe about love. I guess it has tainted me for all time."

"No, not for all time." Marcus fingered the tassel on the end of my scarf. "You just need to know my heart. For me, love isn't precarious or the loveliest bloom on the trellis, far out of reach. For me, it's something you hold on to. My love isn't going anywhere. And as far as money, well, you don't have to worry about me coming after yours. I have plenty of it in my trust. I don't need your mother's fortune either. She's welcome to live to one hundred and beyond. I just want you. That's all."

"Okay. Good speech. I like it."

"But as you know, love needs to be reciprocated if it's going to work right." He rested back in his seat but didn't take his eyes off me.

Oh, Lord, is this the right time to say how I feel? Is it too soon? Too ill-timed? Maybe love was more like being perched on the edge of a rock face with the thinnest of ropes to let us down. "Marcus, even though I wasn't sure how my husband felt or how much he loved me, I always knew what love felt like." *Here we go, Lord, I'm heading over the edge.* "And it looks and feels like I'm pretty hopelessly in love with you too."

"That is good news. The best. Especially after such a bleak house, Dickens kind of morning. You've made my day, Lily, my life."

I rested back in the seat, staring at the muddy-streaked windshield. It wasn't the best time for love to show up, but there it was just the same, improbable and lovely like the flutter of hummingbird wings. "I didn't go to Australia to fall in love, but God gave it to me anyway. To both of us." I chuckled at the sound of it. "Now, will you please kiss me?"

Marcus grasped both ends of my scarf and pulled me over to his lips. As we kissed thunder rolled around us like the applause from an unseen audience. Could it be the angels sounding their joy?

When we'd put the soft murmuring touches on our kiss, the sun eased out from behind the rain clouds, spraying the earth with light, brilliant and promising. The two clashing opposites reminded me of life—the storms and the sun all mixed together. "But there is one thing I need to add to this moment." I cringed at the negative sound of my words.

"One more thing?" Marcus pulled back but didn't let go of me.

"Even though this sounds like a bad movie line, sometimes marriage needs more than love. I mean, if this were to lead to marriage, there're all sorts of hurdles we'd have to jump over."

"Yes, love usually leads to marriage. At least that is what I'm hoping for . . . but what hurdles do you mean, exactly?"

"Well, I would want Julie to grow to care for you too. I would want her blessing. But beyond that, well, God says there's a time for everything under heaven. For everything there is a season. I just don't think this is our season. After what I saw today with your family, and with me just now bringing my sister home, trying to plug her back into my family." *And with her pregnancy and her need for help.* "Maybe it should be a season of sewing our families back together, not a time for us. At least not yet."

"You were right . . . I was going to propose. You got a little ahead of me, but I intended to ask you in a romantic setting, not in the middle of a thunderstorm."

"I'm so sorry." I pulled my hand away. "I was being presumptuous, thinking you were about to propose, since you mentioned love and all. In fact, I'm suddenly a little embarrassed." My face flushed, thinking about my audacity.

"You shouldn't be embarrassed. You just connected the dots."

"But maybe this makes it easier on you, in a way. To say no to your proposal now rather than you having to spend your life savings on a fancy meal."

Marcus shook his head. "The ever practical Lily. I'll bet you get all the wear out of your shoes even if they're pinching the life out of your toes. And I'm guessing you eat the cheese in your fridge even if it's turning fuzzy green."

"Yes on both. I just wear those shoes when I don't have to walk too far, and I scrape the fuzzy green off the cheese."

He grinned.

"Okay, so you've seen behind the curtain. Just for the record, I *did* throw out my cheese when I got home from Melbourne. It was beyond fuzzy."

"Well, you're making progress then. But I'm concerned that it's still the same Lily who won't let herself enjoy wedded bliss until everyone around her is as happy as she is."

"Hmm. Maybe you know me a little *too* well." The real me still had a few closed petals in need of some warm rays. I looked out the window at the concrete beams of the underpass. There they were holding up the bridge, doing their job well, but they were dirty and used and unthought-of, while everyone drove over them without a care. Was I trying to be those beams, holding up the world? My family? And no one had given my needs any consideration? No, that thought had a selfish ring to it, and I would have none of it.

I scooted down in my seat, trying to find a more comfortable spot. "I think you mean well, Marcus, but right now you're being Dudley, the seal pup, in your Horace and Dudley series. He gave profound speeches to his family to get what he wanted. He was very persuasive, just as you are. But I stand by my homily on seasons."

He groaned. "I should never have told you I was Miles Hooper. I thought you'd be enamored with the idea, but you're more interested in using my characters against me than worshiping my presence in your life. It hurts. It really does." He put up his hands, pretending offense, but holding back a grin the whole time.

"Guess it's not fighting fair to slam you with your own imagination. But you're wrong. I am enamored with Miles Hooper as well as Marcus Averill. Sometimes I can hear Miles, the writer, in some of the little things you say. It's sweet and stirring and fascinating to say the least. But you wouldn't want me to marry you for your celebrity."

"Sure I would." He laughed.

I gave his shoulder an affectionate shove. "I know you don't mean that. You will wait for me, won't you? It's always a little scary when there's two of us, you know, Camille and me . . . exact copies." The moment that remark left my mouth I knew I was in for a lecture.

"Surely I didn't hear you right."

"I meant it as a joke. Well, not totally."

"Lily Winter, do you believe in me so little that you'd entertain such a thought?" He stared at me, his expression incredulous. "You're *not* Camille. You both may look alike, but you are not her. You are Lily. You have your very own fingerprint on this world, literally speaking, and in every other way. I like Camille, but I *love* you. Huge difference. How can I make you see? My love for you has fenced me in, and I've never been happier to be ensnared by anything. So, I don't want to hear those words coming out of your mouth again. All right?"

I saluted him. "Yes, sir."

He chuckled. "But in the meantime, while I'm waiting for you, I'll need something to do. So, when I'm not working, I'll be busy trying to win you over. Make you think I'm irresistible."

You already are. "I will enjoy the ride." My heart got all twittery just thinking about all the creative ways Marcus might choose to romance me. Not a bad way to live.

He glanced out the windshield. "Well, I guess the storm has passed over."

"I'm ready. We should head back before it gets dark." I started the engine, and just as I was about to pull out again I put the car back into park.

"What's wrong?"

"You know what? I'm kind of tired, and I need a nap. Do you mind driving for a while?"

Marcus loosened his tie. "You're going to get me back, aren't you? For all those times I forced you out of your comfort zone in Australia."

"Absolutely." I gave the console a sound pat.

"This could go very badly." He rolled his eyes at me, yanked off his tie, and threw it in the back. I went around to the passenger side and he opened the door, got out and let me in, and then shut the door. Then he walked around to the driver's side and slipped behind the wheel.

Just as I surmised, we cruised forward in perfect harmony with the traffic, and in spite of Marcus's white-knuckle grip on the steering wheel, I fell into a deep drowsy mode like a newborn baby with a tummy full of milk. But just before I fell to dreaming, I wondered this—how long would Marcus wait for me? Would he eventually tire of my hesitations and fly back to Melbourne?

CHAPTER
thirty-six

When Marcus and I arrived back in my little neighborhood in Northwest Houston, he turned the corner to my house and there in the driveway was such a surprise—Julie's car. I could barely contain my excitement as I chattered on about how she'd come early and I hadn't even purchased all her favorite foods yet. "She must have gotten finished with her tests early. Won't you come in to meet her?"

"You don't even have to ask. I wouldn't miss this for anything, meeting your Julie." Marcus parked the car. "And please don't wait until I come around to open your door. I know you're anxious to run to the house."

"My thoughts exactly." I paused with my fingers on the handle. "But first let me say, I'm very proud of you, Marcus. You're an excellent driver. I went off to sleep and wasn't worried at all. Really, you're a much better driver than I am, so—"

"Enough about me. I'll let you praise me with a kiss later. Go."

"Okay." I jumped out and ran-walked to the front door with Marcus not far behind me. I fumbled with the house key so much, I rolled my eyes and handed it to Marcus, who opened the door for me.

"I can tell you love your daughter." He handed me the key back and grinned. "Let's go meet Julie."

Once inside, I yoo-hooed, "Julie." No answer. "Camille." Still no answer. "Hmm. Maybe they went somewhere together."

A tiny eruption of giggling came from the kitchen. It was their voices—my Julie's and my twin sister's voices mingling together like stirring chocolate syrup into milk. What a pleasant sound. Marcus and I peeked around the corner into the kitchen. There they were, the two of them, mixing something in a big bowl on the island counter. Probably making homemade cookies—one of Julie's favorite things to do. The scene looked so homey I hated to break it up. It was good for Camille to be embraced by my family, and it was a new and wonderful experience for Julie to have an aunt. Especially since she no longer had a father.

Julie looked so cute and yet all grown up in her figure-hugging blouse over slacks. But the biggest change was her hair. The long wavy locks of her youth were gone. I sniffled a bit.

My motherly whimper was just enough of a sound to make Julie glance toward the doorway. "Mom!"

She ran toward me, and we threw our arms around each other. I held her tightly and kissed her shoulder. "I missed you so, my darling girl."

"I missed you too. You smell like Australia."

"What? I hope I don't smell like kangaroos in the bush."

Julie released me and added, "No, just the chic scent of a seasoned traveler."

"Okay. Good save," I said, using some of Julie's lingo. "And look at your pixie haircut."

"Do you like it?" Julie fluffed the top and turned from side to side, making her feathery earrings dance.

"I love it," I said without hesitation, but for a mother, it would take some getting used to. Amazing that I'd driven Julie to college as a child and only weeks later she'd come home as a young woman. Ahh, the mysteries of life.

Julie gestured toward Camille. "Is this too weird or what, Mom? Aunt Camy looks just like you. Sounds just like you. Laughs just like you. It's spooky and awesome at the same time to have an identical twin. Right? You guys must freak out every time you look at each other."

"We've done a lot of freaking out since we've met." Camille tossed me a knowing grin. "Your Julie is a darlin'."

"Thanks, Aunt Camy." Julie draped her arm over Camille's shoulder. "But I mean, it's like having two moms. I don't know if that's good or bad." She put up her hands. "Just kidding, Mom." Then she turned all her attention to Marcus. "You must be Mr. Averill."

"Hello." He strolled into our warm little circle.

"So, is this the guy you texted me about? You know, a billion times?" Julie asked.

I gurgled out a nervous laugh. Okay, that was awkward. "I don't think it was quite a billion times."

"Mmm, the candor of youth." Marcus grinned, way too widely. "And here I was afraid your mother wasn't all that interested in me."

"Oh, you don't have to worry about *that*," Julie went on to say. "Mom thinks—"

"We get the general idea that I like the man." I set my mortification aside. "Julie, this is Marcus Averill, but what I didn't tell you, because I was leaving it for a surprise, is, well, this man is also . . . drumroll . . . Miles Hooper, which is Marcus's pen name."

"What?" Julie pulled a funny face of disbelief and then astonishment.

"It's true." I grinned. "You're hearing me right."

"So, you're not joshing me? Wow. Gimme a sec." Julie's attention landed on Marcus, and it stayed there. "You mean you're *the* Miles Hooper?"

We all laughed.

"Guilty," he said.

"How ultra cool is that?" Julie leaned against the counter. "Mom and I lived inside your stories when I was little. And that's how I learned to read. Your stories made me fall in love with books."

"What an endorsement," Marcus said. "I should hire you for my publicist."

"One of my favorites was *Toucan and the Sparrow*. Let's see, how does it go? 'Morning arrived at the zoo, and the sun poured over the park like a glass of spilled lemonade. All the animals, big and small, ate their bowls of cold breakfast porridge without a single complaint. Well, maybe one or two grumbles from the gators. But when the park gates opened for the day and the watchers came, the animals stood tall, each trying to look wild and brave in some way. But it was always hard to look noble when one was locked in a cage.' Mom and I always got sad on that part."

"Goodness," Marcus said. "You guys really are big fans."

"We read *Toucan and the Sparrow* until the binding fell apart. I had five favorites, but Mom liked all your books. Well, she fell in *love* actually. Didn't you, Mom?"

I caught her sneaky double meaning, and I flushed hotter than a woman in the throes of menapause. "Yes, we bought all your books, and I loved every one of them."

"Thanks." Marcus flushed. "And it's nice to finally meet you, Julie. Your mother talks a great deal about you. All good and wonderful things."

"Yeah, I know." Julie looked at her fingernails and blew on them. "It's the price I pay for being the perfect daughter."

We all laughed.

Marcus leaned over the bowl on the counter. "Okay, so what are you making here?"

"Aunt Camy and I are making chocolate-chip cookies. Classic, right?"

"Very." Marcus was already rolling up his sleeves and washing his hands. "I'd love to help if you want me to."

"Great." Julie poured a cup of coffee and took a sip. "I'll just sit here with my coffee and watch Miles Hooper bake cookies in our kitchen."

"So, you're drinking coffee these days?" I raised an eyebrow at my daughter.

"Yep. I discovered that I love it. Aunt Camy introduced me to it. Do you guys want a cup?"

"I'll have some," I said. "So, you're going to be one of *those* aunts."

"Probably." Camille gave me a playful poke in the ribs.

How heartwarming that Julie had already started to call her by such an endearing nickname. "Julie, you're plenty old enough for coffee, but be careful not to overdo the caffeine. It can be pretty addictive in college, and it will keep you awake all night if—"

"Ding, ding, ding, ding," Julie sang out in an operatic voice.

I put my hands up in surrender. "Okay, I get it."

Julie chuckled. "That's my bell to caution Mom that she's about to go overboard with advice."

"Good one," Camille said to Julie. Then as if right on cue they raised their hands and gave each other a high five.

Goodness, my sister had dropped into the aunt mode faster than I could have ever imagined. So fast my head was spinning. *God, please don't let me be jealous. Ever. Please.* I was living so many answers to prayer that I'd lost count, and I'd be an ungracious child to feel anything but grateful to the Almighty.

Marcus eyed my coffee. "I only have milk with *my* cookies."

Julie pointed at him, shaking her finger. "Just like Popsy Purvy in *Elephants Love Cookies Too.*" She laughed. "Only he had to have chocolate milk with all his cookies."

"That's right," Marcus said.

When Marcus glanced away, Julie looked at me, her brown eyes sparkling with mischief, and nodded in his direction. I knew what she wondered about—how serious were things between Marcus and me. Little did she know that he'd proposed. Sort of. And that I'd put him off. Sort of. Funny thing—I'd been hoping Julie would get along well with Marcus. Guess I could check that potential glitch off my list.

Camille pulled a cookie sheet from the bottom cabinet and turned on the oven. Then she backed away with a flourish and gestured for Marcus to take over with a spoon. He tied on an apron, which he looked masculine in as well as cute, and began plopping dollops of cookie dough onto the sheet.

Twenty minutes later, we all sat around the kitchen table, laughing and eating hot gooey cookies and totally ruining our supper but totally not caring. I pulled out a Monopoly board game, and we settled in to some serious fun in between popping a frozen pizza in the oven and dragging out some leftover salad from the fridge. We were the Four Musketeers with our swashbuckling camaraderie, and the thought of all of us being together for the coming holidays was a dream I could live with just fine.

"Mom," Julie said, "I have something to tell you about college."

"Hmm?" I asked absently, since my token and I were doing well. "You always do that interrupting thing when I'm winning. And I think you shortchanged me just now, Ms. Banker."

"No." Julie laughed. "I did not!"

I woke up from my board game daze. "What? Nothing bad at school I hope."

"What makes you say that?" Julie restacked the piles of cash just like her Momma always did.

"It was the hesitant way you said it." I took another mouse nibble off Camille's cookie. Accumulating vast properties always made me hungry.

"Well, I hope you don't think it's bad." Julie threw the dice. "I love school, but I don't like my major."

"Oh?" I studied her then. "But your life has always been about music."

"Yeah, I like music, but I guess now that I've had more time to think about it, well, I don't want it to be my whole life. I want music to be a joy I do for myself and a gift to others, but I don't want to do it for a living." Julie zoomed her race car token around the board.

What brought on that change of plans? "Well, what do you want to do with your life?"

"I know how this is going to come off . . . like I'm changing my major because I met Miles Hooper today. Sorry." Julie chuckled. "I mean, Marcus Averill. But I've been thinking about it for the last several weeks, and I want to switch my major to English."

"English? Really? Do you want to discuss this later?" I hoped she'd say yes.

Julie brightened. "No, now is a good time."

Hmm. That's how we ended up with a pet gerbil nobody wanted to play with and a trampoline nobody wanted to jump on and so many other nonessentials through the years. Julie knew I couldn't say no very well in front of other people. But this wasn't her pet. This was her life. "It will be harder to talk about the downsides to an English major with Marcus here. I wouldn't want to say anything that might hurt his feelings."

"Hey, I'm the first to admit that writing is a hard field to break into. The money can be at poverty levels for a long time. I was one of the fortunate few who made it big when I was young. But that's pretty rare." Marcus picked up his cup of milk, gulped it all down—loudly—slammed the cup back down like it was a shot glass, and then wiped off his white mustache.

We all sat staring at him and then burst out laughing.

Marcus shrugged. "Hey, I like cold milk."

Julie dunked her cookie up and down daintily into her coffee. "But you guys are just assuming I want to be a writer. That's not what I meant."

"Oh? You mean teaching or—?"

"No, I like the writing world, but I was thinking of a behind-the-scenes kind of job. Like an agent."

"Really?" I sat back in my chair and really studied Julie.

"I've researched it, and it seems like something I would enjoy."

Impressive. She'd obviously spent some time thinking it over. My Julie was growing up.

Marcus perked up. "I have an agent in Austin. I'm sure she wouldn't mind calling you, and you could ask her a bunch of questions about her career. You know, like what was her major. How she got started in the business. What's required to make it in that kind of career. The upsides, downsides." He tossed the dice.

"Really? You'd do that for me?"

"Well sure. If you're interested, I'll set it up."

"Brilliant. Thanks."

Marcus looked over at me, and his smile spilled all around the table like the lemonade in the whimsical park from his book. Then he scowled as his boot token landed on Go To Jail. "So not good. Hate that spot. Anyway, did you know that in the Aussie version of this game they have a koala bear for a token?"

"Well, this is the *American* version, Marcs," Camille said, "and I'm thrilled to say that you're going bankrupt." She gestured to her own houses and hotels and rubbed her hands together.

I continued to watch Marcus within my little family and found myself falling more deeply in love with him. He was enchanting with Julie, and she obviously adored him already. Camille also kept giving me nods of approval about Marcus. But I knew what Marcus was up to. He was trying to check every obstacle off my list to getting married. And trying to romance me through my family. His sweet diabolical plan was wonderful, but it still wasn't the right time for a proposal.

Camille drew a card and gasped. "I totally forgot to tell you, Lily. But Dragan called."

"Dragan? You mean the woman who wears flip-flops and reeks of rum and whose name rhymes with Fagin?" I grinned. "Sorry, that was unkind."

Marcus chuckled. "Dragan. She's got quite a funky name."

"Not nearly as funky as she is." I gave the dice a good shake. "So, Camille, what did Dragan want?" I blew into my hands as if for luck, just to make everyone chuckle.

"You'll never believe what she wanted." Camille stuffed a whole cookie in her mouth. "These are soo good. And I'm soo hungry," she said between chews. "When will the pizza be ready?"

"Soon." I stopped rattling the dice. "So, what did Dragan want?"

"She said that Mrs. Gray wants us three—" Camille licked her fingers— "you and Julie and me—to come to her house tomorrow for tea."

The dice slipped out of my hand and kerplunked right into my coffee.

CHAPTER
thirty-seven

Hearing about Mother's invitation to tea was like something out of a fantasy movie—it was simply not to be believed. And yet the three of us stood all dressed up fancy on Mother's porch for high tea at 3:00 sharp, waiting for Dragan Humphreys and her red-rimmed glasses, luau dress, and flip-flops to answer the door. Lately life changed as fast as moving around a board game. I only wished that when things got bad you could fold it up and go to bed.

I grinned at Julie and then at Camille. "We'd better be on our best behavior, because I doubt we'll get another invitation like this in our lifetimes." I let out a chortle. "Sorry." I cackled again. "Must be hysterical laughter syndrome."

"Hey," Camille said with a twinkle in her eye. "You're ruining my lugubrious expression."

I spewed a snicker again and then tried to rein it in. But failed.

Then within seconds we both exploded with enough chortles and snorts to make Julie shake her head at us. "You guys are like two little kids. I wonder how hokey you both would have been if you'd grown up together. Unbearable, I'm sure." She grinned.

"Definitely," Camille said. "So, what are you hiding in that paper bag you're carrying, Lil?"

"None of your business." I raised my chin with comedic flair. "It's a surprise."

We tried taking some of the monkeyshine off our grins, and we did just in the nick of time too, since the door opened, revealing

Dragan Humphreys in her getup straight from a King Kamehameha parade.

Oh, to have life lived on a consistent basis. "Hi." I sucked in my cheeks to keep my giggles from exploding out my mouth. "We're here for tea with Mother."

Ms. Humphreys looked us up and down and then opened the door without even greeting us.

Hmm. Bad day?

"Tea is set up in the dining room," she said as she walked us toward the back of the house. Dragan still smelled of eau de rum, but she had a strange glint in her eyes I hadn't seen before. One that gave me the creeps. Wonder what that was all about.

Once in the dining room I was surprised to see that the long mahogany table had been set with lovely tea dishes, lace place mats, and a three-tiered crystal serving tray that was piled high with sweets and savories. A mini-feast for sure. How lovely. Surely Mother hadn't made any of it, but it was equally hard to imagine Ms. Humphreys toiling over such delights.

"Wow, what a spread," Julie said. "I was just a kid when I was in here last. I barely remember any of this."

"I'm starving." Camille reached out to touch one of the tiny cakes and then suddenly drew her hand back as if she'd been slapped.

"This room looks so pretty, and I can't believe Granny made all this for us. Maybe she's changed, Momma, and she's no longer the odious woman you said she was."

"Well, if I am odious," Mrs. Gray said, walking into the room suddenly, "then it's God's fault." She glared at us each in turn, but smiled when she saw Julie. "I see you're home from college. I wasn't sure if you'd be here."

"Hi, Granny. You've changed some since the last time I saw you ten years ago."

"Well, I was old back then," Mother said. "Now I'm *really* old."

Julie laughed.

Mother's face crinkled. "Is that funny?"

"Yes, the way you said it." Julie went over and gave her grand-mother a hug.

Even though Mother didn't embrace Julie, she didn't pull back but let her granddaughter give her a hug.

"I had no idea I was such a comic," Mother said. "Better a comic than being odious I guess."

"Sorry you heard that, Mother," I said, feeling crummy for hav-ing told Julie such a thing.

Mother motioned toward the table covered in dainties. "Please sit down so we can eat this high-caloric food. I don't approve of these kinds of sugary fat concoctions, but there you have it. I wanted to see if I could do something maternal. See if it fit me."

"Of course it does. You have two X chromosomes, don't you?" Julie smiled at her grandmother so brightly that no scowl could dim its intensity.

"The things they teach in college these days," her grandmother said, but there was no growl along with her reply.

Mother walked to the head chair of the long table and then fidgeted with a cane in her hand.

I pulled out the chair for Mother. "I don't remember you using a cane before."

"That's because I haven't *used* a cane before." Mother sat down and scooted up her chair. She handed me her cane, and I leaned it against the table by her hand.

"Did you injure yourself?" Camille asked.

"No, but Dragan thought it might be best to have one, since she seems to think I'm getting frail." Mother fingered the carved rose on top of the cane.

"You don't look frail to me." Camille pulled out a chair and sat down. "You look as strong as an iron pickax."

"Oh, really. Good. Well, at least the cane will work for giving the mailman a good thrashing if he needs it." Mother motioned toward the food. "Eat up. I won't bother with saying grace, so please go ahead and—"

"Well, is it all right if I say grace then, Granny?" Julie asked.

Mother moved her lower jaw around as a sort of disgruntled reaction to the request, but she said, "Go ahead, if you must."

We all bowed our heads, except for Mother.

"Lord, thanks for these fine goodies, which we will enjoy to the max. And thanks that Mom found her sister and brought her home to us safely. She's going to be the best aunt. And thank You for Granny who, if not for her, none of us would exist to enjoy this day. Amen."

We all looked up and had no words for a moment—maybe we felt a little startled with Julie's tender but thought-provoking twist at the end of her prayer—but then with pinkies raised, we dug in. Mother didn't seem to be too displeased, so I took that as a good sign. Maybe I could breathe and actually enjoy some of the tea fare.

"All right now, pour me some tea, won't you, child," Mother said to Julie. "Please."

"Sure." Julie picked up the pot from the warmer and poured her grandmother some tea. "There you go." She came around and poured tea for Camille and me and then for herself. Julie lifted the tray and went around the table offering dainties to each of us, but she served her grandmother first. To my surprise Mother took several treats from the tray, even though she called them obscene indulgences.

When we were all situated with our tea and goodies, I asked, "Did Dragan make all this for high tea?"

Mother snorted. "No, she just called a caterer, and they showed up with it all."

"Oh. Well, it was still nice of you to do this. I've never been to a high tea before."

"To be precise, this isn't high tea. This is really called low tea. High tea was for the lower classes, the working Brits. So, what do you do, Camille, for a career?" Mother asked, taking the conversation bull by the horns and charging forth.

Camille minced around on her petit four, licking off the frosting first. "I work in a grocery store."

Mother's fingers tightened around her teacup. "You mean in management?"

"No, I'm just at the checkout counter, but I like the staff. They're very kind to me. And that means a lot really." Camille took a sip of her tea, but when she set it down it made a crash landing into the saucer, spilling some of the tea on the place mat. "I'm sorry." She righted the cup. "Do you want me to—"

"Just leave it," Mother said.

I stared at Camille, and with bits of facial language, I tried to wordlessly ask her if she was okay. Amazingly, she understood and gave me a quick nod.

"Hmm. Surely with a little ingenuity, you could find a better situation," Mother said. "You seem smart enough to improve yourself."

I was afraid my sister might set Mother straight with a pointed remark, so to neutralize the air, I said, "Camille is being shy about her talent. She's a flutist."

Julie livened up. "Really? Are you good?"

"She's very good. She plays on the streets of Melbourne, and they literally cannot walk away when she starts playing."

"That is sooo cool, Aunt Camy. That we all love music. I can't wait to hear you play. I play the piano and guitar, and Mom can play the piano."

"A little," I added.

"Maybe we could have a little family band." Julie raised her cup to us, looking happier than I'd ever seen her.

"Which brings me to something special." I lifted a present out of the paper bag I had set next to my chair. "I have an early birthday present for Camille, since her birthday is next week. I know I should wait, but I'm too excited to hold back any longer."

"It'll be your birthday too," Camille said, "but I don't have a present for you. In fact, I totally forgot it was next week."

"I don't mind. I have everything I need. All my family is around me. What more could anyone want?"

Mother turned her flashing eyes on me. "I forgot your birthdays were next week."

I could have so easily said, "You've never remembered our birthdays before, so what would it matter now?" But I didn't. I was a good girl and let her comment wash away with the sweet taste of Earl Grey. But I cringed inside, wondering if Mother was about to show her teeth again and if she'd be sharpening them on me.

"We seem to be a musical family. Granny, do you play an instrument?" Julie asked.

Mother fiddled with her lace collar as if it made her neck itch. "No. Well, I used to play the piano, but no more."

"Your grandmother has a beautiful grand piano in the front living room." I tried a bite of the tiny quiche, which melted in my mouth.

"Really? May I see it later?" Julie asked. "It would be wonderful to play on a grand piano. We've never had anything so fine."

"You'd better enjoy it while you can. I was thinking of giving it to Dragan's daughter." Mother took a deep draw from her teacup.

"Really? Why?" At that point we all must have stared at Mother, horrified. What she'd said seemed preposterous—that she would give away an heirloom piano to a stranger when her own granddaughter would give anything to play on such an instrument.

"Why are you three staring at me? You make me feel like one of those primates at the zoo." Mother ran her thumb over the carving on the cane again.

I looked away from Mother, since my glance irritated her. So, Dragan was not only helping herself to Mother's liquor cabinet, but she was encouraging Mother to give up some of her expensive furnishings as well. Before long Mother would be willing the entire estate to her. But since I wanted our teatime to go well, I took the high road and let that argument go. For now. Eventually, though, I was going to run out of high roads. I got us back on track and handed Camille her gift.

"Thanks, Lily. You're so sweet to me."

"You're welcome. I hope I got the right kind. Marcus helped me buy it this morning when we were out and about together."

Camille tore off the bow and the pretty paper, and the moment she saw the instrument case, she gasped. She flipped open the latches and lifted the lid. "Ohh, Lily. What a perfect gift. This is wonderful. It's like you could read my mind, since I'd really been grieving lately over the loss of my flute."

"Did we get the right one?"

"Yes, you did. This is a western concert flute just like the one I had before." Camille put the three instrument pieces together and blew in the mouthpiece, testing it. "Good sound, but it'll take some time for it to come to life properly. All things of beauty take time." She smiled at me.

"What happened to your other flute?" Mother asked.

Camille didn't take her eyes off her instrument as she replied, "My boyfriend threw my flute into the Yarra River."

Mother reared back. "And why would he do a fool thing like that?"

"Because he broke up with me and he was angry. He wanted to punish me." Camille pressed her fingers on the silvery keys.

"What for?"

My sister looked at Mother then, and as if waking up from a dream. "I guess because at that moment I was in his space. I was breathing his air."

"Maybe next time you should put some real thought into who you go out with."

Camille coughed.

Mother coughed too and in the same way.

It was such an uncanny moment that they stared at each other for a second.

"Play us a tune, Aunt Camy," Julie begged. "Just one. Please. I have to hear you."

"Well, maybe one." Camille stood. "I would like to hear the sound of it myself." She held up her flute, positioned her fingers, and lowered her lips to the mouthpiece. For a moment she closed her eyes, pausing as if she were gathering some inner strength or summoning that peaceful garden place that she must imagine when she played—and then she blew life into the flute.

The haunting sound of the Irish classic "Danny Boy" curled its way through the room and then rose, finding its home not only in the rafters of the cathedral ceiling but in our hearts. It took my imaginings on a journey to the verdant valleys and hills of Ireland— a country I'd always wanted to visit but had never seen. My sister had her music back, and I couldn't have been happier.

Engulfed inside the sounds and longings was a desire to see Marcus's face. Maybe I'd been too rash in telling him this wasn't a good time to propose. Perhaps I should have put aside my concerns and married him as soon as I could sign the papers. As fast as I could say yes. Why not embrace joy? But what nonsense. It was just the magic of the music carrying me away.

Julie's eyes grew wide and dreamy and misty—obviously she relished every second of her aunt's playing. She hummed along and then sang along. Her voice, coupled with the sound of the flute, added an exquisite quality to a moment I knew I would never forget. Perhaps Julie had learned the lyrics in choir. So lovely and moving.

I glanced over at Mother, trying to gauge her reaction. Would she at least have some pride in her offspring for creating such beauty?

Mother squeezed her chin until her fingers seemed knobbier than ever. She appeared spellbound, and yet like a murky tide, there was something running just beneath the surface of her expression that seemed foreboding.

I closed my eyes to shut her out, not wanting any kind of sour temper to ruin the pretty moment. I let myself imagine streams in the Emerald Isle, as they ambled through woods and flashed down bluffs and then all joined together into one great river. It was the way I'd hoped our family could be, each of us coming together at last, all flowing into one. But then the tune came to a close, and we returned to our real world.

Camille gazed down and touched her womb with tenderness. I was the only one who knew what was in her heart—she'd not been playing for us but for the baby growing inside her.

Julie and I applauded, while Mother sat, clinging to her cane.

"Your singing is lovely, Julie," Camille said. "We should do this often."

Julie beamed. "I would love it. You're wonderful. I think—"

"Camille," Mother broke in, "why don't you play professionally? Surely you don't want to play on the streets the rest of your life."

"I don't mind it." Camille took a soft cloth out of the case and gingerly ran it along the metal instrument. "It will take a couple of weeks, but we will become the best of friends," she said to her flute. Then she looked at me. "Thank you again, Lily. It's the most meaningful gift anyone has ever given me."

Camille's smile touched me, warming me all the way through.

"But except for tips you can't make any money that way," Mother ranted on. "And it's so beneath a Gray family member to play on the streets."

Camille took the instrument apart and settled the pieces in their velvet nest. "I have never thought of where I play my music as demeaning, and my tips are sometimes four hundred dollars a week. With my music and job I've been able to get along. I'm not getting rich, but then that was never my goal. I just wanted to use the gift God gave me. To create something lovely in a cold world."

"Bah." Mother raised her chin. "God. I see. Can't you do it for yourself?"

"Would you like some more tea, Granny?" Julie asked.

"No, thank you, dear," Mother said. "I think I've had enough."

"Are you okay, Granny?" Julie's face lit with rosy innocence, unaware that her grandmother's temper could be as volatile as a volcano's and her words could pelt her with burning lava at any moment.

Mother's expression dissolved into a scowl, a routine that her flesh must have been accustomed to. "Of course I am. I'm fine."

Camille started to take a bite of her quiche but she set it back down. "And I know it embarrasses you for a Gray to play music on the streets, but you don't have to concern yourself with that. Do remember. I am not a Gray. I am a Daniels."

"How could I forget? You won't let me," Mother snapped.

"Granny?" Julie lifted the pot, which trembled in her hand. "Are you sure you don't want some more tea or sweets?"

"No," Mother said. "Stop asking me that."

Oh, Lord, give me calm. I could see it already, that slow descent into a sad and lonely place. My Julie, who had started out by being herself around Granny, and almost winning her over, was now hedging and flinching. My Julie was starting to walk on the eggshells that my mother invariably put out for her entertainment. Or because her misery could offer nothing else. I could handle the badgering, but the sight of my Julie being mistreated was more than sad—it tore me to pieces. "Mother, don't snap at my daughter. It's not a—"

"Déanaim cad ba mhaith liom i mo theach féin." Mother's jaw gyrated in a hard line.

My fingers ached to pick at my skin, but I refused to give in to it. I no longer wanted to torture my flesh for my mother's failings. I instead rested my fingers on the edge of the table and squeezed.

"I'm sorry," Camille said. "I need to leave, Lily. I'm not feeling well. But first, where's your bathroom?"

"It's the first door on the right." Oh dear. Did she have nausea?

"What's wrong with you, girl?" All the pretense of teatime etiquette had now vanished like a sweet breeze consumed by a foul breath.

Camille stared at Mother. "If you must know . . . I'm pregnant."

CHAPTER
thirty-eight

I swallowed my gasp. Why would Camille tell Mother what she'd hoped to keep a secret? Probably she felt desperately cornered.

Mother's face blazed red. "Who's the father? Was it that ridiculous boyfriend of yours who tossed your flute into the river?"

Camille covered her mouth with her napkin and ran from the room.

Julie looked at me—confusion and fear consuming her lovely face.

"It'll be all right, Julie, but I need to see about Camille." I gave Mother a sharp look, not caring in the least if it upset her sensibilities. I rose, slapped the napkin on the table, and stormed out of the room.

I heard a chair move behind me. Julie must be following me, since she was surely afraid of staying in the same room with Mother when she was in such an agitated state.

When I got to the bathroom door I tried the knob. The door was locked. "Camille, please let me in. I want to help."

"I'll be all right. I'm just sick at my stomach." Her voice sounded weak and desolate.

Oh, Camille. I'm so sorry I brought you to this house, to America. I had wanted all to be well, for us to be a family. Would it never be? "I'll stay right here if you need me."

Julie joined me by the bathroom door. "Mom, is Aunt Camy going to be okay?"

"Yes." But really, I had no idea if my sister would be all right. Since Camille was ill on and off, I had no idea what a pregnancy would do to her weakened condition.

Cane in hand, Mother came marching full throttle toward us like a locomotive.

I shuddered at the sight, since I knew she was about to spew more of her bile.

"Please move out of my way." She waved her cane at us, but I didn't move an inch.

Julie stepped aside.

Mother banged on the door with the top of her cane. "What do you mean, you're pregnant? How could you be so promiscuous?" she hollered through the door. "Here you've played your flute, trying to make me think you're somebody special. You're nobody. Worse than that . . . you're a tramp. But then I guess you're used to being on the streets."

If blood could boil, mine was at a full roll. At that moment I wanted to rail and scream at my mother—maybe even smack some sense into her. I couldn't believe she'd said such unthinkably cruel things to Camille and in front of my Julie. "Mother, that has to be one of the most vulgar and heartless things I've ever heard a mother utter to her daughter."

Mother hissed, "She's not my daughter."

"You're right." I nodded. "Nor should she be. You're the last person on earth who deserves her."

"Bah. I should have listened to Dragan," Mother said. "She told me it was a bad idea to have this tea."

"Oh she did. Well, I can tell you, I've heard enough about that woman. And just so you know, Camille is not promiscuous. Her former boyfriend raped her! But you would never know that, since you toss vicious accusations without care or concern for anyone. You live your life in judgment of your family without an ounce of love or mercy. I guess it's because you've saved it all up for the hired help!" By the time I was finished, my breathing was raspy, and I felt dizzy. But I never should have told Mother that Camille was raped. It wasn't my place to tell her, and it was certainly none of Mother's business.

Julie took another step back. Perhaps I had frightened her. Well, I had frightened myself. Mostly likely I'd unleashed forty years of repressed verbal abuse all in one sweep. It felt good and horrible all at the same time.

Mother moved in closer to the door. "You should go home, Camille. Your sister will take you. Come out now. You're so quiet. I know you want to punish us, but it would be better . . ." She rattled the knob again. "The lock on this door has never been right." Mother yanked on the doorknob and then shoved on the door with her shoulder. "I'm coming in." The door burst open but stopped midway as it slammed into Camille full force.

The thrust of the door made Camille stumble forward onto the sharp edge of a standing towel rack. She screamed and crumpled to the ceramic floor.

I ran to Camille and knelt down next to her. "Camille?"

Julie put her arm over her face and began to cry.

Camille clutched her lower abdomen, writhing on the hard floor. "Something's not right. I'm feeling a contraction." She looked up at me, her eyes filled with fear.

I took hold of Camille as if she were a small child. "I'm right here. We should go to the hospital."

"No, I won't go." Camille grasped my arm. "Mom died in the hospital. I won't go. Please don't make me go."

"Okay. All right." That decision seemed far from wise, but I hated to argue with her in such a frightened state. I swept the wispy curls from her cheek and rocked her back and forth. "I'm right here."

Julie stood in the doorway. Mother stood next to her, rigid and silent.

As I whispered to Camille and hummed a lullaby, a spot of blood appeared on her dress. Then the stain turned into a coiling ribbon of blood across the floor.

"Oh, dear God in heaven," Camille said. "The fall. There's blood. I'm going to lose the baby, aren't I?"

"I don't know, but we should go to the hospital right now." *God help us.*

Julie stood next to me. "Mom, please let me help. What can I do?"

"Call 911. Now."

"I will." Julie pulled out her cell phone and pushed in the number.

Mother stood in the doorway, watching us with an expression of terror. She stepped away from us, looking white as death and murmuring one word. *"Adongo."*

Camille mashed the back of her hand to her eyes. Mascara-stained tears ran down her face. "Lily, I wanted this baby so much. If it'd been a girl, I would have named her Anne from your middle name. After you. Little Anne was my last chance to make a family." She burrowed her face into the folds of my dress. "My last chance."

"It's not your last chance. And you will always have me and Julie. You'll always have us." I continued to rock her in my arms. "We love you dearly."

Perspiration trickled down her face as her eyes became glossy with tears. I knew Camille hadn't cried in a long time. But she did now. She cried for her baby.

"You won't leave me too . . . will you, Lils?" she asked in a child-like voice.

"No, I'll never leave you. Nothing will ever tear us apart again. Okay?" I stroked her damp curls away from her face. "But we have to go to the hospital in a minute. The ambulance will be here soon, and they'll try to save the baby."

"Do you think they can?" Camille suddenly looked up and tugged on my dress.

"I don't know, but we have to try."

"Yes, we have to try," Camille whispered.

I held out my right palm, and she her left, and we met palm to palm. But this time I laced my fingers around her hand and didn't let go.

"Maybe we should pray," Julie said softly.

"Yes, pray, Julie," Mother said. "It's all we have left."

CHAPTER
thirty-nine

Reclining in the hospital chair, I half-opened my eyes to make sure Camille was still asleep in her bed. Earlier, she'd tossed and turned, looking exhausted, but now she seemed to have drifted off. I tucked my blanket around my neck, hoping to get a little shut-eye, but the odds weren't in my favor. With my worry over Camille, the itchy woolen blanket, the antiseptic smells, and the not-so-amicable chair, sleep was unlikely. But I wasn't going anywhere.

It had been heartbreaking to see Camille's grief during the loss of her child and then the D&C that the doctors had to follow up with after the miscarriage. To watch as her hope got snuffed out was unbearable. In my blind optimism, I'd had such expectations in bringing her home from Australia. And that hope had ended in tragedy. She had trusted me that I would help her, keep her safe. And even though the fall had not been from my hand, I felt somehow it was my fault. That I had failed her as a sister, and that I no longer deserved her trust.

Mother sat by Camille's hospital bedside, refusing to take a break, even when I insisted. She was as stubborn as always but in an entirely new way—a way I'd never seen before nor could have even imagined. Mother said little, but her hands wrung into knots on the railing. Although there were many reasons for her torment, it was most likely connected with Camille's fall and the loss of her baby.

Outside a storm brewed with bouts of rumbling thunder. Raindrops ran down the windows in twisting rivulets. The gentle sounds

of the storm along with the steady beeping of Camille's heart moni-
tor made me sleepy again. That is, until I heard Mother speak up.

"Camille, I know you're asleep or too groggy from the medicine
to hear me," Mother said, "but I have to say these things or I may
lose my mind. Please, can you ever forgive me? I have not been a
mother to you. I have been . . . odious. It's true. And now I've failed
you again, because I failed your baby. My own grandchild. Your
child's death was my fault, and for as long as I live, I will never forgive myself for what I did . . . for what I've become."

Since I'd never heard my mother utter such apologies I strained
to hear every word. I didn't rouse from the chair, though, since I
didn't want to break the flow of her repentance.

"First," Mother said, "I know how much you love music, so if
you don't mind listening to an old woman sing, I have this cradle
song I want to share. It has always been my favorite. I can't carry a
tune worth anything anymore, but I'll try." Mother paused and then
in a soft voice, sang,

"Sleep, my babe, lie still and slumber,
All through the night
Guardian angels God will lend thee,
All through the night
Soft and drowsy hours are creeping,
Hill and vale in slumber sleeping,
Mother dear her watch is keeping,
All through the night
God is here, you'll not be lonely,
All through the night
'Tis not I who guards thee only,
All through the night
Night's dark shades will soon be over . . ."

Mother stopped singing, her voice choked with emotion. "I forgot the rest."

Her gray hair, taken down from its bun, now spilled around her
shoulders. In all my years I couldn't remember ever seeing Mother's

hair in such a relaxed style. It was wonderfully bewildering to see the changes. Not just in her hair but in her spirit.

She cleared her gravelly throat. "I know there can be no justification for how I've been all these years, but I wish you could know a bit of me. Of my past. Maybe you will see how I came to be the way I am. Something I've kept hidden, and something I've spent my whole life guarding, trying to forget. But it's always been there in the dark corners of my mind, like a devil lurking in the shadows, ready to devour me. If you could only know how it has chased me and hounded me like a beast." Mother coughed and took a sip of her water from the nightstand. "After I graduated from college, but before I married, I was a missionary in Kenya. Hard to believe, I know." She chuckled.

My ears perked up until they ached.

"I was dedicated to Christ," Mother said, "and even though my parents were against my career choice, I went to Africa anyway. I was as headstrong back then as I am today. But different in spirit. Very different. I settled into a village there, helping as a teacher and as an assistant to the nurse. There were so many needs. But the people, they were grateful for everything and eager to know about my life and my God. It became a joy to share. They took me into their hearts, and I did the same."

When Camille turned over, Mother wiped a lock of hair from her cheek. Then she clutched the railing and continued her story. "But then one stormy day, very much like this one, as the children were singing together, making such a joyful noise that I knew heaven had heard us and was singing along . . . there was a massacre. A warring tribe swept through the village like a black flood. The men came with machetes and spears, and they brutally killed most of the people in our village. I'm not sure how I escaped, since I stayed to help the children get away. But my efforts failed. The Kenyan military came in, but they were too late. I heard later that this unspeakable violence was because of a dispute over land. Imagine."

Mother shook her head, her tears turning into quiet sobs.

The sight of my mother in such an emotional state made my stomach constrict into a ball.

"I remember holding one of the littlest ones as she died that day," Mother said. "Her name was Adongo, which meant second of twins. She'd survived the birth, but the first twin had not. And since Adongo was considered a curse in her culture at the time, her mother had fled with her, hoping to save her from being killed. And she had. Adongo managed to survive it all . . . until that day."

Mother plucked a few tissues from the box on the nightstand. "I had grown to love all the children, but she had been special to me for so many reasons. I held Adongo that dreadful day as the blood flowed from a wound in her neck. I pressed my hand there, trying to stop it, but the cut was too deep. I held her to me as the tears and the rain and the blood got mixed together, and the big brown eyes of Adongo lost their light. As the life drained out of her, some part of me died that day along with her."

Mother covered her face. After a moment she raised back up. "I went home to recover but never returned to Kenya . . . to the place and the people I loved. I'd come to believe that if God could allow such horror in the midst of my selfless deeds, then He was of no use to me or to anyone. Not worthy of love or trust or worship. I became disillusioned and despondent, but when I came out of that fog, a new philosophy emerged. Since living for God had no value, I would embrace a new theology . . . by living only for myself. Through the years since then, I haven't been able to stand the sounds of singing. The lovelier the song, the sharper the flash in my memory of the children singing. Of her. All I wanted to do was forget."

Mother blew her nose and wiped her eyes. "When I gave birth, I resented having children. And, you, Camille, you were the second born of twins. You were like Adongo, and in my twisted thinking, I got it in my head that God was punishing me for disowning Him by making me conceive twins. You were a constant reminder of my past, that I was running from my faith. Then when my mother came up with the idea of adoption I gave in to it. I thought it was a way out, but in reality it kept me forever locked inside my misery.

"And then when I saw all that blood flowing from you like Adongo, it was like I came to myself. And I knew what I'd become." Mother rested her head on the railing, whispered something, and then raised back up again. "I could not have loathed myself any more than I did in that moment. The very evil I questioned God about, that I had shaken my fist to the heavens over, was inside me, not God. The very evil that I detested and fled from, well . . . I could see it in me."

Mother took Camille's hand in hers, pressed it against her lips, and then placed it back down on the sheet. "*Codladh samh a stór.* Yes, my little treasure. Your hand is so pale, and there's so little strength left. I wish I could give you the last of mine. I'm not sure I even want mine. I certainly don't deserve it. I'm the old woman who turned her heart away from all that is good and lovely. Just as God turned away for a moment from the sin that Jesus bore, maybe Christ should look away from me. Maybe it's too late for redemption, for someone wicked like me."

It felt unsettling to see Mother dissolve into a pool of helplessness. But the sight was also restorative. It was God's hand reaching across the past. It was His rescue, His remolding, His mercy. "It's not too late," I whispered.

Mother turned back and looked at me, her eyes red from crying. "You heard all that?"

I nodded. "If I haven't turned away from you, I know Christ hasn't."

Her shoulders heaved a sigh of relief then.

"But why didn't you tell me this a long time ago?"

Mother glanced at the rain outside. "I don't know. Well, pride, I suppose. I hated looking weak." She coughed and took another sip of water. "I've seen you and Julie and your sister be so vulnerable together. I've seen you pour out your affection on each other. Your light glows all around you, and I guess you could say that it has illuminated my darkness. You turned out well, a good mother to Julie, not because of me, but in spite of me."

Camille roused from her sleep, and this time her eyes seemed clearer as she stared at us. "I feel a little better." But lingering in her expression was the sorrow of what had happened. The loss of her child—the emptiness of her womb. The pregnancy may have come from one man's sin, but the child was no less precious—no less made in the image of God and worthy of grieving over. It would take some time to say goodbye.

Mother rose from her chair and hovered over Camille. Then she burst into tears again.

Julie came into the room, witnessed the amazing spectacle of her grandmother's tears, and eased over to the other side of the bed as if walking on a fragile sheet of glass.

A nurse stopped in, witnessed the scene, and quietly backed out of the room.

Mother didn't seem embarrassed by her tears. She didn't stop or even try to justify her display of emotions. She took hold of Camille's hand and brought it to her cheek.

Julie and I drew closer and held hands by the bed. Then when Camille pulled the oxygen tubes from her nose and broke down in tears, it seemed to open the floodgates of our emotions as well. The rain continued to fall outside, coming down more heavily and looking very much like tears as it ran down the windows. Maybe all of heaven was weeping with us.

We all cried softly around the bed, and in those precious moments, healing came to our family. In the midst of our loss God had come near—a divine moment had arrived. I embraced it and took a mental snapshot of the scene, so that I could bring it back whenever I needed to see it again, to be encouraged by our miracle.

And I prayed for my mother, that devils would no longer lurk in the shadows of her soul.

CHAPTER
forty

After a while the tears subsided.

Mother sat down in her chair next to Camille but didn't let go of her hand.

Julie went over and gave her grandmother a hug. This time Mother hugged her back. Then Julie whispered to me over Mother's shoulder, "Marcus is here."

"Marcus? Where is he?"

Julie released Mother and circled her arm through mine. "He didn't want to interfere with our family time, so he went to the chapel."

Oh, the enduring kindness of Marcus Averill. "Thanks, Julie." Camille had drifted back to sleep, so I turned to Mother.

Before I could even ask, she said, "Go to Marcus. It'll be a good break for you."

"But what about you?"

Mother looked at me, really studied me as if seeing me in a new light. "I want to stay with Camille for as long as she will let me."

I nodded, understanding her. "Okay."

Julie sat in the recliner where I'd been resting, pulled out her phone, and began texting someone. Then she stopped, stared at her grandmother, and put away her phone. She too must have realized what a profound family moment we were in the middle of—something not to be taken lightly, not to be missed.

I left Camille's room, passed the nurses' station, and then found the elevator. When I made it to the first floor I saw the chapel sign and took a long corridor to an arched door. The sanctuary was empty, except for Marcus, who sat on the front pew. I stepped across the threshold. The amber light streaming through the stained-glass windows, the candles flickering across the front of the chapel, and the faint sounds of Gregorian chants gave the chapel an old world feel. It was a place of quiet reflection and of Christ's hope, the only true hope this weary earth would ever know.

Marcus looked back at me when I entered the room. That face—such a great face.

I smiled at him, glad to see him. We'd only been parted for hours, and yet it had seemed much longer. Wishing I looked better, I tried smoothing my hair. My makeup had long since melted away, so Marcus was going to get his first dose of me looking untidy as well as mournful for my sister's loss. Marcus didn't seem to notice my disheveled appearance as I walked up the aisle and sat down next to him in the pew.

He took my hand and cradled it in his. So warm and welcoming.

"Thanks for coming."

"I'm really sorry Camille lost her baby."

"Yes, it's a terrible thing."

We sat quietly for a moment. The silence didn't feel empty, though, but full of comfort.

"How's your mom?"

"Devastated. I can hardly believe I'm saying those words, but she is. I've never seen her like this before. She broke down and cried earlier, and I've never seen her cry in my whole life, not even when Dad died."

"I know a little how she feels. From what you told me on the phone, your mother and I now have something in common. Because of a grave error on our part, someone has died on our watch.

It's not anything you ever recover from. You go on with life, and you do the best you can, but you never truly mend."

I tugged on the cuff of his sleeve. "Especially when you have a father who is willing to remind you of your error at every possible opportunity. Maybe it's not my place to say it, but even though I feel sorry for him, it's not right what he's doing."

"He will forgive me someday."

I stared at the ornate cross, which sat in front of us just beyond the altar. "I'll remember your words as we build a relationship with Mother. Forgiveness has begun, but it will take more time, especially for Camille." I rested my head on his shoulder. It seemed like the most natural thing in the world to do. As if I'd always known him, always trusted him with my life, my family. I thanked God that He'd sent Marcus into my life. It was a miraculous event that day in the botanic garden. I needed him during this time, and he needed me. *But please, Lord, let it be more than merely a season of helping each other. I love this man dearly.*

I opened my mouth to tell him those very words when Marcus said, "Lily, you are such a keepsake."

"Really?"

"Yes, really. It's the word that always comes to me when I think of you."

I smiled.

"But I want to talk to you about something."

"Okay." I loved being referred to as a keepsake, but didn't treasures usually get put aside into a dusky trunk somewhere? In a back closet? I laughed at myself for such a gloomy thought, and yet I braced myself.

He rubbed his thumb back and forth across the top of my hand. "You know when we stopped during the rainstorm on our way from Dallas?"

"Yes. How could I forget?" It was when Marcus had first told me that he loved me. Perhaps there'd be more on the subject. The chapel was a good place for declarations of love and promises.

"I wanted you to know I've thought about what you said, and you were right. I got way ahead of myself when I hinted about marriage. It's too soon. I know we spent a lot of time together in Melbourne, and we're certainly old enough to know our hearts and minds. We know how we feel about each other, and we're safe in that for now. But both our families are in the middle of some pretty heavy heartache right now. They need us. That should be a priority for us . . . for a while. Thank you for showing me that."

"You're welcome." I guess. My voice had lost all its buoyancy, and so had my heart. It was exactly what I'd asked him for. Exactly what I knew we needed. But why did I feel as though the bottom of my world had fallen out—like those rides at the carnival that drop you suddenly, and your stomach gets an ugly surprise?

"In fact, I'm going to Dallas fairly soon. My dad called, and he wanted to meet with me. He's pretty broken up about Mom leaving him. He didn't sound like he was in a very good mood, but he wanted to talk, and that's at least one step in the right direction. I want to be there for him. I have to."

"Of course. I understand. You should. I'm proud of you for always wanting to do the right thing." *I love you for it.*

"Thanks. I know I flew over from Australia for us, but—"

I placed my finger over his lips. "No. You came over for your family too. This is a season for mending. Of new beginnings for all of us."

"So, you don't mind that I'll be away awhile?"

"No, not at all." On second thought. "Well, how long will it be?"

"Maybe a few days. I'm not sure. I just want to make myself available to him while I'm there."

I smiled. "It's the right thing."

"So, you miss me already?"

"I do." *Someday, Lord, when it's the right time, I'd love to say those two words to Marcus in a lovely and holy place like this.*

"Mom?"

We both looked back toward the voice.

Julie stood at the entrance of the chapel, staring at us.

"Is Camille okay?" I stood. "What's happened?"

"Yes, yes, she's fine." Julie came up the aisle to join us. "Hey, Marcus."

"Hello again."

Julie sat down next to me. "I came to tell you that Granny is acting sort of weird."

"What do you mean?" I placed my arm behind her on the pew.

"Granny is ordering the nurses around," Julie said, "telling them they're not taking good care of Aunt Camy. And Granny even threatened to fire one of her doctors."

Oh, dear. "What did the doctor do wrong?"

"He forgot that Camille wasn't married, and so he asked if her husband had been in to see her yet."

CHAPTER
forty-one

When Camille got home from the hospital, changes of every kind were so thick in the air that it was like Texas barbeque in the heat of the summer. Marcus had driven to Dallas, Julie had headed back to college, and Mother had insisted that Camille live with her until she could regain her health or for as long as she wanted to live there. Since I still had a bit more time on my leave of absence from work, I decided to see how Camille and Mother were getting along. If they were pulling out each other's hair, or if the transformation I'd seen at the hospital had been lasting.

I rang Mother's doorbell and waited for Dragan the Terrible to answer the door.

The deadbolt unlocked and the door swung open. Ms. Humphreys stood in the entry, looking foreboding enough to play the role of an evil queen at a Renaissance festival.

"Hi. Is everything okay?"

Dragan glared at me through half-lowered lids.

Glad to see you too.

"No, it's not good," Dragan said. "Now I have two invalids to take care of."

Was she referring to my mother and sister? Goodness. "But that shouldn't be a problem," I said, "since you and Mother are such good friends." I tried not to sound too sarcastic. But I failed.

"Right." Dragan blew out some hot air, which she had in limitless supply. "They're both in the solarium. You can find your own way back."

"Yes, I can. I grew up here."

Dragan didn't grace me with further comments—thank goodness—but instead flip-flapped her way toward the kitchen. In her case, though, maybe "flim-flammed" her way toward the kitchen was a more accurate description. I couldn't imagine why my mother continued to keep that woman around. Perhaps Dragan's days in the Gray house were numbered. One could dream.

I made my way back to the solarium. The voices of two women arguing wafted out of the glass room. Not angry voices, just loud. What a relief.

By the time I opened the solarium door, both Mother and Camille were standing by a hibiscus flower in deep contemplation.

"Greetings, Lily." Mother waved me inside. "Come in. Come in. Glad you're here."

"Hey, Lils." Camille's face had a little more color, and it didn't appear to just be from the dispute.

"Grab a health nut cookie on the table, dear," Mother said. "Wholesome roughage for the constitution. Keeps the bowels persuaded to do the right thing."

I gaped at the cookies. Somehow putting the two words *bowels* and *cookies* together didn't inspire me to take a nibble. "Sounds frightening."

Mother and Camille chuckled.

I ignored the pile of cookies.

"We need your help to settle a debate." Mother worked her mouth like she was chewing on something. Probably one of those ghastly cookies. "I'm busy trying to convince your sister that she couldn't be more mistaken about—"

"Mistaken my eye." Camille grinned through her frown. "Lils, please tell Iris that you really can make paper out of the hibiscus."

I put up my hands. "I have no idea. You guys are on your own." My stomach growled. Hungry, I stared at the miserable plate of health nut cookies, at the bits of nuts poking out their hapless little heads and arms like they were trying to escape from the dung-like cookie. Hungry or not, guess I'd pass.

"Paper . . . how preposterous." Mother turned the potted plant this way and that.

"But I'm only talking about one species, the hibiscus canna-binus. It's commonly used for paper. Everyone who knows angio-sperms is aware—"

"Shouldn't you sit down, my dear?" Mother asked. "Camille, the doctor said to take it easy."

My sister looked over at me, rolled her eyes, and grinned. Then she sat in the wheelchair Mother had rented for her. Camille snug-gled under the quilt, looking more content than I ever imagined.

"I'll have Dragan make you another veggie shake. I'll have you in excellent working order before you know it."

"I appreciate the raw juice, Iris, but if I drink one more kale and spinach drink I'm going to turn permanently green." Camille made a platypus kind of expression with her lower lip.

"Oh, you are so funny. Then how about some hibiscus tea? Even if people can't make paper out of hibiscus they can surely make tea." Mother chuckled. Then she plucked one of the biggest hibiscus blooms off the plant and slipped it into Camille's hair. "There, that looks pretty, doesn't it?"

Apparently, Mother was going to squeeze four decades of nur-turing into a week. But what an exquisite sight, watching my sister and my mother go after it in an almost musical dance of affectionate disagreement. It had to be the sweetest wrangling I'd ever witnessed, and it did my heart good to see it.

Mother swiped at a housefly that buzzed around our heads. "By the way, where is Dragan?" She picked up a swatter, gave the fly a good smack when it landed on the table, and then scooped it off onto the floor. "I asked that woman for some hot tea an hour ago."

Dragan was suddenly "that woman." Guess Mother was still making some serious progress.

"Humph. I'll go and see about it." Mother hurried out the door with her cane dragging behind her.

When Camille and I were alone in the solarium I asked, "So, how are you and Mother doing together?"

"Not bad actually."

"Mother is trying hard. I've never seen anything like it. Ever. It would give me the creeps if I didn't love it so much."

Camille laughed. "Yes, I know. It's so sweet, sometimes I find myself getting all misty-eyed. And I don't generally cry, but lately everything seems to bring on the waterworks."

"You've been through a lot." I made little circles on her back. "If you need to cry, let it out. Take your time. I heard Mother say that she hopes you'll live here for good."

"Yes, she's told me that, but I don't want to impose."

"You wouldn't be. There's a whole other wing of the house that never gets used for anything. It would be nice to have a little life and laughter back in this huge empty place."

"Well, when you both put it that way . . . maybe." Camille looked up at me. "I called the grocery store where I worked and told them I wasn't sure when I was coming back, if ever. They were fine with it. I liked the people, but it's not like I had a big career future there."

I leaned down and looped my arms around her neck. "We're all hoping you'll call America your home. You are a citizen here, after all."

"Maybe I will."

"We'll just hug that nomadic lifestyle right out of you." I gave her quilt a pat and chuckled. "Say, look at us. We're both wearing floral blouses. We blend right in with Mother's solarium."

"I noticed."

"And from the looks of it, Mother has some caregiving instincts beyond just taking care of flowers."

"Although the mossy drinks and bark cookies are really giving my gag reflex a workout."

I laughed.

Camille pulled the hibiscus from her hair and twirled it in her fingers. "This morning Iris said she only had two flowers that mattered to her now . . . her Lily and her Camille Violet. Yeah."

I grinned.

"I missed my mother terribly when she died. I was so young, and you know I didn't get much of any fathering. So, this does feel good for a change, this intense mothering . . . even though Iris's change of heart came at a great cost."

"Yes, it did." A great cost indeed.

Camille said nothing for a while, so I milled around the solarium.

I fingered a long-stemmed rose, bent it toward me, and took a whiff of its heady fragrance. The solarium was friendlier, more than I ever remembered it, since now it was being used for pleasure rather than experiments. "I'll be glad for someone else to be in this house besides that miserable Dragan woman. It's obvious that she's no real friend to Mother, and I worry that Mother is being taken advantage of."

"We'll just have to convince Iris."

"By the way, there's something I wanted to ask you. When you were in the hospital, Mother told a story of her youth, her past, that explained a lot of whys when it came to your—"

"Sorry to interrupt you, but I already know what you're going to ask me." Camille gave me a sheepish grin. "I heard the whole thing."

"So, you weren't really asleep?"

"I was drifty from the meds, but I heard it all."

"Well, maybe that helps us both to know. Like Mother said, it doesn't excuse her actions, but it helps us to understand."

"It did help, but I had a pretty dreary night when I first came here. I kept playing that scene over and over in my head . . . the one when Iris shoved open the door and I fell. I know what happened was an accident, but I couldn't get it out of my head. If I hadn't fallen, I'd still have my baby. I mean, we don't know for sure, because of my age and health, but I had a fighting chance. My baby had a chance to live. So, it was hard not to hate her even with the tragic story she told us in the hospital."

Camille ran her hands along the arms of the wheelchair. "But I knew if I didn't find a way to forgive her, I'd eventually end up like Iris. That is, the way she'd lived her life until now. Let me tell you, it was enough to scare me into forgiveness."

"I'm sure."

"But some of my anger that first night was inspired by Dragan."

"Why doesn't that surprise me?" I crossed my arms. "How do you mean?"

"Well, after Iris went to bed, Dragan came in to check on me . . . to ask me if I needed anything before she went home. It sounds thoughtful, but before Dragan left she said she was sorry that my mother could have done such a thing. Bring about the death of her own grandchild." Camille set the quilt to the side and stood up. "I don't need this wheelchair, but it makes Iris happy, so . . ."

"Dragan actually said that? How awful."

"Yes, especially since I'd just come home. And Dragan had this strange twinkle in her eyes as she was saying it. That woman wasn't sorry for me or the baby at all. She just wanted to stir up trouble to make me angry enough at Iris to leave."

"I'm sure that's true. But you can't let her win." I drummed my fingers on a worktable. "I should find Mother right now and demand she fire Dragan, but I don't think she'd do it. Dragan has some kind of strange hold on her."

"But there's more to my story. About Mother anyway. This morning I felt kind of woozy, so I got up and lost my way a bit, since I'm not used to the house. But I heard someone crying, so I followed the noise to Iris's bedroom door. I leaned in to listen. It was Iris weeping. I guess she was grieving over what happened. But her tears made me curious. Well, you might as well know . . . I'm kind of a snoop." Camille grinned.

"Me too. Julie hates that about me. I was always reading her diary. I just couldn't help myself."

"Yeah, well, I can relate. So much so, that I went into Iris's bedroom while she and Dragan were eating breakfast."

"Really? That was sneaky." I took a few steps closer to her so we wouldn't be overheard. "What did you find?"

"All kinds of stuff for older ladies. Foot powders and arthritis cream. But on her nightstand I saw this book entitled *101 Ways to Mother*. And she was being meticulous about it. Writing the ideas down on a notepad and making little scribbles. Like she was going to be tested on it." A tear ran down Camille's cheek. "Look at me." She swiped the tear away, wincing and laugh-crying. "I'm some kind of human sprinkler head. I can't even talk about this without boohooing."

"It's okay. Believe me. I know how it is to cry over everything. I used to—"

Somewhere in the bowels of the house a door went shut with an echoing slam.

"Must be Dragan. Wow, somebody's cranky," I singsonged. "Maybe she didn't want to bring us our tea after all."

Then someone hollered. *But it wasn't Mother's voice.*

"Let's go see what's happening," Camille whispered.

She followed me out of the solarium and into the main part of the house, where the voices of two women arguing became clearer. I certainly didn't want to get into a verbal tussle with Dragan, so we tiptoed into the back of the entry, which was far enough away not to be seen, but close enough to see and hear what was going on.

"It's as if you've struck me with a rod," Mother said to Dragan, "the way you've treated me after all I've done for you. I let you have pretty much free rein of the house, in exchange for a little help here and there. But you threw my generosity and even my friendship back in my face. I can tolerate your slovenly attitude and even that ghastly muumuu of yours, but I will not tolerate your thievery. And on top of that, I don't like the way you talk to Lily or Camille."

Dragan cocked her head. "Camille's not really your daughter. Why do you care so much now?"

"Because I've had a heart transplant," Mother said. "I highly recommend it. Unlike insurance companies, God works just fine with our preexisting conditions. And as far as my daughter, I gave birth to two girls. Camille had a good mom, but now I've been given a second chance to make some things right. If both of my daughters will let me, I will spend the rest of my life reminding them how much I love them."

"What a nice happily-ever-after." Dragan's voice came off steeped in acerbity. "But well . . . I am sorry I stole from you." She sniffed the air and rocked her head like it was quite the imposition to offer such an act of contrition.

"Uh-huh." Mother's voice was steeped in disbelief. "I think you're mostly sorry you got caught."

"Yeah, that too."

Mother held out her hand for the feather duster that Dragan had in her steely grip.

"We had some good laughs, though, didn't we?" Instead of handing the duster over to Mother, Dragan nervily set the duster on the entry table.

"Yes, we did have a few good laughs." Mother opened the door for Dragan and made a sweeping gesture for her to leave. "I'm sorry you messed that up."

"Look, I only took an old set of vases you didn't need anymore." Dragan made no move to walk through the open door.

"Actually, they were hand-blown in Italy and worth a small fortune. Family heirlooms, you see, and I planned to give them to my two daughters as gifts for their birthdays." Mother smiled.

"Oh? I really am sorry then. Forgive and forget?" The woman opened her sleepy eyes and tried on a repentant expression. The contrition on her face fit as well as a size five shoe on a size ten foot. "I'm sure you're expecting me to say more, but that's all I've got," Dragan said.

"I forgive you," Mother said, "but you're fired. I'll mail you your last check. I do have a going-away gift though."

"Oh, really?" Dragan livened up a bit. "What's that?"

"This silly thing." Mother lifted the cane over to Dragan as if she were holding a dead rat. "I don't need it. Can't even imagine why I let you talk me into buying it. But I know you'll enjoy taking it to a pawn shop and seeing what you can get for it."

Dragan gave her a scowl as dirty as her flip-flops.

"Now, please go before I call the police," Mother said plainly as she opened the front door a little wider. "I'm sure you're expecting me to say more, but that's all I've got."

And then that was it—the fire-breathing Dragan Humphreys left the premises and our lives.

CHAPTER forty-two

Camille murmured to me, "Guess that wasn't in the *101 Ways to Mother* book."

I stifled a chuckle. "No, but it should be." Hmm. What a great life moment.

To say the scene between my mother and Dragan brought me joy was truly an understatement. Once again, as at the hospital, I still felt like Bob Cratchit seeing the transformation of Scrooge's heart.

When the door shut, Mother turned around and looked right at us in our little niche. "You girls. You seem to think I'm hard of hearing."

We laughed as we came out of our hiding spot. "You knew we were here?"

"Absolutely. Everything in here echoes." Mother chuckled and then pointed toward the front door. *"Níl easpa ann cosúil leis an dith chara."*

When Camille and I both looked clueless, Mother said, "It's an Irish saying. It means, 'There's no need like the lack of a friend.'" She shook her head. "And I have been needing a real friend for a long time. I thought I could buy one. What a fool's errand, eh?" She waved her hand at the door as if shaking off any remaining Dragan dust and said to Camille, "Say, do you think you could order me another one of those Aussie jammyton things?"

"You mean lamingtons?" Camille asked.

"Yes, that's it. Lamington."

"Sure, I'll order some online." Camille grinned. "How many did you want?"

"Oh, a few dozen ought to do it." Mother slapped her hands together. "Now I feel like celebrating the firing of Dragan Humphreys. Who wants to celebrate with me?"

"Got ice cream?" I asked.

Pretending offense, Mother replied, "Of course I do."

"You actually keep ice cream in the house?" Camille looped arms with me and let out a chortle.

"I have three flavors." Mother tilted her head at us. "But I can always make some prune compote to put on top if we need it."

We chuckled.

"And we can eat it while you help me to plan a dinner for your fortieth birthdays."

"Sounds like fun," I said.

"I'm not sure I know how to make anything fun," Mother said, "but you two can help me. By the way, I found something."

"What did you find?" Camille and I said it at the same time and laughed.

"Something in the attic, and I wondered if you two would want to look at it while we eat our treat." Mother looked back and forth at us with an almost childlike pleading.

I tightened my grip on Camille. "Oh?"

"It's an album of photos. Of you both together... before I... before I gave Camille away to Naomi." Mother's voice choked on the last words. "But I wasn't sure if you both were ready to see them."

Somehow I felt it wasn't my place to answer. It was up to Camille.

Mother and I waited for her response.

As if our lungs were tied together and we were breathing as one, my sister and I took in a deep breath and exhaled.

Camille smiled. "It's always the right time to be a family."

CHAPTER
forty-three

Four weeks later I stood outside Terminal C at Intercontinental Airport to say goodbye to Marcus. It was one of those bittersweet moments in life when one had to say a temporary farewell so there could be a bigger, more permanent hello. I clutched at his lapels and then examined his face to read every nuance of his expression. His eyes were full of affection as usual and something else—grief? Good. I wanted him to miss me like a crab would miss its shell. "You'd better come back, or I'll have to come and get you."

"The thing is, I have a great affection for Australia, but that great vast land is missing one important thing for my survival . . . you. So, Love, I'll have no choice but to come back here to live."

Marcus said the Aussie endearment, because now it never failed to make me smile. I loosened my grip on his lapels and then let him go. "So, am I still your treasure?"

"More than ever. I will only be gone for a couple of weeks. I just need to pack up my things and have them shipped here. I need to say some permanent goodbyes to my church friends. I need this time to shut down my life there. Then I'll be back." Marcus kissed me on the tip of my nose. "I also hope you'll be wretchedly miserable while I'm gone. Promise me."

"That's a promise that's easy to keep."

"We have some time before I have to go. I'm early for my flight, and it doesn't appear that anyone is trying to give you the boot out of this parking space, so hold my hand a bit longer. Please?" He took my hand in his.

It wasn't a very romantic spot with the exhaust fumes, honking horns, and busy travelers, but being closer to Marcus was always a good thing, especially since in a matter of seconds, he would walk through those sliding glass doors and be gone from me.

"We did what we set out to do, didn't we?" Marcus squeezed my hand. "We gave our families priority over our relationship. It has been a time of mending."

"It was the right thing to do. So, did you hear anything recently from your mom?"

"We talked awhile this morning. Mom still hasn't agreed to move back in with Dad."

"The counseling hasn't helped then?"

"It has," Marcus said, "but it's going to take time to rebuild their relationship. I'm grateful that Dad actually agreed to get some counseling. That's a miracle in itself. *And* they both seem pleased that I'm moving back to Texas." He grinned. "And even though Dad isn't singing my praises about my work, he talks to me without looking like he's going to have a stroke."

"That's a good start."

"I'm glad we gave our families some time to breathe. They were worth it. But now, Lily, when I get home, I'm hoping this will be our season. *Our* time." He lifted my hands to his lips and gave them a kiss so sweet and solemn, it was like a vow.

"It will be. I'll let you take me to concerts and museums and movies. And I'll make you picnics by the fire. Thanksgiving won't be terribly far away by the time you get back. Won't that be lovely? I'll make you a huge turkey feast, and we'll both eat so much we'll have to put on pants with elastic around the waist."

"And we'll nod off and take long snoring naps like an old married couple."

I grinned.

Marcus touched my chin with his knuckles in an affectionate gesture. "But I can tell something is bothering you. What is it? Tell me before I go."

"You know me so well. But I don't want to bother you with—"

"You're my love. Please tell me."

I looked away but then back at him since I knew he wouldn't let me go until I'd confessed my worries. "Okay. I'll tell you. I had such a nightmare last night. Well, one I've had on and off for months. I woke up gasping for air. I dreamed that my husband was alive, and he was still having an affair. And that Julie found out. It made her so stressed she became ill and had to leave college. I felt so trapped in *his* sin, in his choices, that I felt myself sinking into a blazing pit along with him. It felt so real and—"

Marcus drew me to him. "It's all right. It was just a dream. However . . ."

I pulled away. "However?"

"Look, I don't want to start a tussle right before I leave, but now that you've mentioned this nightmare I feel I must say something. I know you didn't use our families' struggles as an excuse to put our relationship on hold—"

"Of course I didn't." *Did I?*

"And I know when I first arrived here, we were rushing things between us. No, I admit that it was me . . . *I* was trying to rush things. But we've had more time together now, and we know what we're about—"

"Yes, and I did promise to—"

"Lily, my darling, I haven't made my point yet."

"Okay." I pressed my lips together, trying to squelch my nervous chatter. "I'll be quiet for a moment."

"I think with all of that progress, my point is . . . there is still something missing between us."

My spirit trembled. "What do you mean?" I tried not to pout.

Marcus took hold of my arms. "You're assuming the worst right now, but I'm trying to find a way to help you. I'm just doing it very badly. What I'm trying to say is that something still needs mending, and this time it's not the other members of our families. It's you, dear one, who needs restoration . . . healing. The bottom line is, because of your husband's transgression, you still don't trust me."

"That's not—"

"Now, now." Marcus placed his finger ever so gently on my lips to shush me. "I don't think you trust men in general. You think I'll be loyal while things are fresh and new between us, while the blush is still on the lily, but when age comes or when times get tough, and they do sometimes get tough as you can see from my parents, that I might be tempted to be unfaithful to you like your husband. That I'll find someone else to share my heart with . . . my bed with. Am I right, Lily girl?"

Who me, afraid? Guess that was still the story of my life. But did it have to be? Couldn't I change my story? And couldn't God? "Well, when you put it like that . . ." I took in a deep breath. "Okay, so maybe you have something there. A valid point. But I don't want it to be that way. It's not my intention. I want to put away what happened in the past. But it's like trying to hide a gorilla in my closet. I close the door and forget about it most of the time, but the silly thing keeps thrashing about, trying to get out. Sometimes it's more than I can handle."

"I thought so. But I think I have the answer to this dilemma."

"You do?"

"You've never had closure. Because of your husband's death, you didn't get to spend time with him, talking the affair through. Yelling it through or whatever it would have taken for you to move forward. I'm not sure marriages can ever fully recover from a breach in trust like that, but talking to him would have helped."

One by one, my mind flashed the memories, especially the dreadful moment when I first found out about the affair. My stomach churned all over again. It was still so near the surface. Marcus was right. I had yet to move on. "Yes, I do wish I could have talked to him, but it's too late now."

"Didn't you tell me that you knew the woman's name? That it was someone your husband worked with?" Marcus asked. "Do you still know how to get in touch with her?"

I looked around. It seemed like such an odd place to talk about my husband's affair and the woman, but since Marcus brought it up I said, "My husband accidentally left her address on his writing desk. So, unless she's moved, it would still be possible to meet her. But what would I do . . . go scream at this woman? Stomp my feet?"

"No, but you could talk to her . . . if she'll let you. Who knows, maybe she'd like the opportunity to ask for forgiveness. You never know. Maybe you could finally ask the questions you wanted to ask . . . face that beast of adultery that keeps showing up in your nightmares. And maybe by going to see this woman it will give you some closure."

"Yeah, it could be a good thing I guess, as long as it didn't dig up enough sharp emotions to keep me awake for years."

"It might. You're right. It is a risk." Marcus fiddled with the handle on his suitcase as if he were about to go. "You know, a long time ago when I was younger and more daring I went zip-lining across a canyon. I don't remember a whole lot about the experience except something the guide said to me before I stepped off my safe little perch to fly across the canyon. He said, 'Trust the harness.' And that helped me to let go. I wasn't nearly as afraid when I went across that chasm. You need to trust me, Lily, but more importantly you need to trust the One who made you. The One who has you safely in His arms . . . sort of like trusting that harness. It really makes the letting go a lot easier."

"So, I can fly across the canyon and into your arms?"

He chuckled. "Well, that's a fine idea."

"You're a good man, Marcus." I placed my palm over his heart. "You reached out to me when I was needing to find my sister, and you've proven yourself to me in a lot of ways. But I admit, I still have this problem. You're right. I appreciate you bringing it up . . .

sort of." I grinned. "And bringing it up at your own peril, I might add, since you didn't know how I would react. But I'm glad you haven't held this against me, this lack of trust. Since, well, you've done nothing wrong."

"You helped me work through my problem. You know, of not being able to have anyone else in the car when I was driving. I did it because of your push. Now, I'd like to help you."

"I'll think about your suggestion, and I'll ask God about it."

"I know you will." He straightened the bow at the top of my blouse. "Take good care of yourself."

"I will."

Marcus pulled out an orange piece of paper from his pocket and held it up.

"What's that?"

Marcus folded the paper here and there, with a few squashes and creases in between until I realized what he was doing. He was making an origami lily. Then he pulled out a pen from his pocket and used it to curl the paper petals. When he'd finished it, he handed it to me and said, "Never forget that you're my lily. I know I won't."

"That's beautiful. Thank you." I twirled it under my nose even though it had no scent.

"Whenever I miss you I'll make one of these. And then I'll call you."

"But not too often. The calls will cost you a fortune. It would be cheaper for you to make the lily and text." My words sounded so boringly pragmatic. "No, I don't mean that. If you want to call . . . just call. I can't hear your voice when you text."

He grinned. "These two weeks will be the longest in my life. So, right now before I go . . ." Marcus got that look.

"Yes?"

"I'm going to kiss that pretty lipstick right off your mouth."

And I was happy to let him.

CHAPTER
forty-four

It was an early November evening when I sat in my sedan, staring at her house—Vontella Quinn's house to be exact—the *other* woman. Vontella Quinn sounded like the name of a movie starlet or the name of a woman who wore greasy overalls and worked at an auto repair shop. Could go either way.

I lowered the rearview mirror to gaze at myself. I'd fixed up more than usual and reapplied lipstick too many times to count. I had no idea why I'd gone to so much trouble, except that if Vontella turned out to be the starlet type, I couldn't stand for the woman to think I was the clichéd housewife who'd let herself go and who tooled around the house in a tattered duster. Yes, I had become that shallow.

Who knew, maybe I had become that kind of housewife. Then again, Marcus didn't seem to think so. Marcus had even told me I was beautiful.

You're just stalling, Lily. Get out of the car. Even though the daylight was fading, Vontella probably saw me from the kitchen window. But my body refused to move. I'd prayed every kind of prayer I knew. I had a level of peace, and yet my hands trembled.

The past visited me as it always did when I didn't want it to. I remembered Nanny Kate and how she'd coax me out of the car with the promise of ice cream. She'd used that ploy for everything because it worked. It was how she'd gotten me to go on one of our many nature outings. On one of those day trips, Nanny Kate showed me that trees would grow even in the rocks. That nature would fight for life, that it struggled to live. So, when had I stopped fighting to live life to the fullest? When had I become a walking shadow of gloom? I knew the answer in that moment, sitting there in front of Vontella's house. It was the day I saw the letter from my husband's lover, hidden inside his desk.

From Vontella.

Even though the promise of ice cream did little to encourage me now, I knew I needed to do this thing. I had to confront Vontella— since I didn't want my fears to overtake me. I no longer wanted to be a child in search of hiding places. I would do it for Nanny Kate, wherever she was. Perhaps she had her own family now, her own struggles to overcome. Perhaps from time to time she thought of me with fondness, and maybe she would be proud of me as I unlocked the car and pulled the handle.

For all of Nanny Kate's rallying words and for Mother's courage to change, I let the door swing open wide. I stepped out, planted my feet on solid ground, and began my march up the walkway toward the house. Now I was committed. No turning back. The woman's car sat in the driveway. Perhaps she'd just gotten home from work. The house appeared warm and uncomplicated, the landscape tidy. Just the right kind of a house to stage an extramarital affair. Or perhaps it had taken place in a hotel room. Or even my own bed!

Now, Lily. Not a good way to start. At this rate I would want to wring her pretty little neck right after ringing the doorbell. "Lord, please let my words and meditations be acceptable, because I'm starting to feel villainous about now." My thoughts were getting as foul as dung.

I had wanted to face this woman ever since that first day I found out about my husband's affair. I'd just never had the courage until now. Or the stupidity.

But what if the woman was married, and her husband an-swered the door? What would I do then? Before I could chase that potentially formidable rabbit trail, the door opened. Vontella Quinn, or the woman who surely must be Vontella, sat before me with a puzzled brow. The woman sat because she was in a wheelchair. Now, that was the last thing I would have expected. She wasn't a glamorous woman but handsome enough with her buxom body and thick mane.

"May I help you?" she asked.

"Yes, I'm sorry to bother you. I'm . . . well, I'll say it straight out. I'm Lily Winter."

"I know who you are." Surprisingly, the woman didn't look irritated, but more weary—like a woman with baggage that was too cumbersome to carry.

"You do?"

She nodded. "Your husband showed me a photo of you."

"He did?" Now why on earth would he do that?

"Yes. I know that must seem odd."

"It does . . . seem odd."

"I was sorry to hear about it . . . when Richard died," she said. "I didn't go to the funeral, as you know."

"Yes, it was a rough time." My hands fumbled around until I slid them into my coat pockets. "Look, I realize this is terribly awkward, but would you mind if we had a brief talk? I promise I'm not here to make a scene or anything. I just want to understand things better. After my husband's death I'm still struggling. I need some closure."

"And you think talking to me will give you that."

"Maybe. I don't know for sure, but I felt it was important enough to try . . . if you don't mind."

"Well, that sounds honest at least." The woman opened the door and moved her wheelchair back to let me inside. "Come on in. I see no reason not to talk to you."

"Thank you."

"I'm Vontella Quinn, but you probably already know that."

"Yes, I know."

She motioned for me to sit down on the couch, which seemed to be the only new piece of furniture in the living room. The rest of the house was a hodgepodge of furnishings, and when I breathed in, my nostrils were accosted by the pungent smells of musty fabric and cooking grease. "He suspected you found out about us. So, I always wondered if you wouldn't stop by someday to drag me over the coals."

"No coals, I promise." I smiled, even though I didn't feel like it. But it was impossible not to wonder what my husband had seen in this woman. Had I failed our relationship in some way to make him flee into her arms? Was it a midlife crisis, or had he had a moment of weakness? I didn't take off my coat, since I didn't intend to stay that long. "I'm sorry if you've been in an accident recently."

She scrubbed her hands along the arms of the wheelchair. "No accident. In the last few months I was diagnosed with rheumatoid arthritis, and sometimes it gets bad enough to keep me from walking. Now I use the wheelchair when I'm having a flare-up."

So the wheelchair was a more recent addition to her life—something Richard had never seen. My hands flailed around; I took a throw pillow and fiddled with the corner tassel. "I'm sorry. It must be painful."

"It is . . . very painful." The woman took a deep draught of me, even though her eyes were at half-mast. "But you didn't come here to discuss my ailments. In fact, I would think that my suffering would bring you joy. You know, my just deserts and all."

"I'll try not to rejoice in your suffering, and if I do, I'm sure I'll repent about it later." I smiled, trying to lighten our discussion. If things spiraled into anger, she would mostly likely ask me to leave. That was the first and the last thing I wanted. I guess extramarital affairs made for complicated emotions—like gasoline and lit matches. Bad combo.

"Humph." Vontella splayed her fingers over her cheek and pursed her ruby-painted lips.

The thought that those lips had kissed my husband's with passion made me crazy with disgust and anger, so I dismissed the image as best I could. "The thing is . . . my husband died before we had a chance to talk about this. I guess the biggest question that has been burning a hole in my spirit is . . . why. I know you two worked together, and it's not uncommon for men and women to meet at work and form a bond that could, well, blossom into more, is a nice way to put it."

"If you're referring to love, that's not what we had. At least it wasn't for me."

"Oh." I waited for her to go on, but perhaps she felt too embarrassed to talk about the other "l" word—*lust*. She deserved to face her shame. It would be good for her to feel its teeth.

"The affair was centered on God or, more accurately, the absence of Him."

Curious woman. "What do you mean?"

"Years ago, your husband tried to witness to me. I'm an atheist, and I didn't appreciate his proselytization at work, although sometimes I admit it was entertaining to watch him try to match wits with me concerning religion. I even felt sorry for him, since I felt like a cat batting a mouse around."

She raised her chin. "I was on the debate team in college. Anyway, after one of his particularly self-righteous sermonettes I got it in my mind that I would find a way to bring him down. To show him he wasn't all that righteous after all. I knew one way might be easier than others, since men tend to be . . . well, thirsty if you know what I mean. And they like their egos massaged. They like to be king of the mountain. And so over time, I meticulously worked from that angle. It became an obsession for me to work the chain, until I found the weakest link in your husband's scruples."

That it wasn't love or even lust on Vontella's part was a concept I hadn't considered. Richard had been a handsome man, so I couldn't imagine that homing in on my husband came from some anti-Christian obsession. "Why was winning so important to you? If all religions mean nothing to you, and you're confident in your belief, then why did you work so zealously to prove him wrong? Especially since the affair could make you both look unprofessional at work? Seems like a lot of risk just to prove something to yourself."

"Yes." Vontella shrugged. "Maybe I was bored too. I needed something to do."

I tugged on the pillow tassel, nearly snapping it off. Come to think of it, I would like to have torn up all the pillows in her musty little living room and then flung the stuffing around the room—especially the fluff from the pillows that were used during the affair. But then surely my husband hadn't stayed in this place. "Well, your boredom could have broken up a happy family."

"So, I see you brought your hot coals after all." She lifted a tumbler of amber-colored liquid from the end table and took a sip.

"I'm just stating the facts. Isn't that what you do on a debate team?" I kept my tone respectful and calm, even though I felt like lashing out at her for her actions, which were riddled with foolishness and pride and a hundred other sins conjured up in the darker corners of hell.

Vontella didn't reply.

Rope in the anger, Lily, and remember why you came. "One of the reasons I need closure is because I've been dating a man who is hoping for a commitment from me. Even though I love this man it's been difficult to think long-term because of what Richard did."

She fiddled with her chair, rolling it back and forth. "So, now I'm your shrink?"

"No, but do you mind if I ask how long it took to make my husband give in to this transgression?"

"Almost three years." Vontella seemed to scrutinize me.

"Really?" Was she joking? But it was certainly not a teasing topic. The woman who sat across from me had to be neurotic.

"If it will make you feel any better, know that it took me longer to turn your husband's head than it did for any of the others. So, he does get that prize."

"Others? You mean you've done this before?"

"Several times." Vontella fingered a greeting card, which sat on an end table next to her. The front read "get well" in big pink sparkly letters.

I wanted to say something truly nasty but bit my lip. "So, this is a game to you?"

CHAPTER
forty-five

"Sure, why not?" Vontella pushed on the front of the greeting card with her fingernail until it fell over onto the floor. She didn't bother picking it up.

"Wouldn't you want to be known in your life for more than that? You have the potential to do good. You were made for so much more than this—"

Vontella gave me a wave like she was swatting at a mosquito. "Please don't you start with your religious babble. If this is all there is, then what does it matter what I do? All our good or bad deeds will come to nothing. None of it matters, except to get the most out of each day. I have faith only in the here and now. If you want my advice . . . you should marry this man who wants you. Enjoy him for as long as you can. Before you get bored or he finds—"

"Before he finds another woman like you?" My mouth said it before I could think of anything else.

"Yeah, something like that." She picked up the glass, clinked the ice around with her finger, and then took a deep swig. Some of the whiskey splashed onto her pantsuit, but the stain it left didn't seem to ruffle her.

"But if this is all there is . . . even if the thrill of another sexual conquest doesn't really matter, I'm surprised you don't promote suicide."

"I wouldn't go quite that far, although I've considered it for myself, especially now that I'm sometimes confined to this infernal wheelchair. The pain and depression that promise to come with this disease will eventually make me seek that kind of end. But I won't tell you to take *your* life."

"Why not?" I lifted my shoulders nonchalantly.

Vontella looked at me. She was trying to figure me out. How much was twaddle and how much might be something else—something real? "Well, you wouldn't follow my advice anyway."

"My husband certainly followed your advice." I had no idea where I was going with the conversation, but I felt edgy and tempestuous and maybe a little bit sorrowful about her plight. I wished Vontella could see beyond the hopeless world she'd created.

"Yes, Richard did take my advice. Not right away, but in the end he did."

"So, why won't you suggest that I kill myself?"

Vontella glowered at me, her eyes glistening and her cheeks rosy from the liquor. "You won't give this up, will you? I don't know why I won't advise you to take your life. You're probably just pulling my leg with all this claptrap, but since I don't really know what you're capable of, I have to tell you, you're scaring me a little."

"Why?"

"What do you mean, why? In case you're nuts and you really do go home and take your life. That's why." She slapped her hand down on the armrest but missed.

"But if this really is all there is, then none of that matters, even this conversation. Even your affair. Even what we do when—"

"I won't tell you to commit suicide . . . just in case," she said in a whispery slur.

"In case of what?"

"Leave it be, woman." Vontella mumbled a curse.

The alcohol was making her more angry than mellow. Or maybe I was upsetting her. Maybe the irritation came from the inconsistencies in her faith that had been brought to light.

"If you must know," Vontella said, "I won't convince you that suicide is good, just in case there is something out there. I wouldn't want your blood on my hands. Adultery is one thing, but . . ."

"So, you have your limits on how far you'll take your lack of faith."

"I have my limits, so sue me." Vontella lifted the tumbler off the table and tossed back the last of the whiskey, wincing as she swallowed.

She looked "full as a boot" as Marcus might say in his Aussie vernacular. I set the pillow aside and leaned forward, more curious than ever. "You must be a doubting atheist then."

"Aren't you a doubting Christian?"

"At times. I've had a few doubts . . . like when I found out my husband was having an affair."

She chuckled. "Right." Her laughter became a rattling cough.

"Somebody must have really hurt you in the past."

"For me to be such a malcontent, you mean? Maybe. Well, my father was a lout. So, I don't have a very high opinion of men."

I could have guessed that one.

"It's also hard to look up to a heavenly Father when your earthly father decimated your childhood." Vontella's eyes drooped even more. "I'm beginning to feel tired now. This disease doesn't give me a lot of energy. At least wives will no longer have to be afraid of me. No man is interested in me now."

If it were true, I couldn't say that I was sorry about the last part. "I'll go now." I rose from the couch. "I do have one last thing to say."

"Oh, yeah? What pray tell is that?"

"I forgive you."

"Yeah, well, I don't want your forgiveness." Vontella spat out the words. "I have no use for it."

"That's fine, but your spirit might accept what your mind rejects."

"Odd little aphorism. Like a pretty box with nothing inside." She shook her finger. "That's the same kooky thing your husband wanted to do. After our one-day affair, he asked for my forgiveness like he'd been the one to do something wrong. I didn't give him the satisfaction of saying I would forgive him. Guess I should have, since he died. But that was all there ever was between us. That one day."

One day. It had only been one day. "I give you my forgiveness anyway, even if you don't want it. Freely given, with no hot coals attached." I picked my purse off the floor.

Vontella chuckled and shook her head. "If there is a God, He threw away the mold when He made you. 'Cause you're one crazy chick."

"True. I am." I gave my purse strap a good twisting in my fingers. "There is a God, because He's the One who's kept my hand from slapping you, my mouth from screaming at you, and my heart from despising you."

"Well, I'm glad for that at least." Vontella followed me, rolling her way to the front door. "So, you're not going home and kill yourself?" she added with a smile, but there was a hint of concern in her voice.

"No, this crazy chick is going to start a new life." I smiled at her. "I'm going to propose marriage to the man I'm dating."

CHAPTER
forty-six

Later at home, the many scenes and conversations that I had been repressing, with Mother, Camille, Vontella, Marcus, everyone really, came frothing up in my emotions, threatening to smother me. I rubbed my neck and then unbuttoned the top buttons on my blouse. A dizzy buzz filled my head. Maybe I needed to eat, and yet I wasn't hungry. So much had happened. Tragedy, miracles, betrayal, fury, and forgiveness, even for those who didn't deserve it. What to do with it all? Maybe I could funnel it into art rather than have a nervous breakdown.

Perhaps the confrontation with Vontella was like the last mile of the traveler after a long journey. I felt grateful that Richard hadn't given in to sin easily, but hearing about the details of his unfaithfulness was like touring Dante's inferno. I knew that the seedy realm of adultery existed, and yet I had never been forced to see it up close. Until today.

In an attempt to escape too much reality, I went into my small music room—a place I rarely visited—and ran my fingers along the polished wood surface of my Baldwin Acrosonic piano. Dust collected on the tips of my fingers, and I fluttered it off. The room smelled unused as though no one was home.

But I was home now.

I sat down on the bench. Perhaps God had given us the arts to lessen the blows of life, to bring heaven close—at least as close as we mortals could get.

It's been a long time.

Before I even played a note the music came to me, as it always had—but I'd learned to repress even that, even God's inspiration, His music.

But no more.

I would call the piece "Haven"—a place where God meets us here on earth. There'd be green pastures and still waters in my piece, and it would be juxtaposed with dramatic chords, echoing the human condition. My melody would reflect the hope of redemption for Vontella, the prayer that I would fully forgive Richard, and a look at my own transgressions. Those daily offenses that separated me from God—the things that made me step away into the shadows, away from the brilliance and warmth of His perfect love. And lastly, the haven that would help me to find my way into the future, into that holy place called matrimony.

I lifted the lid and rubbed my hands together. I played a note and then another until beauty formed from chaos, just as it did that first day of creation. The passion of my soul flowed onto the keys. The melody started out wispy like the tiniest flutter of a petal, and then it became intoxicating mixed with thundering fury, and then finally satisfying, with a resolution, just like the release that comes from forgiveness.

As I finished up the last notes of "Haven," I had a sense of freedom. In that liberty of spirit I could see a future scene playing out before me—I would run into Marcus's arms, and this time, we'd both hear the merry chatter of guests—the guests who would attend our wedding.

In Melbourne I'd said, "You have to know yourself to have hobbies . . . be a friend to yourself." Maybe I knew myself a little better now. Maybe I could be a friend to myself. But I did know this too—I wanted the piano to be more than a hobby.

I ran my fingers across the keys like a breeze flowing over silk. "My eighty-eight little black and white companions . . . how I've missed you."

CHAPTER
forty-seven

Forty-eight hours after my confrontation with Vontella, I stood in front of the magazine shop in Terminal E just outside of security at Houston's Intercontinental Airport.

I knew what I was about to do. It was an extraordinary step for Lily Anne Winter. I would tell Marcus I not only loved him, but I was ready to marry him.

Today. Now. Whenever he wanted.

Only one hitch remained. Marcus was late. Thirty-one minutes late to be exact. I'd checked my watch, and it was correct. I'd checked the board for flights, but the information had disappeared off the screen. If the plane were merely delayed, it would still be listed. Wouldn't it? Had he come in early, and I'd missed him? But he would have texted. We both knew where to meet. There could be no misunderstandings.

I slid my coat off and sat down on the bench outside the store, but my twinge of panic got bigger and scarier like those blow-up monsters on people's lawns at Halloween. One ugly thought played over and over in my head—Marcus had changed his mind.

Maybe he'd gotten back into his routine there, met with his friends, got involved with his church, and Melbourne had worked its way back into his heart. He'd canceled his flight and stayed. Perhaps he thought I hadn't proven, after all, that I could be the kind of person who could ever trust again. Maybe he thought I was a lost cause. That my husband's infidelity had ruined my faith in men and in the loveliness of married life.

With jittery fingers, I texted Marcus—again. If he'd decided to stay, wouldn't he have called or texted? Maybe not. Maybe he surmised that a clean break was the only way. But did people really disappear into foreign countries? Marcus had done that very thing a year ago.

Wanting to feel closer to him, I felt around in my pocket for the origami lily he'd made for me. It had been the last thing he'd touched. I pulled it out and twirled it under my nose as I did the day he'd left. What had he said to me? "Never forget that you're my lily. I know I won't. Whenever I miss you I'll make one of these." How many flowers had he made while he was in Melbourne? I wanted to envision his apartment full of paper lilies as he packed his belongings. Marcus had also promised to call, and except for the last few days, he'd been faithful. Eventually, though, his communications had dwindled to a brief text or two. Perhaps he'd just gotten busy with wrapping up his life there, tying up loose ends.

I slipped the lily away into my pocket and gripped the edge of the cold metal bench. Funny, we'd begun our life together on a bench. Now I prayed this wouldn't be the place where it would end.

But I'd been mistaken about so many things—I was notoriously wrong, in fact—even about Richard. Although what my husband had done with Vontella had been a painful breach of trust and a terrible sin, I'd thought he'd given in to adultery easily with little remorse. But it had taken Vontella three years of manipulations, a master plan, to make Richard fall. And then he'd obviously felt terrible enough about their one-time fling that he'd begged her to forgive him. I would like to think that he was asking for my forgiveness in a way. Perhaps he would have done that very thing had he not died of a heart attack. Yes, I would give Richard the benefit of the doubt. Something I hadn't done before.

My hands ached, so I let go of the bench. The warmth of blood made it back into my hands, and I relaxed a little. Marcus had turned out to be one of the kindest, most down-to-earth, most amazing creatures God ever made. And if that weren't enough, he'd even been Miles Hooper thrown in the mix. He'd made me fall in love with him, so deeply and dearly. But what if it all ended with me on this bench?

And I was left alone—without him?

Oh, Lord, could Marcus have come into my life just to be a friend? True, he'd shown up at the perfect time, when I needed help, and he'd been suffering with the same issues, which was an uncanny turn of events. Miraculously, we'd worked it out together. It seemed like the perfect divine setup. Jesus with skin on as they always said, and now was it time for him to go?

Oh, God, please don't let it be. I love him.

I checked my phone for texts. Still nothing. I glanced around at all the people, zooming around. All going somewhere important. Many of them headed into the arms of someone they cherished. Hadn't Marcus used that very word with me? Cherished? A person like Marcus doesn't leave someone high and dry after making that kind of declaration. Then I remembered the last thing he'd touched—it hadn't been the paper lily—it had been my lips. And in that kiss had been such promise. It couldn't have been a final goodbye. The kiss hadn't merely embodied the joyful remnants of our past days together, but it had celebrated our future. Hadn't it? *Oh, Lord, this constant vacillation is driving me crazy.*

Trust.

That one word echoed in my mind, so I invited the word into my heart. Just as I had gotten over my fear of flying and moved on from empty nest and so many other travails, I also had the ability to learn to trust people again, even after a heartbreaking, life-changing event. People had the potential to let me down again, but the One who held the controls never would. Since faith was a choice, I would choose to trust the harness. I would trust the One who was love and who'd made me for love.

And I would start now.

Next stop—I would head to one of the airline desks and see what happened to Marcus's flight. He loved me, and I would choose to believe him. Just as I rose from my seat, determined to follow through with my plan, I saw the outline of a man, silhouetted by the light, who looked a lot like Marcus. When the light hit his face, I saw that smile of his—the kind of smile that gave the sun something to be envious about. Yes, it was Marcus, my Marcus. I walked and then ran toward him.

He let go of his luggage, dropped his carry-on backpack, and pulled me into an embrace. He gathered bunches of my hair into his hands and brought it around to frame my face just as he had done when he left. Then he kissed me so warmly I knew we'd surely drawn a crowd. I didn't mind. Not one bit. In fact, let them bring out the confetti and celebrate with us. I savored his warmth, his kiss. All of Marcus Averill.

When we parted briefly, Marcus whispered, "I don't want to ever be that far away from you again."

"Just a heartbeat away?"

"That's right." He chuckled. "I really did miss you something fierce, just like I said I would."

"Did you make lots of origami lilies?"

"A whole bouquet, and they were all in full bloom I might add. But they didn't help me. They only made me miss you all the more."

That made me smile.

"But I'm so sorry I'm late. My flight came in early, but a couple that I'd befriended on the flight had quite a frantic few minutes when they couldn't find their four-year-old. So I helped them. All is well, but I'm so sorry I didn't call or text. I should have."

I smiled, taking him in. I should have known. "No worries."

"So," he asked, "you missed me then?"

"Something fierce."

"Good. I knew you would."

I chuckled. "And did you get your life wrapped up in Melbourne?"

"Yes. I love Australia, always will, but this is my home. You're my home." He grazed my cheek with his finger.

"By the way, I did what you suggested. I went to see the woman . . . the other woman. And we had quite a visit."

"You did?" Marcus motioned to the bench. "Let me sit down for this."

When we'd moved his luggage, and we were settled on the bench, Marcus asked, "So, what in the world did she say?"

"Quite a bit actually. Enough to give me the closure you'd prayed for."

"That is good news."

"And I've gone back to the piano. I know what I want to do now. I'm going to stay on at the oil company part-time, but I'd like to teach piano to children. What do you think?"

"I've never heard you play, but something tells me you're wonderful, Love."

"Oh, how I've missed you calling me by that name. I've missed your smile. Well, all of you." I scooted closer to him. "Does this mean we're no longer Leroy and Zelda?"

"Yes. We'll be Marcus and Lily."

"Okay, so you know that question you were hinting at during the awful rainstorm under the bridge?"

"How could I forget?"

I took his hands in mine. "Well, if you could hint at it again . . . this time, I think you might get the answer you were hoping for."

He suddenly got all hushed on me.

I continued. "You know, I think it might go something like, 'Will you marry me?' Uh, this would be a good time to say something." I caught his mischievous gaze. "Marcus?"

CHAPTER
forty-eight

Marcus made me wait a whole day before he would respond to my proposal of marriage, but since he'd taken me to Galveston I was fairly certain I knew what his answer would be.

The late autumn chill in the air didn't stop us from rolling up our pant legs and strolling along the beach. After a while we settled ourselves on the sand, snuggled into each other's arms, and watched the waves roll in and out like a pendulum swing. Mesmerizing. "That was dreadfully mean, you know," I teased him, "to make me wait for your answer."

"But I knew you'd forgive me."

"Always so sure of yourself, Mr. Averill?"

"With you I am." Marcus bundled my sweater around me and ran his finger along the curve of my cheek. "I wanted to do it right. I'm old-fashioned that way. *And* I didn't want to share such a sanctified moment with a bunch of noisy, sweaty travelers."

I laughed and glanced around. "So, how did you manage to keep the noisy, sweaty travelers at bay today?"

"Not sure. Maybe they can sense that we need a moment to ourselves." Marcus kissed the tip of my nose. "And it could be because it's cold out here."

I grinned. "True."

"Look at those waves."

"Yes?"

"I've always been fascinated by waves. Did you know that when two ocean waves collide they influence each other, but once they pass over each other they go on about their business as if they'd never met?"

"Well, that's a sad thing to think about."

"Isn't it? And not very romantic. But I'm not quite finished. In some cases the waves do come back. They are forever changed."

"And when is that?"

"Well, in one case, it's the waves in a bathtub."

"So, are you saying our love is like the water splashing around in a bathtub?"

"Yes, but in other ways it's like the ocean. Deep, beautiful, and full of surprises."

"Oh, I like that part. You're definitely warming up now."

Marcus's grin looked full of mischief. What was he up to?

"Do you remember a book I did a long time ago called *Pockets*?"

"I know it made me misty every time I read it. It was about a boy named Sebastian Pepper."

"Good memory."

"And let's see . . . Sebastian would dump out his pockets into his toy box every night with all his treasures. Then as he would finger each memento we would learn about his daily adventures along with his hurts and secrets and joys. It was a brilliant idea. What made you think to write something like that?"

"Because that boy was me."

I smiled.

Marcus leaned back and pulled out everything in his pocket, making a little pile of treasures on the sand.

I chuckled. "So, what do you collect?"

Marcus motioned for me to sort through the heap. "Be my guest."

Among the items were acorns, lip balm, and seashells. I pulled out the two mollusk shells from the stack. "There are two here. Does that have significance?"

"Everything has significance." He lifted up the two shells. "See, if you place the two halves together like this . . . they make a home." Marcus fitted the two shells together. "The way God intended."

I rested my head on his shoulder. "That's as sweet as the marshmallows I used to eat. But what else do we have here?" I eased away and fingered through the mound again. Something shiny winked at me from within the tiny mountain of treasures. "What do I see?" I knew immediately what Marcus was up to, the darling rascal.

He watched me intently. "You tell me."

I moved a few items, uncovering the shimmer. A diamond ring flashed in the afternoon sunlight.

Marcus picked up a penny from the heap and placed it next to the ring. "Penny for your thoughts."

I turned the ring in the light. "My thoughts are . . . this ring is gorgeous and unique, just like you."

"Well said."

I laughed.

"So, will you, Lily Winter, be my wife?"

"I think I'll have to."

"And why is that?" he asked. "I want details. Metaphors."

"But you're the word person."

"Come on. Give it a whirl."

"Okay." I pursed my lips, but it didn't help my brain. "Let's see. Because you, Marcus Averill, are the sunlight shimmer on my seashell."

"Good alliteration."

"Thank you, but I'm not finished. Let's see. You're the moonlight . . . on my wave. And I don't want to live without that light. Not ever."

"I'm impressed."

"Thanks."

Marcus took the ring and slipped it on my finger.

"Lovely." I turned my hand. "I promise I'll never tire of gazing at it."

"I'm glad you love it."

"I do." The salty surf foamed up around our feet, tickling our toes. For a moment I turned my attention to the edge of the earth, where the sea touched the sky. "You know, on that first day we met . . . I wondered what was just beyond the horizon."

"Obviously, there were very good things, just waiting for us." Marcus lifted my chin so that our lips were a whisper apart. "And do you remember my reply that first day we met?"

"You said we'd just have to use our imaginations."

"What a good idea," he said.

Like birthday candles all aglow, my whole being did a little melting thing as women do when they know they're about to be kissed by the man they love.

We did, of course. We kissed beneath the autumn sun, the circling gulls, and the heavens. And in the midst of our sweet alliance, I knew somewhere up there, God was surely smiling.

CHAPTER
forty-nine

"*Lily's veil looks a mite askew.* Don't you think?" Camille turned her head this way and that, gazing at me from a distance with an eye for perfection.

"Yes, I think it is." With Julie's help, Mother lifted the tiara with the long trail of tulle and repositioned it on my hair.

"That vintage gown and tiara make you look like a princess, Momma," Julie said.

"See? I have a superb taste in gowns, don't I?" Mother donned a smug grin. "Maybe I should have been a wedding planner."

"It's never too late, Mother. But I would have been happy in a clown costume as long as I get to take home the prize."

We all laughed.

As if on cue, the four of us turned to face the mirror. What a sight that was. Three generations of Grays—smiling, laughing, and attached to each other like brand-new strips of Velcro. I looked upward. *Oh, Lord, You really are good to me.*

Yes, many times through the years I'd walked away from life, too afraid to journey into the hidden places. But once inside, I found there were still mysteries to unfold, secrets to marvel over—some wonderful and some not so wonderful—but there was always love to be discovered.

While reflecting over my long journey, Mother did something I could only have imagined in a dream. She cradled my face in her hands and said, "You are one of my two precious mustard seeds, and because of you and your faith, we are all reunited. I am proud of you. And now you have been blessed with Marcus. You were wise enough to know that the Irish saying is true. *'Níl aon leigheas ar an grá ach a phosadh.'* It means, 'The only cure for love is marriage.'"

She smiled. "I will pray God's love enfolds you, and that you and Marcus will know joy all of your days." She kissed my cheek and then turned to Camille and to Julie, christening them with more words of affection.

When Mother concluded her tributes, we huddled amidst the gossamer tulle. I could feel it in my spirit—we four had become a special delight to the Almighty—we were a family in love.

Later when everyone in the chapel was seated and more than ready for a wedding, my mother offered her arm, since she was going to be the one to give me away. We walked up the aisle to the recorded sounds of The Highland Bagpipes. It had become one of my favorite instruments—right along with the guitar, and the flute, and the piano.

Spring had come and a good portion of it had been brought inside the chapel. Sprays and baskets of every blossom imaginable filled the sanctuary with a profusion of colors and scents. Some of the flowers arrived from a local florist, but the prettiest and biggest blooms—the white lilies—came from Mother's solarium. I whispered to her, "Your lilies stole the show."

"We only need one Lily to do that," she whispered back.

I grinned. After giving Julie and Camille—my two bridesmaids—a wink, I took my place by Marcus's side.

My groom gave me his signature smile and snuggled his hand into mine.

When the vows were repeated, the unity candle had been lit, and the holy seal of matrimony was upon us, the pastor said an Irish blessing over us.

"May God be with you and bless you.
  May you see your children's children.

May you be poor in misfortunes
and rich in blessings.
May you know nothing but happiness
from this day forward."

Sniffles could be heard all over the chapel, but this time, no tears came from me. I was too busy kissing the groom.

EPILOGUE

Summer came and Mother and I found ourselves standing next to a taxicab—the one that held our Camille. Mother clung to a little Irish flag while I clutched a wad of tissues. Marcus had wanted to be with us for our goodbyes, but he'd had a previous engagement—a signing in Austin for his latest picture book. He'd wanted to cancel his event, but I wouldn't hear of it. Mother and I would have enough tears for all of us.

"You should see yourselves." Camille grinned. "You're about to make this poor cabdriver tear up."

The man turned around and winked.

"Lily, you found your destiny in Australia," Camille said. "In more ways than one. Maybe I'll find mine in Ireland. It's our homeland. Good things are bound to happen there."

"But it's quite a leap to travel there just from a letter," I said. "Are you sure you want to go all that way because of some sweet words from a man you knew years ago?"

"But you took a chance," Camille said, "a big one, because of a letter."

"Yes, I guess that's true." Hard to argue with that.

"And a man named Hugh O'Callaghan may change my life. He did once a long time ago in small ways." Camille grasped the edge of the cab window. "Now I have to find out if he's the one who can change my life in a bigger way. If he's the one."

"I wish you'd at least let us drive you to the airport," Mother said.

"I'll take good care of her," the cabby said.

"You'd better." Mother gave the man a fierce glint like she meant business. "Or you'll be answering to me," she added in an Irish brogue.

The man chuckled.

"I cry too easily these days," Camille said. "I don't want to make a scene at the airport."

I crossed my arms. "I'll tell you right now that if you don't find what you're searching for, and you don't come back home . . . well, I'll be traveling to Ireland to find you."

"I believe you, Lils." Camille grinned. "I do."

Mother stepped forward. "Let us know the second you land. I'll be worried until we get that text." She reached out to Camille, clasped her hand, and kissed it soundly. "I know you girls must be getting tired of my Irish sayings, but I do have one that is a favorite. *'Is é níos fearr iarracht a dhéanamh na dochas a bheith agat.'* It means, 'It's better to make a try at it than to just have hope.' I'd rather lose you for a while to pursue this dream than keep you here and have you always wonder what could have been. I can't do that to you."

"Thanks, Iris, for understanding and not trying to talk me out of it . . . like Lils has been doing."

"Oh, I've wanted to talk you out of it quite a few times," Mother said. "But I also know you can be as headstrong as I am when you set your mind to something." She sighed. "But I'm fiercely proud of you for it." Mother handed Camille the little Irish flag. *"Dia duit . . .* God be with you."

"I'll be back . . . Mother," Camille said softly. "No worries, okay?"

"Okay." Mother's voice trembled.

It was the first time Camille had used the word *Mother*, and I knew the endearment would be enough to keep her going for a long time.

I handed Mother my wad of tissues. She would need them now.

"Take good care of yourself." Mother tried to sound like a fortress of strength, but it was no use. She raised the tissues to her face.

I held out my right palm to my sister, and then Camille reached out her left to me. We met palm to palm as we had grown accustomed to doing. But this time I laced my fingers around her hand and didn't want to release her. Moments later, though, I did. I knew I had to let her go.

Mother—who was such a lover of all things Irish—wasn't the only one who knew a saying or two. As the cabdriver whisked Camille away I thought of a phrase that fit her journey well. "It takes time to build castles." But even though love did take time—as I'd learned from Marcus and my family—it was always a castle worth building.

ACKNOWLEDGEMENTS

Many thanks to my editor, Deborah Keiser, at Moody Publishers, for her kindness and her wonderful editorial expertise in making this book a finer read.

Also thanks to editor Cheryl Molin for her wise assistance.

Cheers go up to my husband, Peter, for his thirty-three years of love and support.

Much appreciation goes to Sandra Bishop at MacGregor Literary Agency for praying for me and believing in what I do.

In addition, I'm grateful to Debby Hartzell for her valuable input, and to Faber McMullen for his knowledgeable advice concerning the Gaelic language.

Lastly, appreciation goes to the fine folks of Melbourne, Australia, who were so helpful and welcoming. I fell in love with your enchanting city.

Any errors in the text are solely the fault of the author.

A Note to Readers

They say art reflects life. In fact, life and art are like two vines on a trellis, getting so tangled that you can barely tell which bloom comes from which stalk.

The idea for *Winter in Full Bloom* started when I took a trip to Melbourne, Australia. I traveled across the globe to stay with my husband who on a work assignment there. When I departed from Houston to the Land Down Under, I had to leave my daughter, Hillary, behind during her first days of college. The heart-trials of my empty nest and saying goodbye were as traumatic for me as it was for my heroine, Lily. By the way, Hillary, who was getting a music major and later switched to English, just like in the story, attended the same university as my heroine's daughter.

In addition to other similar life/art elements not mentioned here, I too like Lily had a fire-breathing fear of flying. I hadn't flown in fifteen years. I eventually got over those anxieties as did Lily, and I now travel with my husband domestically and internationally. I just wish there had been a real Jenny on that maiden voyage to Australia to talk me out of my crazies, especially when the captain announced that we'd be flying around a tropical storm while over the Pacific!

One major difference in my story versus real life was that my husband and I had to cut our stay in Melbourne short because Hurricane Ike had hit Houston. We rushed home when we found out that our house had sustained internal as well as external damage. It was a mess, but with God's help and the efforts of some kindhearted neighbors, we got through it.

So, does art reflect life? Most definitely. And you, the reader, are truly appreciated in taking that art-life journey with me!

ANITA HIGMAN

Bestselling and award-winning author Anita Higman has thirty-three books published (several coauthored) for adults and children. She's been a Barnes & Noble "Author of the Month" for Houston and has a BA in the combined fields of speech communication, psychology, and art. Anita loves good movies, exotic teas, and brunch with her friends.

Please visit Anita online at anitahigman.com. Feel free to drop her a note by clicking on the "Contact Me" button on her website. Or visit Anita on her Facebook Reader Page at https://www.facebook.com/#!/AuthorAnitaHigman.

Some of Anita Higman's more recent books
Texas Wildflowers
A Merry Little Christmas
Where God Finds You